CATACLYSMIC MISTAKES

MCFADDEN AND BANKS™ BOOK 7

MICHAEL ANDERLE

LMBPN Publishing
PMB 196, 2540 South Maryland Pkwy
Las Vegas, NV 89109

Version 1.00, June 2021
eBook ISBN: 978-1-64971-862-4
Print ISBN: 978-1-64971-863-1

THE CATACLYSMIC MISTAKES TEAM

Thanks to our Beta Team:
Jeff Eaton, John Ashmore, Kelly O'Donnell

JIT Readers

Deb Mader
Dave Hicks
John Ashmore
Peter Manis
Jeff Goode
Diane L. Smith

Editor
Skyhunter Editing Team

DEDICATION

To Family, Friends and
Those Who Love
to Read.
May We All Enjoy Grace
to Live the Life We Are
Called.

CHAPTER ONE

"Heads up! We have movement on the perimeter."

"Let me guess—more of those bastard sneak moles," Murphy responded as he snapped instinctively to attention and adjusted his rifle when the warning brought him out of the reverie he'd been in.

He didn't waste time on personal recriminations. It was hard to stay focused for so long, and most of the other guys were already being cycled out to rest while the new rotation took their places. As the captain and the man who was mostly in charge, however, he was expected to be on the ground as often as possible. Dalbert's hours of sleep since the whole clusterfuck had started were in the single digits. He was running on fumes and whatever preservatives they pumped into the coffee at this point.

It didn't surprise him at all that a week or so after the Japanese base had been reclaimed, he continued to direct the mop-up operation on the front line. With his last name and hard-nosed determination to get the job done right, his particular brand of Murphy's Law was still in demand in the field.

Once he was sure he hadn't ignored any gun safety basics in his sleep-deprived state, he moved to join the rest of the gunners as they took up their positions.

"You'd think these fuckers would know when to lay down and die," Saddler muttered and ran another quick scan.

"They don't care," Murphy reminded him. "They'll throw themselves at us until we run out of bullets or they run out of...well, whatever the hell makes them spring up out of the ground the way they do."

For not the first time, he was immensely relieved that Dr. Sal Jacobs had shared footage he'd received from Taylor McFadden which provided some warning about this New Zoo addition and how one could kill them. The leprechaun and his team had encountered them out in the Sahara after they'd escaped the so-called "New Zoo." The mutants were particularly lethal because they could hide so thoroughly in the sand and launch their ambush attacks in seconds.

"There are spirals up ahead," Murphy called and highlighted the places where faint swirls in the ground indicated that something waited for them under the surface. "Make sure the perimeter is clear of any of the usual nutants and drop the grenades. I don't want us to fight them if we also have other monsters to deal with."

They'd tried that once. It hadn't ended well and proved to be the engagement with the most casualties since the fighting was technically supposed to be over. Of course, as it turned out, the mopping up had proved to be as difficult as the fighting had been.

The jungle might have lost the battle but it certainly seemed determined to win the war. Vegetation appeared overnight as if to rally the Zoo to expand again and had to be systematically destroyed. Murphy and his team were there to escort the men bearing plasma throwers to burn the rest of the New Zoo down and give them as much space as they could to do their thing.

The trees had begun to resist the plasma throwers, but whatever the planes were dumping deeper into the vegetation appeared to help and slow the growth so it now burned faster than it could recover.

With no sign of any other mutants in the vicinity, he motioned for the teams to prepare their grenades. Half of them would lob the explosives while the others held their firearms at the ready to gun down any creature that launched out of the sand.

The grenades were thrown and Murphy stepped forward, drew a deep breath, and felt the adrenaline spike as he moved closer. The blasts kicked the dirt up and the monsters roiled beneath.

Six nests were hit but two hadn't been seen and he highlighted them hastily as the mole beasts thrust out and lashed viciously in an attempt to catch anything that was nearby. None of them was close enough, though, and the men had already opened fire to eliminate the two almost immediately before they could pose much of a threat.

He nodded approval. His team had dealt efficiently with this new Zoo monster but they had encountered enough of them during the past few days that they should have mastered the drill. The first time one of those mole creatures had launched from below the surface, panic had ensued and even the guys who carried the plasma throwers had joined in.

In retrospect, although McFadden had warned them via Sal Jacobs about them, most people had somehow assumed that they wouldn't be found in the business side of the Zoo. This had no basis in anything as no one had real data, but an insidious complacency had crept in around the vague supposition that they preferred the desert to the jungle and so wouldn't be an issue where the more traditional Zoo environment was present.

With that said, there was honestly also no way to prepare for the first time. He was sure there would be no end to the vids that proliferated about their overreaction, but at least it drove the point home and no more people would die unnecessarily.

The area was clear and Murphy took a second to reload and check his equipment and their surroundings before the throwers began work again.

"Captain Murphy!"

He started and registered a handful of new signatures that had appeared in his HUD. The fact that he needed a moment to realize they were not in any actual danger but were instead being greeted by the new team come to start their shift was an indication of his utter exhaustion.

"You guys are here a little early," he pointed out as their throwers moved in to take position.

"Franklin sent us in. He said he wants to see you."

"I won't look a gift horse in the mouth," one of the

members of his team shouted and the others were only too happy to get off work a little early.

Still, if the US base commander wanted to meet with him, Murphy was well aware that his time on the clock was far from over.

It was a short walk to the Forward Operating Base, where the rest of the crew quickly settled in for what little rest time was available to them. He moved directly toward the command tent and grimaced as his gaze noted far more activity than Franklin generally liked to have around him.

Not much could cause that and if he had to guess, he would have said it meant a group of the base commanders were all present to inspect the progress of the cleanup. There had been surprisingly little dick measuring and bickering about responsibility and territory allocation since the attack began. It would start eventually, but he was at least thankful that they had understood the danger that all bases were in if the situation was not contained quickly.

Sure enough, a group of men in different uniforms was present around the displays, which showed real-time feeds from high-altitude planes and satellites that all maintained a bird's-eye view of the situation on the ground.

Even he had to concede that it was a pretty piece of tech, one that Franklin had likely been aching to break out for all the other commanders. It was subtle but there would always be that little one-upmanship between them. Still, the fact that this was the so-called New Zoo was the only reason they were able to use it effectively. While no one voiced it, everyone accepted that if brought into play over the "Real Zoo," the interference would inevitably render it useless, however technologically advanced it was.

The captain recognized most of the European uniforms —French, German, and British—along with the Russians and Japanese. Given that the Russian base was closest to the incursion and the Japs' base had been overrun, having them present to coordinate on the mission was expected.

But the Sahara Coalition had tried to avoid involvement with the situation, which made their presence a little more surprising.

Murphy came to a halt at the door of the tent, stopped with his hands behind his back, and waited respectfully to be noticed. Franklin was the first to do so and approached the door as the captain snapped a sharp salute.

"You look like shit, Captain," the commandant said.

"I feel like it too, sir. I was told you wanted to see me?"

"Yes. We need a report from the ground. While we can look and watch from above all we want, it doesn't give us any idea of what is being dealt with in the actual combat zone."

"We've pushed the New Zoo back on schedule." Murphy moved to the display and felt the gazes of all those present suddenly locked onto him. "I'd say the Zoo has tried to adapt to our efforts, but the combination of the chemical drops and the plasma throwers on all sides have been effective. We've reduced the total invasion area to under twenty square kilometers and are closing fast. The troops on the ground are hampered somewhat by the presence of live cryptids still defending the area, but the New Zoo remains cut off from the original. I believe these few mutants are either those that were missed during the initial push to the base or have been produced out here. In both cases, the new jungle is not able to reproduce these in sufficient numbers to slow us beyond schedule."

"We could always simply drop the bombs and turn the area into a crater like you Russians did the last time," one of the men muttered. He recognized the uniform as belonging to the Nigerien military, one of the higher-ranking members of the Sahara Coalition.

"The walls still in place are all that is preventing the New Zoo from connecting with the Old," the Japanese representative noted in good English. "If the bombing compromises the wall structure, we could be looking at a second attack and one worse than the first."

The captain nodded. He would also have preferred to bomb the shit out of the place but he heard the guns on the walls going day and night to prevent the original Zoo from pushing forward to join the fight. That was a decent enough compromise.

The Japanese commandant was still recovering from the injuries that occurred when the base was taken, which meant that his second in command, a young major, had taken his place. Any questions about her competence were set aside after Jacobs had very clearly stated that her involvement was the reason why they'd managed to reclaim the guns.

"That brings me directly to the point of this gathering," Franklin interjected and zoomed in on a hot spot that appeared suddenly and where they could barely make out the heavy suits powering hard into a surge of mutants that attempted to push out from the tree line. "The work on the second wall has unfortunately slowed. We need to resume it again before another base sees an attack like this."

"It will involve considerable financial implications." The Libyan commander folded his arms and studied the display curiously. "Especially if we move forward with building it in the model the Japanese have used here, which I believe is the standard designed for the wall structure at the outset. It's effective enough when it works but we will have to ask our respective governments to commit billions to a project that has already been shown to fail."

"The failure was an isolated event," the Russian commander stated quietly. "As far as our intelligence shows, the incursion coincided with an unrelated hack on the AI that operated the security systems."

"Do you mean to say the Zoo hacked the systems?" The Libyan commander looked confused and more than a little alarmed.

"The hack was unrelated, aside from the timing," Franklin answered. "Human error was also involved."

Of course, the fact that Solodkov knew about the hack was an interesting development. Sal had told Murphy about the theory based on what his and McFadden's tech experts were able to find out about it but as far as he knew, it was not common knowledge. Either the Russians had experts who had come to the same conclusion or the man had all kinds of ears in all kinds of places.

In all honesty, he always gave Dalbert the creeps. He had little to no military experience and it was a poorly kept secret that he had been in the FSB before he took control of the Russian base. That led him to wonder if the appointment had serious political implications and when they'd raise their ugly heads to disrupt what was already a complex situation.

"How are we to know there will not be another failure?" the British commander asked, her features contorted in a deep scowl.

"If you're doing the building, you'll be responsible for the tech put into it," Franklin pointed out. "Going into this project, a condition of every sector's involvement was that the wall would follow a standard design and layout that would optimize both safety and efficiency. I regret to say that this has not been adhered to across the board—an issue that will have to be addressed at the very least."

He paused, his expression hard and unyielding, to let the full meaning of his words sink in but ignored the somewhat uncomfortable reaction the truth had elicited.

"If nothing else, we can learn from this incident. The Japanese base conformed fully and was backed by top-of-the-line additions and improvements. If it could fall to a Zoo invasion, the rest of us who have not met that standard are woefully ill-equipped to withstand a concerted push."

"But again, if this base fell, what is the point of adding the bells and whistles and going to the unnecessary expense?" The German's defensiveness gave his tone a surly edge.

Franklin smiled but it lacked humor. "Let me be clear. The Pentagon has already begun to put pressure on various governments to compel all member nations of the Zoo sectors to meet the conditions relating to the construction requirements of the wall. In essence, discussions around that are moot at this level, although we will be expected to ensure that the requirements are identified and met.

Thereafter, what you choose to add to your defenses is entirely at your discretion."

This last statement drew nods and some measure of relaxation from the delegates. Murphy could almost hear them counting what savings they might be able to glean to offset the construction costs.

Franklin must have seen that as well as he smiled and shook his head. "Although if you're looking for suggestions, I would recommend putting a slew of big fucking guns on the top—" He paused when the Japanese Major cleared her throat. "You know, within reason. Let your engineers make the decisions on how big the guns are and where they are positioned. That aside, you should also know that the Pentagon has recently been given the green light by the US Congress to start on what we're calling the Zoo Containment Protocol, and there's considerable language in there to involve anyone who chooses to be included."

This was the first Murphy had heard about this ZCP but if he knew Franklin at all, he could assume it was the reason why this meeting was called. Close to the incursion, it would make every commander extremely uncomfortable with how close the Zoo could get to everyone and more amenable to what might well already be innumerable changes in the pipeline.

"We've been in contact with ENSOL International," Franklin continued. "It's an independent international engineering and construction company. They will conduct the full evaluation of what we still need to get Wall Two finished and up to standard and will be in contact with any and all of the parties involved. I hate to say it, but we need every sector here to do its part to address the situation. One weak point in the wall will be enough for all of it to go to shit."

It felt a little like bullying tactics, but Murphy could see a hint of desperation in the man's eyes. It was his job to ensure that the Zoo didn't pose a greater threat than it already did, and he needed to rely on everyone else doing their part toward the same goal.

"We all know something is changing in the Zoo now," Major Murakami stated. "The status quo does not satisfy it any longer. We need to adapt our tactics accordingly or our base might not be the only one overrun. It is better to have all bases coordinated than to stand and fight on our own. For myself, I know I would not be alive if not for the rapid mobilization to recover our base."

"Agreed." Franklin nodded and it seemed clear that Murakami and he had discussed this already. "It's critical to close all doors before the Zoo finds another egress point and we have to do all this shit again. I know that no one here is in a position to make any decisions on your own, but I hope what you take away from this is the desperate nature of the situation we're in. All we can hope for is that our actions do not come too late."

His voice rang through the suddenly silent tent and for a moment, they all stood without saying a word. Murphy could see the calculations running through their heads and the conclusion they came to—they didn't want what happened to the Japanese to happen to them.

"I have to make some calls," the Nigerien commander stated and left the tent quickly, followed by other commanders a moment later, all likely heading off to make the same calls.

Franklin was right when he said that none of them were in any position to commit their governments to the kind of expenditure that was being suggested but hopefully, they would broach the topic while the full impact of the Japanese tragedy added a little enthusiasm to their efforts. The people writing the checks would have to listen to them, at least, and the pressure brought to bear by the Pentagon might well push the matter forward when emotions cooled and saving costs while reaping greater rewards took precedence again.

"Are you still at that strip mall?"

Taylor could feel Niki's glare on him before she turned to the screen.

"Yeah, Jennie, we're still at this godawful strip mall."

"You might want to make your feelings about it a little more obvious," he suggested. "There's no need to tone it down on my account."

"Exactly like the sarcasm in your tone, then." Her snark had become predictable by now. While no one ventured to mention it out loud, her ongoing tension—like she teetered constantly on the thin line between being in control and a full-blown meltdown—was evident to everyone.

"Jesus Christ." Jennie sighed and rubbed her temples. "You two are bickering like an old married couple. I guess you'll talk about how you're not fucking anymore."

"No, it's made it more fun," her sister snapped in response. "There's no sex like angry sex."

For once, she didn't grin when her cousin gagged in the background.

"I think I need to join Vickie in saying eecchhhh." Jennie gagged with her tongue out like she was about to throw up. "Keep your personal lives private. We're here to talk business and I'm still at the office, so topics need to be safe for work, unfortunately."

"Boring!" Niki protested, but her attempt at humor held a sharp edge that made it fall horribly flat. "Do you guys have any updates for us? If it has to be all work and no complaining, we might as well get on with it."

"I have worked on getting the dummy AI in place," Desk announced over the shared line. "But it should be obvious that this is only a play for time and little else."

"We need every second we can get." Taylor leaned back in his seat and folded his arms. "Anything to keep Desk and Nessie away from the assholes who have given us problems over the last few months—as much as it amuses me to hear the story of how Desk went all Skyfall on that one dumbass."

"It's Skynet," Vickie corrected. "And I think you know that."

"Sorry." He cleared his throat.

"What about the property you have in DC?" Jennie asked as she tapped her keyboard. "Do you have anything there that might be a problem for moving our AIs to Italy?"

"I was diligent in erasing any sign of my presence on those systems," Desk announced quickly. "You'll be happy to know that the location is very easily covered by a security company while we're away. It's always a good idea to have a location in the DC area."

"I'm a little more concerned with the safety of our Vegas property holdings," Taylor said and winced at the words. He sounded a little too much like a millionaire who was trying to get his money to the Caymans before the IRS came knocking. "Not that I think Desk would have left any trace. It's merely an overall worry about how much money was spent on them and how we'll simply leave it all behind."

"You don't need to be concerned about that." Bobby rocked back in his office chair, rolled his shoulders, and looked a little uncomfortable. Taylor had tried to ease up on him in their sparring session but he'd gone a little too hard around the ribs. He made a mental note to suggest that he see a doctor once the meeting was over.

"What do you mean?" Niki asked.

"Well, Tanya and I have been looking for a while for somewhere with a little more space. We could rent one of the smaller houses on the property and make sure everything's on the up and up."

"It seems like a fair amount of work," he muttered.

"Sure, that's what you hire people for. And we'll keep an eye on the people in exchange for a reasonable rent."

Taylor's eyes narrowed. "How reasonable?"

"Very reasonable." His friend grinned.

It wasn't very like the mechanic to volunteer like that and he could see that even Tanya was a little surprised by it, but it did offer an alternative.

He took a deep breath and toyed idly with his beard as he considered the possibilities.

"And why would you pick that kind of responsibility up for me?" he asked finally.

The other man shrugged. "I have my reasons."

This came as another surprise. Bobby Zhang was not the kind of person to keep things to himself.

Before he could press him for more answers, however, his phone buzzed in his pocket. He made a face immediately when he saw who was calling.

Niki knew the expression a little too well. "Marino?"

Taylor nodded. "I'll take this in the next room. One second."

He moved into the other room and made sure to close the door before he accepted the call.

"I didn't expect to hear from you again so soon," he said without so much as greeting the man.

"I'm all for pleasantly surprising you guys," Marino answered with a laugh. "Besides, I know how much this move to Italy means to you so I wanted to make sure that you're kept in the loop on everything that's happening."

The fact that the mob boss was getting such a kick from their business together only made it worse, but Taylor forced the sick feeling down and nodded.

"I appreciate that. Is there any news?"

"Well, all the security you wanted is already up. Of course, it did belong to one of the most paranoid dons of the region, so almost everything was already there. All we have to do now is upgrade a few places and repair others. The residence itself didn't need that much in the way of renovations, although I will make sure that they do more than simply the minimum needed. It should all be ready to move in shortly from what they tell me but might still be happening should you choose to move sooner."

"And you trust what they tell you?"

"I trust that they understand not to fuck with me like I've learned not to fuck with you. Things are moving along quickly. You and your people should prepare yourselves at an equal pace."

"Don't you worry about us," Taylor answered.

"The thought never crossed my mind. I'll let you know if there are any other updates. Have a good one."

The line cut and he was left with the familiar sick feeling in his stomach again. Something slimy about Marino always reminded him about what the mob boss did for a living. Being tangled in his business again wasn't a pleasant development but getting Desk and Nessie away from the wrong hands was worth whatever nausea it caused.

Taylor breathed deeply and savored the few moments of privacy. The move couldn't happen soon enough as far as he was concerned, but he had a more pressing issue that needed attention. Niki was trying but failed miserably to cope with being confined to a home base she utterly hated. That was the only reason he hadn't lost his patience with her.

Still, it was only a matter of time before something blew up in a spectacularly ugly fashion. The inaction resulting from no jobs on the horizon didn't help matters, and it had begun to wear at him as well. They both needed a break—something simple and non-threatening that would enable her to blow off steam.

Maybe, he thought wryly, a night out for drinks and a

meal at a rough and rowdy venue might work to alleviate the stress. It would, he mused, have to be somewhere they weren't known given that she seemed to have a fair amount of venting to do. Perhaps Desk could do a little research and find what he needed, but it should happen soon before the proverbial hit the fan.

CHAPTER TWO

Nothing was more natural than the sight of two old friends having coffee together. They had not seen each other in a long time. Meeting by chance at a family gathering or a quick commitment like this one was perfectly normal and wouldn't raise any questions.

It was the kind of thing that happened every day all over the world and meetings like these were what coffee shops made their bread and butter on. The kind that had tables and a place to sit usually offered a quieter ambiance. Those that prioritized getting the coffee quickly to people on the move were often frenetic and others that were a little more hybridized to cater to both tried to juggle what was essentially a balancing act to achieve the best of both worlds.

Their chosen venue provided for people who wanted to linger for a while with numerous tables, comfortable chairs, and thick, appealing mugs to serve their beverages in.

Eben had settled for black coffee and sipped it slowly

while he watched the traffic outside. He'd already picked up all the anti-surveillance software he could take with him without questions being raised by the FBI, all to ensure that no one would be able to listen in to their conversation.

It was unlikely that anyone would expect him to be involved with anything other than meeting an old friend for coffee, but given the people they were dealing with, he preferred to not take any chances.

His friend showed no signs of similar caution. He arrived in a bright yellow Lambo and looked like a movie star as he handed the keys to one of the valets from the up-market restaurant next door. It wasn't a stretch to assume that he was a regular customer there and had no doubt greased the palms of the staff enough to expect a few favors in return. He smiled and pulled his sunglasses off as he entered the coffee shop, scanned the area calmly, and moved to join his friend.

"It's good to see you again, bro." Shane patted his shoulder as one of the baristas approached the table with a tablet in hand, ready to take his order. "Hi, a large caramel, creme de menthe, white chocolate powder, butterscotch, English toffee, peppermint, and white coffee, thanks."

The girl was a professional and punched the order in quickly before she beat a hasty retreat.

"That's not coffee," Eben pointed out. "That's a dessert with a hint of coffee in it and doesn't even have the ingredients needed to call it a coffee cake."

"Who the hell cares?" The man shook his head. "Were you followed?"

"Of course not."

His friend caught his glance at the Lambo.

"People expect me to be a flamboyant asshole all the time," Shane explained. "Changing that would only trigger suspicions."

He hated to admit it but the man had a point there. By acting as he always did, he wouldn't raise as many eyebrows as he would have otherwise.

"I've made sure no one's listening in and there are no cameras in this area of the shop, so you don't need to worry about that either." Eben leaned back in his seat and took a sip from his coffee while his companion's diabetes-in-a-cup was delivered. "You said there was word from your man?"

Shane nodded. "Ghosteye reported in but there's no good news. He said there's no evidence of an AI on their systems."

"What?" He placed his cup down and tried to not show his annoyance too blatantly. "Are you sure?"

"That's what he said. Almost verbatim."

"And you believe him?"

"The guy is the best in the market so I'll take his word on the matter. It doesn't mean your people don't have the AI at all, only that they were able to wipe it from their systems without leaving a trace. If they had an AI and knew they were being watched for that kind of thing, they would be able to do that, right?"

Again, Shane was not wrong, but something about the situation rubbed Eben the wrong way.

"If the best couldn't find it," the other man continued, "what chance do we have? If they moved the AI on, sold it, or hid it, it's irrelevant at this point. The evidence suggests that they no longer have it and unless we have concrete proof that they have simply hidden it somewhere, we're both left with empty hands despite the massive investment I put into this."

The guy had a way of bringing up the obvious in the most annoying way possible. As much as Eben hated to admit it, he did owe him for his investment, big-time. The kind of investment that would see results, one way or another.

"What are you talking about?" he asked. It was always better to make sure everything was said aloud to ensure there were no implied and open-ended debts hanging around.

"Well, it was an investment, right?" Shane sipped his drink. "And an expensive one. Still, you brought it to my attention that we could both profit from this so you did us both a favor by getting me involved—the kind of favor friends do for each other. Sure, people will ask questions about where the money went but I'll write it off as consultant fees or some bullshit like that. In the meantime, you know I'll take any advice you have to offer me as I did before and vice versa."

Implied or not, there was no question in his tone that Eben was tied to him. The kind of favor he would want in the future would no doubt put his career in jeopardy, and if any part of it was made public, he had little doubt that the man would turn him over to the wolves for an easier sentence and a few months spent at a resort turned into a minimum-security prison.

This was the kind of deal that many in Shane's business sphere were more than willing to make.

"Do you think you'll keep searching for it?" his friend asked once the silence between them lasted a little longer than he was comfortable with.

"Call it an obsession but I honestly don't think free-lancers with the kind of history McFadden and Banks have should be in possession of something as dangerous and powerful as a combat AI." He swirled his coffee in his cup and studied the black liquid with a deep scowl painted on his features. "There's no way to tell when or if they will decide to use it for something other than killing cryptids—and that's assuming they haven't already used it for illegal purposes."

Shane chuckled. "You truly are in law enforcement because you believe in it, aren't you?"

"Not really. But I do have a moral compass and I've seen the kind of damage freelancers can do when they're left unchecked with as much power as they want."

"I can't argue with that. So, you're merely out there, saving the world one errant freelancer at a time."

"I would be. One thing they never talk about when it comes to law enforcement is the sheer amount of paperwork."

"Which is what generally drives people to the private sector. Not that there's no paperwork but there is usually less of it. And most is done by lawyers anyway."

Eben nodded. "For now, though, I'll have to wait for the people working in the FBI and DOD who are still poking around. I guess even they are bound to get lucky eventually."

"Well, let me know if you have any updates on that

front." Shane finished the last of his coffee. "And I'll be in touch if there's any business we can do in the future."

"You do that."

He tried to keep the disgusted look from his face until his friend was in his Lambo. The asshole had left the bill for him to pay, of course. It wasn't like he was broke but it was a solid reminder of the fact that he was in the mother-fucker's pocket now for better or worse.

More than ever, he needed to find that bastard AI or Shane would come up with something that would derail his career more than it already was.

As a favor, of course.

There weren't many benefits to rising too early in the morning. Badawi had never subscribed to the ideal that being up with the sun for its own sake was a good idea. Some people reveled in it and others even seemed to need it, but if he could avoid it, there was time to wait for the sun to rise a little before he did the same.

But there was one good thing that came from the concept, at least on this particular morning. It was ridiculously early, of course, and the desert sun still struggled to surge upward and the air was chilly, but his anticipated meeting would not be conducted in the unpleasantly debilitating Saharan heat. He had always preferred the cold. One day, he promised himself, he would live somewhere colder that would allow him out into the sun without the threat of being burned to a crisp.

As the SUV pulled up to the meeting location, he saw

that his counterpart's arrival was recent from the dust the man's vehicles had kicked up. At least he wasn't late. He knew how much Mashoul hated to be left waiting, especially outside the comparative safety of his camp.

The Algerian merc climbed from his car and shivered as a chilly wind whipped around him. He clutched his coat a little tighter as the Nigerien stepped out of his vehicle as well. There wasn't much that could make the man feel cold by the looks of him. Arms as thick as tree trunks and powerful shoulders defined a man who had worked a great deal with his hands.

Although the growing belly spoke of time spent away from hard work—or maybe a little too much beer on the sly. Badawi wasn't much of a fan of working with people who did not adhere strictly to their faith but there was a soft spot in his heart for the hard hitter out of Niger. He hoped that if he was indulging, he wouldn't be caught. Perhaps that was the appeal of a mercenary camp—it was a remote location where one could indulge one's sins relatively safely.

"It is good to see you again, brother," Mashoul said with a broad grin and shook his hand firmly.

The calloused grasp made him try to rub some feeling into his hand once it was released. "It is always a pleasure to do business with you, Mashoul. You said you had news to share?"

The Nigerien brushed his fingers over his bald head and nodded. "Word has reached me that the Sahara Coalition will join the efforts to build the second wall around the Zoo. I cannot blame them, given what I saw of the damage caused by the jungle to the Japanese base, but it will cause problems with our supply. As a result, a limited window of opportunity has opened to make as much money as we can before the governments step in and enforce stricter measures."

"I am always happy to hear of windows of opportunity for money to be made." Badawi motioned for his man to approach with a small thermos and two cups. Even if they were meeting in the middle of the desert, there was no reason why manners could not be followed. "Coffee?"

"Please."

Both cups were filled and the men paused their business talks for a quick sip of the fragrant, thick liquid. It wasn't quite as good as when it was fresh but still the perfect way to greet the sun on a cold morning. His wife certainly knew how to make it and the thought made him wonder if he shouldn't make a short trip home. She would never tell him her secrets but it was something that gave the visits something extra to look forward to.

"Now then," Badawi said once they'd had the chance to enjoy the brew. "Tell me about the business you had in mind."

Mashoul handed the empty cup to the waiting man. "I have a contract with a company overseas. They are buying panther pelts at a premium now that the other supply chains are cut. With that said, I need additional manpower to make a couple more concerted drives to hunt the creatures and meet the order quota we agreed to."

"I guess you agreed to what you could provide before this whole mess with the Japanese base. All the mercenaries were paid a premium to help there."

"Exactly. Still, I am convinced we will be able to meet it

if we can bring in outside help. I'm willing to split the profits from the next shipment and if you're interested, keep you involved in the shipments in the future. We're talking two hundred grand per pelt and a delivery of thirty pelts per shipment."

"Two hundred thousand. American?"

"Hell no. Euros. But around these parts, that can be better."

That was true, especially if they were dealing with clients in Europe instead of elsewhere.

"They will pay even more for komodo skins if we can find them too."

Badawi nodded and stroked his beard pensively. "There are many risks involved in this kind of business. Khaled remembers well the type of problems that can arise from dealing with the monsters of the Zoo. We had some difficulty with that already in the past."

It was difficult to forget the kind of trouble they ran into with the Sustainagrow situation, but his boss had managed to protect them from the bigger problems. Still, the money now on the table was such that a little extra risk was acceptable.

Business was business, after all.

"Do you need to send word to Khaled?" Mashoul asked.

Badawi shook his head. "I know he'll turn the money down. He's afraid of the Zoo these days. No, I think he's better off not knowing why our little camp is so profitable these days. Besides, if the shit hits the fan, this is your project and all the blowout will be on you and yours."

The Nigerien laughed. "You are a devious little fuck. My kind of people."

Badawi shook the man's hand again. "Drop a message as to when and where you need my men. They'll be there."

He'd endured a long ride across the blazing heat of the desert to reach a city glittering with all kinds of lights. Logan had always had a visit to Vegas on his bucket list but never quite like this.

There were many reasons why the head of the Lynch clan had put him in charge of their little venture into the desert and gambling was not one of them. Even if he did play a mean hand of poker.

No, he wanted him at the head because some kid with roots in the Guardian Angels Chapter in South Boston couldn't be tied to him if shit went sideways. He knew that from the start. He was practically in Vegas on his own to work against the groups that were already in place in the hope that he could destabilize them. Once that happened, Miles would dispatch his "army" to make a clean sweep and oust the current major players.

If there was enough profit and they managed to elimi-nate the competition, an actual chapter of the GAMC would be established in Vegas. If not, the little offshoot would be forgotten quickly and the people who avoided death and prison time would return to their Southie buddies.

This was make-or-break time for him, though. Logan had worked up the ranks of the group but there was only so much he could do without serious connections. This kind of opportunity would put him in the good graces of

Miles Lynch. While it didn't guarantee an easy road ahead from that, it was a good start.

He killed the powerful engine on the Harley he was riding, settled on the comfortable leather seat, and narrowed his eyes as he inspected the location chosen by Cody. It certainly wasn't the Ritz, he decided sourly, given that it looked like the building was about three weak gusts of wind from total collapse.

As a starting ground for the Dopplers MC, however, it would have to do. Even if the premises was a nightmare not only for a city inspector but in terms of any hope at security.

At least the assholes hadn't parked their bikes out where they could be seen from a mile away.

Logan started the bike again and the motor thrummed between his legs as he twisted his wrist enough to get the heavy ride going and circled the building to a small parking lot where the bikes were parked.

Once situated, he stood for a moment before he walked to the door where he could already see one of his boys waiting outside, taking a smoke break.

"If you've got time to smoke, you've got time to work, Murph," he snapped but the man raised a middle finger in response. Murph had been a Guardian Angel for longer than Logan had been alive. He had all the attitude to show for it, the skinny shithead, but he'd forgotten more about running an MC than the younger man would ever know, and he was a crack shot with that rifle of his as well.

He was Logan's first pick for second in command, but politics had gotten in the way of that.

"Cody's waiting for you upstairs," Murph muttered from around his cigarette.

"Where's upstairs?"

"Two floors up. I hope you like walking up stairs."

As it turned out, he didn't, but crying over spilled milk wouldn't change anything. Still, as he began the rickety ascent, he made a mental note to find a clinic that provided people with tetanus boosters just in case.

When he reached the third floor, about a dozen men wearing the GAMC's colors were already setting beds up in the open space. They'd taken one of the walls down to join two apartments and create one shared space where they could work from. It was a far cry from the bar they'd operated from in South Boston. Still, that would come and one day, they would all watch Patriots games while drinking copious amounts of Irish whiskey in a bar they owned in Vegas.

Cody stood from his seat, where he'd been eating a sandwich purchased from a nearby deli, and moved to where Logan stood.

"You got here about a day early," the man commented as he wiped his hands clean on a cheap napkin. "We'd have had all this shit looking a little more presentable by then."

"Well..." He shrugged and ran his fingers through his short blond hair. "How much work would it take to make this place even halfway livable?"

"Too much. And the whole building is earmarked for demolition, so it was always purely temporary but it's the only location we could find on short notice. Most of the other gangs in the city are well-entrenched and if we were to push into their business before we're ready, we would start a conflict with them I had a feeling you would want to avoid until we're ready for it. Still, there are premises in the city that would be a better base for our little endeavor if you're interested in talking about them."

Logan sat on a handy overturned crate and studied the activity in progress. Most of the crew who had been brought over were either focused on the attempt to create a decent base from the dilapidated structure—and a few basic repairs that would accomplish this—or simply ignored the chaos while they set up the electronics they would need going forward. GAMC had brought specialists in who knew how to tweak and upgrade the hardware they needed for Wi-Fi and other connections in the craziest places and while he didn't understand it as a concept, it sure as hell worked.

The best part was that it would be easy to move once they were out of the location that even the slumlords of Vegas couldn't turn a profit on.

"I still don't understand why my dad put you in charge of this venture instead of me," Cody commented as he sat on a dilapidated chair and returned to his sandwich. "It might have looked a little like nepotism, sure, but it's not like I couldn't run an expansion."

"He's hedging his bets," Logan replied. "He wants you here so you can get the experience to run shit later on but if it fails, he doesn't want you to be remembered for it. If all goes to the crapper, I'm the one who is killed or gets a nice long prison sentence."

Of course, the whole venture had been Logan's idea in the first place. To put someone else in charge would have been the pinnacle of idiocy, given that he was the one with the connections and was also who would make the gun and drug sales in the area. But excuses needed to be made and while his logic was sound, he was in this to prove himself as well.

"So, tell me about these other properties we can move to," he continued and frowned as he tried not to look too closely at their surroundings. "Any more time in this dump and I'll have to Google whether you can contract tetanus from inhaling dust."

"The one that caught my eye particularly was a little strip mall near Sam's Town on the East Side." Cody pulled some pictures up that had clearly been taken from Google Maps. "From what I've been able to find out, it looks like the local Cosa Nostra and the Thirteens avoid it for some reason. Even the cops give them a wide berth."

That generally meant it was a good idea to stay away from the people involved, but he wanted to see why he thought it had the best potential as a headquarters for them.

"Who owns it?"

"It's a repair shop. Honestly, the owners are a couple of vets and they're armed, so maybe that's why the cops don't want to get involved. Next thing you know, someone gets a warning shot in the back and everyone involved goes on involuntary paid leave while the media throws a hissy fit. That said, it seems like a location ripe for protection, and given that most of the premises is still empty, we could double it up."

It wasn't a terrible idea, of course, and it was the kind of concept he would prefer to be involved in. Despite this, if the local criminal gangs avoided the group, he wanted to know why. It was possible that his second was hiding something from him for whatever reason, so there was no point in making any assumptions.

"Well, take three of our best with you to give the asshole the good news."

"Good news?"

"Yeah. That we'll improve his income by renting his unused space and that we'll provide him with the protection he is so sorely lacking."

CHAPTER THREE

"Relax," Taylor told Niki, who squirmed continually in her seat and glanced either in the passenger mirror or over her shoulder. "You wanted time out of the strip mall and this is it. Sit back and enjoy it, for crying out loud."

"Have you forgotten why we're in that goddammed dump in the first place?" He scowled at her and she shrugged. "Safety in numbers had something to do with it, as I recall."

"And better defense possibilities."

"Right. It only drives my point home. Here we are, out on our lonesome, while the rest of the team—"

"They waved us off with as much enthusiasm as Disney put into Aladdin's homecoming. Face it, they couldn't wait for us to get out of there. I think if we'd delayed any longer, they'd have got down on their knees and begged me to carry you out."

"That," she said sharply, "was plain mean." Still, it drew a glimmer of a smile which he decided to take as a good sign. "But you get my point. I feel like we're driving around with our tails in the wind."

"First," Desk interjected, "you're technically driving somewhere, not around. Second, your tails are covered. I am monitoring you and there is no sign that anyone has chosen to follow you—although I cannot comment on why that might be the case given their tenacity and determination to watch your every move. Better still, the route I added to the GPS is one that avoids street cams so anyone who might be inclined to follow you digitally will have lost you a couple of blocks away from the strip mall. Not only that, but I've hacked the cameras in the venue as well."

"Fair enough," Niki responded begrudgingly and peered out the window. "But you can't honestly tell me this is a safe neighborhood."

"Maybe not," Taylor agreed and suppressed a sigh. "But it's a safe-for-us neighborhood because no one will know who we are. We can relax and have a few beers and a meal, and the worst we might encounter is a couple of rough types who should know better."

"So where are we going?"

"Right here." He swung into a large parking lot that was perhaps half-full.

Niki frowned as she studied the somewhat shabby building emblazoned with *Back Door Bar* over the closed and barred front door. "It's closed."

"Nope." Taylor pressed the window button and the insistent thud of heavy metal swept over them. "It's the Back Door Bar."

"I don't get it. Why use the back door when there's a perfectly good front door?"

"I believe it's biker terminology," Desk explained. "The name is a gimmick, basically. Back door is a term that refers to the rider at the rear of the pack according to my research, usually the most experienced of the group."

"Well, shit." Niki shook her head as a group of riders roared past them and around the corner of the building. "But as long as the beer is good and food is decent, I won't complain."

"That's my girl," Taylor quipped and ignored her scowl as he parked and stepped out of the truck. He'd half-expected her to refuse and decided to not waste time but get her inside with a beer in her hand.

The interior was about as dim and rough-looking as a dive bar could be but even through the smoky haze and the low lighting, it was very evident that it was clean and well-maintained. They found a table at the window and a server appeared almost immediately. His long hair had been untidily braided and he was dressed in black jeans with a matching denim vest emblazoned with various patches. The rolled sleeves of the shirt he wore beneath the vest revealed a multitude of tattoos that would require considerably more lighting to identify the details.

"Oh yeah," Niki murmured, an edge of genuine approval in her tone. "Rough and rowdy—my kind of place."

"I suppose it's too much to ask you to behave?" Taylor asked with a broad grin.

"Who knows? I won't start anything, but I sure as shit won't complain if someone else does."

The server laughed, took their order, and placed a

menu on the table before he wove through the tightly packed tables toward the bar.

There wasn't much of a selection to choose from, but a glance at the other tables assured them that while variety might be lacking, portions and appeal certainly were not. If the enthusiasm with which the patrons attacked their meals was any indication, the food would easily pass the taste test too.

When their beers arrived—chilled and opened in front of them—they both ordered mixed grill with all the trimmings and Taylor was relieved to see that Niki had already begun to relax a little. With any luck, they might see the evening through without any shenanigans, although he decided to keep an open mind. A good old-fashioned humdinger with the right people might add considerable fun.

Almost as if he'd conjured their arrival, the door was thrust open and a group of five bikers stepped in to shouts of welcome that indicated they were both popular and regular patrons. Their jeans and leathers were scuffed, but the overall impression lent them a hard-core edge that spoke toughness and arrogance.

Niki grimaced at the way they swaggered through the crowd greeting everyone and plainly enjoying the attention. A table was soon cleared for them—the one directly beside her and Taylor, which turned her grimace to a scowl —and she rolled her eyes as they shared a few lewd jokes with the server while they ordered.

"Bikers," she muttered acerbically but he made no response. It seemed wiser to finish his meal as quickly as possible.

Almost half an hour passed uneventfully and he felt almost hopeful that the seemingly inevitable clash might be averted. Niki had carefully avoided even looking at their neighbors and they finished their meal and he signaled the server for another two beers.

An odd lull settled in as the kid placed the drinks on the table and opened them before he hurried away with a slightly nervous glance at Taylor.

"So, sweetheart, what's your ride?" The question carried despite the loud background music, and Niki frowned and took a swig of her beer before she turned her head slightly to look at the greasy-haired individual who seemed to be the leader of the group.

"Seriously?" she asked waspishly. "That's your line?"

"Yeah. It's not a hard question, honey. A girl like you looks like she likes it hard and rough."

"Maybe so and maybe not," she snapped. "But it has fuck all to do with you what I ride and how."

"Hey now, missy," one of his friends interjected with a smirk. "There's no call to get all uppity. You clearly don't know who you're messing with here. Dwayne's a main man and you don't want to get on the wrong side of him."

"That's beside the point. I don't give a rat's ass who he is."

Dwayne stood, his expression set in a scowl. "One ride with me and I guarantee you'll change your tune," he boasted and before she could respond, he snaked his hand out, grasped her upper arm, and hauled her out of her seat.

"Let go of me, bozo," she said with ominous calm but he missed the warning in her tone and simply leered at her. She yanked her arm free and before he could react, delivered a solid right hook that caught him squarely on the chin.

The blow was backed by all the pent frustration of the past few weeks and Taylor grinned as the biker staggered, entirely unprepared for the strike, and managed to upend the table as he flailed to regain his balance. A chorus of curses and protests followed from his friends, none of whom bothered to brush the spilled drinks and food from their clothing before they surged forward.

"Well," Taylor said laconically as he slid from his seat. "I guess that's my cue."

"Bozo's down for the moment," Niki responded with evil glee. "That leaves two each."

The other patrons scrambled hastily away from their tables and dragged them aside while they yelled encouragement to the home side. At the bar, the bartender and the server simply leaned on the counter to watch, seemingly unconcerned by the brawl.

Niki was the target of the four men who launched a combined attack but Taylor stepped in, grasped two of them by the back of the neck, and pounded their heads together with a satisfying crunch.

The third man reached her a moment later and she uttered a battle cry fit to curdle the blood and drove her knee into his crotch before he could block. He yelled in pain and as he doubled over, she linked her hands behind his head, stepped forward, and raised her other knee as she yanked his head down to meet it.

"You bitch," his friend bellowed as he plowed into her and knocked her off her feet. She landed with sufficient force to knock the breath out of her but rolled instinctively as he tried to straddle her.

Behind her, Dwayne had extricated himself from the furniture and showed signs of joining the melee, but Taylor stepped into his path.

"Shit," the man said as his gaze traveled upward to measure the full height of him. "What in God's name did they feed you growing up?" he asked as he threw a series of punches almost reflexively

"I'm fucked if I know," Taylor responded cheerfully and blocked the attack with relative ease.

His opponent's eyes narrowed and he whistled shrilly. "Some help here, boys," he bellowed, and three men stepped out of the crowd to join him.

"What's the matter, Dwayne? First, a girl floors you and now, you need your friends to defend you?"

"Fuck you, asshole."

"That's my job," Niki yelled as she rolled the other way to evade her attacker. "Get off me, you ball-brained asswipe." She raked her nails down his face and when he flinched, followed the girlish action with a hard punch to the side of his head. His teeth snapped as he jerked with the force of it and she used the opportunity to straddle his chest, grasp his ears, and thunk his head on the wooden floorboards a few times. In moments, the man was out cold.

Taylor studied his four opponents quickly. Dwayne seemed a little unsteady on his feet thanks to Niki's solid blow and his encounter with the furniture. The others were three sheets to the wind—the reason for their bravado, no doubt—and while they bristled with both arrogance and hostility, he doubted that they had what it took to deliver any significant damage.

"So what'll it be, boys?" he asked with a grin. "One at a time or a good old gangbang? I don't mind if you think you'll have a better chance as a group." He gestured at himself. "It's understandable if you don't feel up to taking this on man to man."

With a belligerent growl, one of the three newcomers lunged toward him, goaded into the attack as Taylor had hoped would happen. He sidestepped as the man reached him and as he passed, turned and delivered a solid kick to his rear end that launched him into the stacked furniture.

The second man thought to make the most of what he assumed was his distraction but he spun, caught hold of the fist that powered toward him, and continued his turn to swing his opponent after his cohort. At the same time, he snatched the third by the collar, hauled him close, and lifted him so his feet flailed a few inches from the floor.

"You're a drunk fool," he said curtly and flung him aside. Unfortunately, the man careened across several tables, and plates, drinks, and food slid in all directions and caused a loud chorus of protests from those bystanders unlucky enough to be in their path.

He turned his attention to Dwayne, who gaped at him with an expression that seemed to veer between fury and disbelief.

"Your turn," Taylor said and fixed him with a hard look.

"Nuh-uh. My turn." Niki stepped up beside him. "I need to finish what I started."

Before either man could argue, she powered her fist into Dwayne's solar plexus and he gasped painfully for breath as he folded. "Stupid-ass biker punk," she snapped as her other fist drove into his nose with all the force she could muster. He sagged to his knees, then toppled onto his side with an odd gurgling sound. "I suggest someone makes sure he doesn't choke," she said loudly and the bartender hurried forward.

He cast her a belligerent look which she ignored as she downed half her beer.

"Are you done?" Taylor asked.

"Yeah, I'm done," she responded as the wail of sirens overrode the music.

"It sounds like someone called the cops."

"Yeah," she agreed after another sip. "But only after the home team went down. I guess they don't play nice unless they win."

A moment later, two uniformed officers walked in and paused to survey the chaos. Dwayne, by this time, had been eased into a seated position and propped up by a chair, four men were still unconscious, and the three Taylor had hurled into the furniture sat around a broken table.

"It's time to talk to the nice men in uniform," he said with a smirk, took her beer, and placed the bottle on the table.

"Hey, I didn't finish it."

"Pretend you did. I think we overstayed our welcome." He slung his arm around her shoulder and guided her to the counter where the officers were in discussion with the bartender. "Here," he said, and placed a few notes on the counter. "This is for our share of the damage. Those idiots started it so I sure as shit won't pay for their portion."

"That's not—"

"You're Niki Banks, right?" one of the officers asked and cut the other man's protest off.

"Yeah," she said reluctantly, not sure where this was going.

"I never thought I'd see an FBI agent in a biker brawl."

"You know what? Neither did I. The strangest shit happens when you're incognito."

"FBI?" The bartender had paled noticeably. "Were you… uh, working a case?"

"I can't answer that," Niki responded, her expression deadpan. "But you might want to pay a little more attention to the people who frequent your establishment." She turned to the officer. "Can we go now?"

"Sure, if your friend is right and the others started this." He glanced at the bartender who nodded enthusiastically.

Taylor guided her out the door before she could respond and was relieved when she made no effort to speak. They reached the truck and scrambled in and as Niki closed the door, she gave up all attempts to restrain her laughter.

"You lied to a police officer," he said calmly, which set her off again.

"No, I didn't," she responded finally as she wiped her eyes. "I merely let him think what he already believed—and it worked, didn't it?

"Yeah, this time." He laughed as he started the engine and eased out of the lot. "You're impossible, you know that?"

"And you know exactly how to show a girl a good time," she retorted cheekily. "We make a damn fine team."

"Say what you want about these criminal masterminds but they do know how to create a decent security setup," Vickie muttered and rubbed her chin in irritation.

"There is a good reason for that, of course. They face the very real prospect that literal assassins might wander in so it is absolutely in their best interests to be at the cutting edge of the security game."

Desk did have a point there. Of course, so far, the McFadden and Banks team had only managed to stick around this long because Taylor happened to be equally as paranoid as everyone else and far more competent besides.

"Still, if you look at these plans Marino sent, you have to think this boss guy believed that someone would target him. And for all we know, he might have been in the middle of a bickering fit with another mafia boss, and those guys are known for settling their grievances with hitmen."

"Well, his paranoia was justified. Someone did target him," Desk pointed out. "Merely not the person he expected. And when it comes down to it, there isn't much in the world that can save you from either an infestation of cryptids or an angry Taylor McFadden powering a couple of tons of battle armor."

Both were good points and Vickie wondered if the old don had any inkling whatsoever of what had awaited him. Probably not, she decided and leaned a little closer to the screen as she called up the upgrades that were being installed on top of what was already functional on the property. Marino had made certain promises and given how much she trusted the guy—which was to say not at all—she would make damn sure that she verified even the smallest details.

"I don't suppose it's important to note that we have had a greater number of people watching the strip mall over the past few days?" the AI asked.

"We've had people from agencies spread across all the letters of the alphabet watching us these days. I shit you not. I picked up on people from the Office of Naval Intelligence who tried to set taps up around our building, for fuck's sake. I thought they were only supposed to focus on naval situations, and we could not be farther from the ocean if we tried."

"Maybe ONI is trying to determine if our usage of a combat AI could be considered a threat to their naval forces."

"Or they're merely greedy for the AI tech themselves." The hacker called the scans up and tilted her head. "I'm not sure who those guys are, though. We might have to extend our line of worry to all the independent parties out there that have a hard-on for you and Nessie. It's about time we move you guys out of the country."

"Which brings up the question of how soon we will be able to set up the servers in our new abode," Desk agreed. "We do need to push our move to as soon as possible."

"We might need to do a little more than that." The hacker rubbed her temples. "We need something to distract all these assholes around here—some kind of big contract that'll distract everyone so you and I can get on with our prep work."

"It might interest you to know that Taylor has already

been in contact with Marino and Gallo and is using them to push through all the red tape required. We have to get the IT aspect resolved as quickly as possible so we can move the moment we get the approval."

Vickie continued to study the teams that seemed to be working around the clock to keep an eye on McFadden and Banks. It was one thing if they only tried to keep tabs, but this had begun to border on the excessive. She wouldn't push for them to leave since that in itself would be a little suspicious, but there was the question of whether or not they realized that other people were doing the same thing at the same time. Efficiency did not seem to be the motto of any of these agencies.

"I don't suppose we can tap into their intelligence reports and see if they're keeping track of all the different people who are spying on us?" Vickie was already working on calling up her backdoor into the FBI's servers. "That way, we don't need to do any of the work since they're already on it for us, right?"

"Do you trust them to provide us with reliable intel?"

"Not really, but they'll know what the other agencies are doing and if there are independent parties at play, the chances are they'll start their own investigation. It makes sense that if they are doing the work anyway, we might as well take advantage of it, right?"

"It's a solid idea and worth the attempt. I'll get to work on that."

The hacker switched screens as Desk took over delving into the FBI servers. She would be able to do it much faster and with less chance of getting caught.

"I'll see what I can do about getting us work that'll get all the assholes off our backs," Vickie muttered.

"Already done."

"Right. Then I'll...uh, get caught up on my Netflix queue then."

"I've already done that as well."

"You can't watch something for me, Desk. That's not how it works."

"What if I could beam everything directly into your head? It would be more efficient."

"And also impossible with current technology. Besides, it would probably give me a stroke or something. Or... whatever happens to people when they get a sensory overload."

"Seizures?"

"Yeah, that."

"I could have medical professionals on the way when it happens to mitigate any possible medical problems that would result."

"But again, it's not possible."

"Not with our current technology."

"Okay, it's a little creepy and I'm totally here for that. Do they...are they working on brain chips that allow you to stream information directly to the brain?"

"Unfortunately not."

"Maybe I should start working on that." Vickie folded her arms. "I'd need to come up with a name for it."

"You might want to reverse the order of priorities there."

"That's not how creativity works. You have the idea for

the product and the name, then you start work on the product itself."

Desk paused for a moment. "I am fairly certain that is not how it works."

"Probably, but who gives a shit?"

CHAPTER FOUR

Sam Jackson shifted in his seat and stared out the window at what was, to him, an entirely alien environment. It was somewhat humbling for a man whose brilliance had earned him the moniker "the fixer"—one now so entrenched that most people who knew him well simply called him Fix—to encounter something that left him with a distinctly uncomfortable feeling of being out of his depth.

That sensation was strong enough that a part of him was relieved that when they had said they didn't need an escort on this kind of assessment, the assertion had been taken with a quick nod and a wink and the escort had been assigned regardless.

The fact that they had a troop of American soldiers to accompany them to what they were told was the Middle Eastern base wouldn't be the cause of any tensions—or so they had been assured. Sam decided to take that with a grain of salt.

"This must be a treat for you," he told the young-looking Asian kid seated across from him in the Hammerhead. "All that chatter about the Zoo in your free time and now you'll see it up close."

"Not too up close, we hope," Elke interrupted before Chen could answer.

The youngest of the trio looked up from his phone and removed his earbuds. "Shit, did you guys say something?"

"I merely said this must be a treat for you, getting so close to the Zoo."

Chen nodded and peered out the small windows of the vehicle. "Yeah, it's a sweet treat. Not anything I would be able to film and put up on my ZooTube channel or anything, though."

"Well, you can at least see the jungle out the window there."

"So can everyone. This is the kind of view all the news cameras get when they do a report on the Zoo although sometimes, they try to put someone in a uniform in front of the camera to talk about it so there's a little more legitimacy. Being up close and personal to it is interesting but not the kind of footage my viewers will be interested in. I'll do a short vid when we get back to the base to share my experiences."

Sam nodded. He'd never been much for the whole ZooTube craze but it was good to encourage Chen in his hobbies, especially since they made him far more efficient in his work with ENSOL. His skills in 3D engineering had been what had put the company on the map, after all. His new software allowed for more efficient distribution of prefab and was likely the reason why people thought they were the right people to call to help with their construction of Wall Two.

He'd seen some of the vids too. What got the most viewers was when the kid put in the physics design and development to make 3D replicas of Zoo monsters to move the way they did in real life. These made his short story vids about the stories of what was happening in the Zoo uncanny in their realism.

With all that said, it was a little beyond his realm of expertise but it was always a good thing to encourage others in their passions.

"How long until we reach the wall?" Elke asked the driver of the Hammerhead.

"Fifteen minutes, Miss Muntz," the soldier answered without looking back. Of course, they were all used to conversing over the commlinks their suits shared, but it was still something that took a little getting used to for the three engineers and co-owners of ENSOL International.

None of the engineering team had been given real combat suits. The lighter suits allocated to them had some power functions but were relatively simple in their design, although the military had subjected them to fairly rigorous training in their models over the past few days.

"What were you working on when you were putting the suit on, Fix?" Elke asked. "From what I could tell, they handed the suits to us in decent condition, right?"

"Sure, but it doesn't mean everything was as good as it could be, which is a great shame. The hydraulics on these were outdated three years ago. All I did was put in some upgrades that'll make them a little easier to move."

"I don't mind a little extra exercise." She grinned at him and he could see that Chen was laughing a little too.

"I guess it's my fault that I'm surrounded by athletes." Sam shook his head and shifted a little in the suit when the Hammerhead began to slow.

"You should join us in our athletic pursuits one of these days," the other man commented. "We want to run the half-marathon in Berlin in July if you want to train with us."

"Thirty minutes a day on my treadmill while listening to my podcasts every day is enough exercise for me, thanks." He shook his head.

"Every day?" Elke raised an eyebrow. "Seriously?"

"Okay...five times a week. Four if I'm feeling lazy. That's enough to keep me healthy."

"Sure. But you don't get to complain about a little extra exercise later on."

"No, that's why I put in the effort to fix the suit. But no, you keep walking around in that bullshit serviced by Neanderthals. See if I help you fix it."

Both were laughing again when the Hammerhead came to a halt. He couldn't help the fact that he could feel a clunk in the wheels. The breaks were a little worn but he now realized that almost everything in the military was on the ragged edge of functional, especially this far from civilization. It did beg the question of how many people were dying because their equipment was absolute shit.

They climbed out of the vehicle. Sam was the last of his team to exit and he stopped the moment his boots met the sand. His eyes widened when he realized that the jungle was considerably closer than he imagined it would be.

"Holy shit," he whispered.

"Yeah," Chen agreed and cleared his throat. "That's…uh, much closer than I ever wanted to be to the Zoo."

"I thought you were one of the fanboys," Elke responded although she sounded like she wanted to be anywhere but this close to the jungle ahead of them.

"Sure, I'm a fan of the concept of an alien jungle. It doesn't mean I want to be close enough that one of the cryptids can have a taste."

"Cryptids?" Sam asked.

"Yeah, that's the official term. It seems the higher-ups think that calling them monsters is a little too aggressive or something."

"That's dumb."

"Hell, cryptid sounds much cooler so you won't hear me complaining."

Still, the presence of the jungle was not something Fix had ever thought about when they considered taking the work offered to them. It was easily their most profitable contract since they'd founded the company and there he was in full view of an alien jungle, already behind the wall they were supposed to complete.

"This is why you need an escort," one of the soldiers noted, drew the assault rifle he carried on his back, and aimed it at the sections where they could see dozens of teams on the ground, working to burn the Zoo away where it had crept across a wide section of the desert buffer between it and the wall. "Besides, that's where your camp might be if you need to work on this section in the future and I don't need to tell you that it's not exactly the most secure of locations."

Talk about understatement, Fix thought waspishly.

Pressed against the wall was a small building, still intact but with no signs of any other protection. He tried not to think about the fact that the Japanese base, according to Franklin, had recently been overrun and mop-up operations were still underway. By all accounts, that had been what some called a model base, completely to spec and with additional armaments that were reputedly top-of-the-line. It left the lingering question as to what would happen to the other bases that didn't meet the same high standards.

"I'm very sure we could do all of our work from home." Fix nodded firmly. "They managed to do that in the early 2020s, right? We could simply do all this from far, far away."

"I'll be honest with you, I agree," the soldier stated. "This is a war zone and bringing civilians into the middle of it is asking for serious trouble. No offense."

"What's your name, soldier?" Elke asked.

"Corporal Ewan Donnelly."

She nodded and didn't say anything more than that. It was an odd interaction, but Sam knew she would make notes about who to thank. She was a thoughtful woman like that, although people tended to think she was a little severe. Mostly because of the accent, he assumed, but she was the sweetest person and the most thoughtful.

Although she could be severe too. He didn't like talking about the time when he accidentally took her food from the fridge even though it had been clearly marked. In his defense, he hadn't had any coffee at all that day but it took her weeks to forgive him for the slight.

"We have movement to the northeast," one of the soldiers said sharply and it was impressive to see how quickly the team reacted to the warning. They suddenly went from relaxed and joking into bristling and ready for a fight and moved immediately between whatever movement there was and the engineers.

"For shit's sake." Donnelly growled his frustration. "Ground Team Bravo-Niner, this is Echo team. We have a swarm of locusts breaking from the tree line and heading our way. We need active support."

"Roger that, Echo team. We have a read on the swarm but I don't think we'll get to you in time. You'd better get ready for action over there. Good luck."

It wasn't the words they wanted to hear, although Sam couldn't see the swarm they were talking about. Maybe it was farther away than their tone indicated and they were trying to be extra safe with the civilians around.

All such thoughts were put aside when he realized that he could almost feel the beating of wings in the air. They weren't flying too high or they would have seen the creatures already, but a chill rushed through his body as the massive assault rifles the soldiers carried suddenly started firing.

He jerked his hand instinctively to draw the sidearm they had all been outfitted with, even though he hadn't so much as gone to a gun range in his entire life. Fix always liked to think of himself as a pacifist, but no instinct in his body told him that he couldn't defend himself against the damn aliens. It truly was weird how that worked out.

The soldier in the single heavy suit among them stepped out in front and the miniguns mounted on his shoulder kicked into life as the first of the cryptids surged into view and tried to fly over the solid line of armor suits in front of them. The miniguns were likely set to target anything that tried to get up and over the firing line held by the other six men, and it certainly looked like it did the most damage.

They had glimpses and images of the insane creatures that somehow looked familiar and yet so very, very alien. He could see that Elke and Chen also had their sidearms drawn, although they seemed as uncomfortable carrying the weapons as he was.

One of the men stumbled back with a shout and Sam gaped when he realized that one of the creatures had practically tackled him and now used its mandibles to try to pry his armor open. Another one of the creatures pushed through the hole in the line, its wings still buzzing like it was looking for something to latch onto as well.

He raised his pistol although he hadn't made a conscious effort to do so, and the reticle appeared on his HUD to ready him for a fight he did not want.

Still, as he looked down the sights, he realized that his finger worked the trigger reflexively to fire at the monster and try to kill it.

It blew to pieces, but not from his pistol. The heavy suit executed a slow turn and the miniguns on the shoulder made short work of the mutant that had broken through.

The man on the ground had drawn his sidearm and continued to scream but more aggressively as he punched hole after hole into the cryptid that attempted to rip through his armor.

"Lopey, are you good?" Donnelly shouted when the sound of gunfire began to dissipate, although more could be heard ahead, likely from the other team that had come to assist.

"It's Lopez, dumbass!" He pushed from the ground and kicked the corpse away. "And yeah. The suit's gonna need time in the repair shop, though."

The corporal seemed happy with that assessment, checked the group, and made sure they were all accounted for before he looked at Sam.

He realized that he continued to pull the trigger of his pistol, even though it was already empty.

"Is everyone okay here?" Donnelly asked as he approached them.

"Yeah," he answered and hated the slight tremor in his voice. "I've...never shot anything before."

The soldier looked at the corpses that had broken through their line and shrugged. "I'm fairly sure you still haven't, Mr. Jackson, but there's no time to focus on that. Let's get you people to the wall. Hopefully, they won't be as interested if there's a little prefab between you and them."

Of course, the bastards wanted him in front of them again. He'd repeated the report time and time again since Franklin had sent it. Corey had the damn document committed to memory by this point, but the Pentagon and the people who signed the checks wanted to hear it repeatedly and to dissect and cherry-pick from what the US base commander had to say.

They all hoped to avoid the inevitable outcome that they had to spend more money on their operations in and around the Zoo if they wanted to continue to profit from the jungle.

The staff sergeant approached and cleared his throat softly and Corey stood from his seat. He straightened his uniform as he was led to the debriefing chamber.

A handful of generals and their aides waited inside, as well as a few senators and congressmen. None of them were familiar but they looked about the same as everyone else. Old men, grown fat from the years without fighting, tried to stare him down as he took his seat in front of the committee.

"State your name for the record," the general who led the session instructed.

Corey leaned forward into the microphone in front of him. "Captain Corey Davids of the United States Marine Corps."

"Thank you, Captain," one of the men not in uniform answered. "As you're aware, we are not a committee deciding whether we're spending too much money on the Zoo."

He tried not to show his surprise as he studied his notes again. The old man was right. They weren't. This was what they called a Zoo 'Thinktank.' He'd met with so many committees over the past week that they had begun to blur together.

"No, sir," he answered and cleared his throat.

"We are well-briefed on the contents of the report you carry with you," the man continued and adjusted his glasses. "Sent by Commandant Franklin, the commander in charge of our base close to the Zoo, regarding his efforts to contain an incursion into the base operated by the Japanese."

"That's correct, sir."

The group exchanged a quick, uncomfortable glance before they inspected their notes again. He knew what they were all worried about. The Zoo had been a massive cash cow for years now, and no one wanted to be responsible for interrupting the flow, no matter what the reason. But they all knew it had to be done anyway, so it was a matter of whose shoulders would carry the blame.

"From what I can see in the reports," one of the four-star generals noted, "it was all down to human error on the Japanese base. Looking beyond that is the kind of erratic and overreaching behavior we are here to make sure won't happen."

"Franklin's stance on the matter is very clear," an admiral noted and ignored a pointed look from the general. "What we're seeing from the Zoo is the kind of behavior that needs to be addressed before it spreads out of control."

"With all respect to the man, he's overreacting. I'm sure that in a few months when nothing comes of this mess, he'll be more than willing to reassess the suggestions laid out in his report."

Corey tried not to let his annoyance show on his face. None of them were addressing him, which meant he had no say in the matter. The point remained that Franklin was not a man given to flights of fancy and if he stated that action was needed from the Pentagon, it was certainly the right thing to do.

The first man nodded and returned his attention to him where he was seated silently in the center of the room.

"We're here to ask for your opinion, Captain," he said. "Your record says you were one of the most prolific operatives in the Zoo until your unfortunate injury."

Corey moved his hand toward his shoulder at the mention of the injury before he jerked it away. "Thirty-six trips in, sir."

"A respectable number, one that makes us believe you know what you're talking about. What do you think about Commandant Franklin's assessment of the situation?"

It was the first time anyone had asked his opinion on the matter, and his response was one he'd been crafting in his head for a while. He was assigned to desk work after his injury because he was deemed psychologically unfit for active duty. Basically, people told him that if he went back in, he would break.

It was not the kindest thing for the ego and it had taken him more than a few months to get over it and bury his nose in the paperwork that kept the military machine running.

Despite the negative side, it paid better and had the bright side of not wondering what time he would come home every night.

Corey cleared his throat and leaned forward, suddenly very aware that all eyes in the room were locked on him. "Commandant Franklin has overseen one of the largest upticks in profit from our Zoo ventures so far. I've worked under him and do not think he's the type to overreact to any situation."

The general shook his head in disagreement but the admiral interjected before he could speak.

"I've heard there's a group of independent scientists who are compiling a fairly damning series of documents to prove that the Zoo is far more dangerous than we have thus far been led to believe."

"Who are they?" the first man asked.

"I've presented their names and findings to the committee already."

"Academics." The general all but spat the word. "None of whom have very much experience in the Zoo or even the Sahara. We can't commit to massive changes in our policies in the area over irrelevant hype. We have no evidence to support any changes to our current policies in the area. Our political and economic interests are engaged to the point where we need real evidence regarding this... this global threat presented before we can pull out or insist on its destruction."

"On that we can agree," the first man—a politician —stated.

Corey tried to bite back any response he had to the issue. As it turned out, nothing had changed. They were still too afraid to commit to anything that would see their political donors lose a cent in profits from the region.

But it wasn't his place to tell them what to do. They had been more understanding than most of the committees in that they'd allowed him to voice his opinion on the matter.

The politician raised a hand before the other two could continue their disagreements. "Thank you, Captain Davis. We appreciate you presenting the report and your opinion."

That was his invitation to leave and Corey rose to his feet and adjusted his uniform. He had three other committees to meet with that day and he had a feeling they would all have the same arguments and the same lack of results.

It was weird to miss the Zoo at this point, but it was very possible that he would break in Washington faster than he would in the Zoo.

CHAPTER FIVE

Three pelts wasn't a bad start to the day. Mashoul had been a little worried that they would have difficulty meeting their quota, but if they maintained this rate, there would be bonuses for all the men involved, himself included.

The sounds of gunshots still rang through the jungle and he motioned the men forward.

"Two men per carcass," he snapped. "Get those pelts off quickly. The rest of you, stay on your guard! The goddammed jungle has ears and they'll attack us soon. I don't want anything to interfere with us getting those pelts."

They jumped into action without so much as a pause and worked two men per carcass to peel the skins off quickly. None of them wanted to be caught out in the open when the rest of the Zoo heard the gunfire.

Mashoul pulled half his suit away, crouched beside one of the corpses, and drew a knife to work at the pelt with his very practiced hands. He'd been a poacher in the past, working in the savannah when that was where most of the money had come from, but a bright new source of income had sprung out of the desert. Many of the freelancers who had the same ideas he had were dead now, but he'd learned to adapt to the jungle faster than the others. It was the only reason why he was still alive while they weren't.

"Shit!"

He snapped his hand away from the dead panther and looked at his bare arm. A spot of blood appeared and a little swelling and he slapped his hand over what felt like a mosquito bite, although he couldn't see the little bugger anywhere.

Not that it was a huge surprise given that without his HUD, the darkness of the jungle made it difficult to see more than three or four meters away.

"Are the mozzies giving you trouble too?" one of his men asked, who had also pulled half his suit off. "You know, you have to consider the larger monsters while you walk around in armor but you forget there are the little bastards all around us too."

"You got bit?"

"A couple of times. I've seen more than my share of them, though. I simply shrug and keep on working."

Mashoul did exactly that. Worrying about tiny insects didn't touch his mind while he was in his suit but they weren't that uncommon in the Zoo. He shook his head and worked a little faster. Mozzies, as he called them, creeped him out, and he didn't want to deal with any more bites.

The pelts were pulled off and sealed in airtight bags before being stored in a cool container that one of the larger suits carried.

"Come on!" he shouted and pulled his suit on. "There is

no time for delays. We keep hunting until we meet our quota."

The troop moved quickly, including those Badawi had sent. The guys were tough bastards in their own right and if all went well, he looked forward to making more money with them added to his team.

Maybe they could be tempted to leave Badawi and Khaled in favor of more profitable work in the Zoo.

There were still many bases that needed to be visited. Sam rubbed his eyes gently as the Hammerhead began to move again after refueling.

The tour was decidedly less adventurous after that first surprising encounter in the US sector and he was grateful for the lack of activity. They could focus on what they did best and from the looks of things, work on Wall Two had progressed faster in the northern sectors, which meant there were fewer Zoo incursions in the region.

Of course, the Russians only a little farther south had been overrun—before they'd seen the necessity of a strong wall—and the Japanese as well, despite their base being one of the strongest. It left one with the nagging question as to the efficacy of the existing system, although it was certainly far better than no wall at all.

"Where are we going next?" Sam asked.

Chen checked his notes. "We're coming into the Middle East Sector."

"Middle East?" Elke asked and narrowed her eyes. "They aren't mixed with the Sahara Coalition?"

After another quick check, the youngest of their group shook his head. "The Sahara Coalition consists of representatives from Egypt, Algeria, Chad, Libya, Mali, Mauritania, Morocco, Niger, Sudan, Western Sahara, and Tunisia —I guess the countries that are within the desert itself or contain some part of it. All the other Middle Eastern countries are part of the sector we're entering now, with the exception of Israel since they share a sector with France and India. The Middle Eastern group has a different approach, though, and has set up a string of bases every three miles along the wall, each one responsible to not only build the wall but to maintain it too. They've done some surprisingly good work."

He handed his tablet to Fix for inspection, but he trusted the kid's assessment of the situation. The walls were mostly built of the same prefab that was being brought in by the ton to build the bases too, which meant he would know a thing or two about how they were constructed.

"You don't have any suggestions for how they might be able to do better?" Elke asked. "They might think we're not worth the money they're spending on our consultancy if we think they're doing a good enough job."

"Good enough, sure, but there's always room for improvement. If we were to make any suggestions, I might say that their engineering staff failed to account for the guns they're putting on the top."

"No, they have all the reinforcement they need to support the weight," Sam disagreed.

"Sure, for the weight of the guns themselves, but what about the recoil from when they're fired?" Chen shook his head. "Even if they're fired under free-recoil conditions, I'd give them only...four, maybe five dozen shots before it starts to strain the foundations. They'll need to reinforce along the lines, maybe lay out test shots for us to see where the stress might come from. And that's not taking into account the additional vibration caused by firing the weapons."

"That's about worth our contract money." Elke patted Chen on the shoulder. "You're a genius, you know that?"

"Would it be a little too cliche to say that my parents never thought so? They wanted me to be a doctor."

"A little."

Sam climbed out of the Hammerhead first as soon as it stopped at what looked like a smaller but more organized base than he had expected. It looked fairly new too, with a few sections still being built. Thankfully, they weren't greeted with the sight of the Zoo at their doorstep this time but a mostly completed wall between them and it, as well as a group of men in uniform.

One of them, taller and fiercer-looking than the rest, stood at the front, his hands tucked behind his arms as he waited for the engineers to approach.

"Good afternoon," Fix greeted him and shielded his eyes from the glaring sun. "I'm Sam Jackson. These are my colleagues Liu Chen and Elke Muntz. We've been tasked with making sure that Wall Two is being built according to the requisite standard."

The man's eyes twitched and a small smile touched his lips. "Sam Jackson? Like—"

"No relation, trust me."

"Of course. As you can see, we've put a great deal of

work into making sure our bases around the Zoo are secured. It feels like the whole jungle has been moving the goalposts, as you might say. I am Major Hakan Cengiz of the Turkish Land Forces. We have been told to expect you."

"We are surprised that you've put the walls up so quickly in your sector," Chen noted with a nod. "From what we've heard, we expected to have to convince people that they need to put a little more effort in."

"While the Turkish Armed Forces provide most of the men and women who man these bases, the UAE has financed the construction of the bases and Wall Two. They had invested a considerable amount even before word came to us of the Japanese base. After what happened... well, they think they are a little too close to the Zoo for comfort."

Sam could understand that, at least, although most of the other countries—especially those in and around the Sahara Desert—must surely feel the same kind of pressure as well.

"We've studied your plans for the walls and while the amount of work your coalition has put in is admirable, there are places where they can be improved."

The major bowed respectfully. "Of course. I have no intention to wake up to find my base in ruin and that fucking jungle upon us."

"It's not the kind of thing most people would have been afraid of only a few months ago," Elke noted.

"People of intelligence around the world are starting to come to an agreement. Something is changing inside the Zoo. No one knows or cares what that something is but they would not see it happen to themselves. Many soldiers here are more trusting of the suits they have been provided with than walls, but I have fought in the Zoo since our first base was set up. Having a wall between us and it will allow me to sleep better, although my dreams will still be disturbed."

He had a way with words that made Sam think he'd maybe gone to a British university and minored in poetry, but he did make an excellent point.

"Regarding the gun mounts—" Chen began but the major raised a hand.

"Forgive me, but I am not the one to speak to when it comes to engineering. The people in charge of building the wall are waiting for you and to be honest, I would prefer to move from the heat."

"On that we can agree." Sam shook his head. "I grew up in Buffalo and while the summers were hot, they didn't hold a candle to what we're feeling here."

He looked at Elke and Chen, who both looked a little confused.

"Hold a candle? Heat?" He sighed. "My excellent puns are wasted on you."

"Perhaps they will not be wasted on the engineers who await you." Cengiz looked like he was anxious to return to where there might be air conditioners waiting for them, and the ENSOL team couldn't help but agree and climbed quickly into the waiting vehicles.

Jennie tapped her desk gently with a spare chopstick and watched the coding sequences scroll on her screen while she checked for any possible errors in her work.

If she'd had a couple of months to work on the dummy AI, it would have been an absolute masterpiece, something companies would fight to get possession of before they realized it was a fake.

Sadly, all she had was a couple of weeks so what few scraps she could put together from her past work and a few notifications were all that could be mustered.

It was some of her best work on short notice, but the short notice put a damper on her expectations.

"Vickie, are you on the line?" Jennie asked as the simulations finished. "Or are you still playing in the sims?"

"I'm here, I'm here." The hacker sounded a little more energetic and out of breath than she usually did, although maybe that had to do with the sims as well.

Jennie had wanted to try them but one trip into the Zoo had been enough for her. She didn't need another taste, no matter how fake it might have been.

"Desk, are you on the line too?" she asked. "I have the dummy AI ready to go but I'll feel better if you run a couple of checks on your side to make sure."

"Of course, Jennie."

"Do you seriously doubt your work?" Vickie asked.

"Hey, I'm fantastic when it comes to making things work at optimal capacity. I'm not super-sure that I'm capable of making something that's made to not work the way people want it to."

"Fair enough. It still seems like you should trust in yourself, though."

"The point is that I want to make sure there's nothing in it that the assholes can use. I want them to find a dummy and spend weeks trying to plug themselves into it, only for it to drop in without anything they can use at the end."

"Do you think they'll work out that it's a dummy?" Vickie asked and sounded like she was munching on chips or something.

"The idea is that they think there's some kind of self-destruct involved that fries their systems a second before they plug in. Of course, leave them for long enough with what remains and they'll eventually realize there was nothing useful in the code, so someone smart mixed in there might realize that something is wrong."

"Do you have any plans to make sure that does not happen?" Desk asked.

"I have a couple of ideas but not anything I can promise. All we can hope for is that you guys are long gone from the country before any of that happens, so there won't be any real consequences involved when I dig through what they might or might not have found."

"You and me both, sister." Vickie crunched a mouthful of chips again. "Okay, I think we're good to go."

"What do you mean?"

"I was running some sims of my own to make sure."

"How did you..." Jennie shook her head. "Okay, neat little trick."

"How else will you learn if I don't point your flaws out?"

"Fuck off. Desk, are you finished with your simulations?"

"There are a few things I would improve but it would

take a while to code. For the time dedicated to getting it done, this will do the trick."

"High praise, I guess." Jennie keyed into her back door to the DOD's servers. The AI was already in and had begun to format the drives to make the appearance of the dummy AI not look like it was a new development. That would raise too many eyebrows.

"All three of us are working on this," Vickie muttered. "You don't think there's that whole thing of too many cooks in the kitchen or some shit, right?"

"I don't think so," her cousin whispered as she watched Desk work. "Desk will do most of it. All we're doing is making sure no one picks up on what she's doing until the appointed time."

"Awesome. Do you watch Esports, Jennie?"

"What?"

"You seem like the kind of person who would follow Esports."

Jennie shrugged. "I followed CS:GO back in the day. I don't think they're still running that league, though."

"No, they moved it to the new edition and all the players left in protest—group of bitches."

She tilted her head. Watching Desk work had once felt like she was watching herself do shit through a skilled interface, but she could see it change and the code becoming more efficient and effective. The AI did things in ways she wouldn't have, but Desk was already a separate entity, capable of changing and adapting like that.

Maybe this was how parents felt when they saw their children doing shit for the first time.

"The breadcrumbs have been laid out," the AI

announced. "I am setting the alarms to go off and advise them that there was a failed hacking attempt from an obscure source. Hopefully, when they investigate, they'll find the traces we left behind and then find the dummy."

"Don't be too obvious about it," Jennie warned.

"Uh...we have to be kind of obvious about it." Vickie sounded like she was shaking her head. "I don't mean to disparage the skills of the people working IT for the DOD, but yeah, they'll need a little extra nudging."

"Fair enough," Desk answered and the traces turned a little more obvious. "Anything else to add?"

"You sound like you're having fun," the young hacker noted.

"I've been on the run from these cretins for months now. It feels good to finally be able to fight back."

"I get that." Jennie watched as the AI withdrew from the servers and erased all signs of her actual presence while she left the traces behind. "Shall we begin?"

Bobby could understand why Taylor and his squad needed time away from the strip mall. The feeling of dozens of eyes on them and watching their every move had begun to tell on everyone's nerves.

A little time away to train with their freelancers would be beneficial for all, not least of all himself. He and Taylor had been sparring almost every day and while he could tell that the redhead tried to hold himself in check, it was difficult to deny that each session left him more than a little sore despite all the padding he wore.

People could say that type of training only made a man harder, but the mechanic was hard enough. He didn't need the giant to beat him into anything more than he already was.

He was tender but not too bad, fortunately. It wasn't like Taylor forced him into the ring every day. Hell, Bobby had insisted on it, knowing that it helped to ease some of the tension. And he knew he gave about as good as he took, which was satisfying.

But maybe they needed time off. Taylor running off to sim with his squad would more than do the trick.

Tanya sat next to him and ran her fingers lightly over his shoulder. "Is everything okay?"

Bobby looked up from his work on the suit in front of him and smiled at her. "Sure. Why would it not be?"

"You look a little…weird."

"I think we're all a little tense. It'll pass once we get the AIs out of here and the agencies don't have a reason to hover over our every move."

"They'll still do it, no matter what we do."

"Sure, but from that point forward, we won't have much to hide from them either."

"Aside from the money still coming in from that time we robbed a casino."

"Sure, but they don't care about that."

She laughed. "Yeah, but if they realize that we don't have what they want, I wouldn't put them above starting to dig into our dirty laundry out of spite."

"My laundry is always clean. That's why we keep sending it to the Sahara—to be cleaned."

At this point, he was very glad that Desk had put in the

effort to protect them from being bugged inside the shop or they would have just admitted to a whole litany of shit that would end with considerable jail time.

"If it ends up being a problem, we'll have no choice but to roll over on Taylor," she commented with a shrug.

Bobby snapped around, ready to growl that it wasn't an option before he realized that she was kidding. Probably.

"He'll be in Italy so it's not like the FBI will be able to arrest him anyway," she continued. "It'll be perfect. He'll be the patsy. And it's not like people won't believe it, given that he's about to take up residence in the house of a mafia don. Seriously, what better patsy could there be?"

"You make a good argument. We'll make sure they all try to arrest the mad leprechaun. I'd like to see how long it takes until they start running away from him."

"You've spent too much time in the ring with the bastard."

"And you've spent too little. Maybe you'd like to go a couple of rounds and remember the kind of animal we've been dealing with all this time."

"Hey, if you two are finished squabbling like an old married couple," Elisa interrupted, "we have movement on the perimeter you might be interested in."

"We've had movement on our perimeter for weeks," Bobby answered.

"Sure, but these guys don't look like they're part of any government agency we know of. Unless the FBI suddenly started decking their agents out in cheap leather and expensive motorcycles. Which...you know, I would absolutely approve of."

He pushed from his seat. "Open the gate. Let's see what they want."

She nodded and the smallest crack in the gate announced that she wasn't wrong about the motorcycles, at least. The belted roar was difficult to ignore and Bobby moved to the gate where four men on the uniquely defined motorcycles pulled up in front of it.

He folded his arms and waited for them to cut the engines and climb off. The one who seemed to be the leader strode forward and looked like he owned the place. Bobby could make out more than a few cheap tattoos—the kind that came from time spent in prison—and a 1911 he carried proudly on his hip.

Nevada was still an open-carry state, which meant the weapon was likely one that he'd bought legally. Still, he had a feeling that illegal weapons were also at his disposal if he needed them.

The visitor pulled his helmet and sunglasses off to reveal short black hair to match his beard and clear green eyes that latched firmly onto him.

"Are you the owner of this establishment?" he asked.

"Yeah. And there are no walk-ins here. Do everyone a favor and fuck right on off the way you came. I don't mend bikes."

"Don't worry, we work on our own rides around here." The guy looked around the shop like he was sizing it up for curtains or something. "Bobby Zhang, right? My name is Cody Lynch."

"My friends call me Bobby."

"And I look forward to being on a first-name basis with you too. I noticed that you have a lot of open space here and I hoped that we could come to some kind of arrangement to rent it. Given that you'll need protection from most of the criminal elements in this city, I know we'll be able to arrange a reasonable rental price."

"Protection?" The mechanic laughed. "I guess you're new in town or you would have heard a thing or two about Taylor McFadden, my silent partner and co-owner."

"I've found a thing or two out about the guy," Lynch admitted. "I've also heard he's been making plans to head out soon, which is why the timing of our arrival is poetic in its perfection."

He was trying to disguise it but Bobby could hear the clear Southie accent. That plus the bikes and the tattoos carried all the markers of a biker gang, the kind that dealt in more than merely owning bars and bike shops.

"It seems like you're in a hurry to settle somewhere," he answered with a nod. "I have the number of a couple of real estate agents who would be able to help you. None of the areas in the strip mall are up for rent while we're still working on renovations."

"We can do the renovations ourselves."

"Don't take this the wrong way but I prefer to do things my way."

Lynch approached him and stroked his beard thoughtfully. "I don't want to cause problems but we like this property. You might want to think a little more carefully before you turn us away. We're paying customers and the kind who won't only pay in cash if you take my meaning."

"Sure, Lynch. But I don't need your cash or whatever else you have to offer. Don't let the door hit your head on the way out. It's the kind that rolls down, not the kind that swings around and hits you on the ass instead."

Bobby shook his head and waited as the other three began to return to their bikes, but Lynch remained a moment longer.

"We'll come around again to make sure you're not interested in changing your mind."

"A man's gotta do what a man's gotta do."

Elisa began to shut the gate again, which made the gangster hustle to get under it and duck before it was too low to get through.

"They'll be back," Tanya muttered. "Do we have to teach every criminal in this city the same lesson?"

"It certainly looks like it. We'll let Taylor know about it when he gets back."

CHAPTER SIX

A taciturn group of Russian soldiers escorted the ENSOL team to the Japanese sector. They had shown little inclination to engage in conversation and even less indication that they understood English. Their visit to the base had been brief but enough to reveal that while the wall was complete at the base itself—and very new—the sections on either side still had a long way to go.

The young lieutenant who accompanied them on their inspection took great pains to point out that prior to the base being overrun by the Zoo, the wall had been all but non-existent, something the new commander had hastened to rectify as soon as he'd taken control.

Fix had sensed that the situation involved all kinds of uncomfortable political undertones and his team wisely followed his lead and avoided embroiling themselves in the morass this might involve. Suffice it to say that they were able to immediately identify the considerable shortcomings of the work in progress, and Chen only looked up from the copious notes he entered into his tablet to find more grist for the mill.

They left amidst considerable mutual relief—the Russians because they could relax and the ENSOL team because they no longer had to avoid possibly thorny issues. When they arrived at the Japanese base, they were greeted by the Russian commander, a man named Solodkov.

Unlike most of the other base commanders they'd been given information on, he did not appear to have much in the way of military history, at least not recently. In fact, there wasn't much about the man that was available for them to look into and it appeared to be intentional.

The Hammerhead came to a halt and Sam was out first again. He grimaced as the Saharan heat scorched the back of his neck almost immediately. The call for serious sunscreen had been a smart one but he still felt like he would come away from this little excursion with sunburn.

Solodkov was already waiting for them with a small escort. The soldiers were armed but they had an academic look about them that made him suspect they were people who spent more time in labs than they did in the Zoo. If he had to make a wild guess, Fix would have explained this as the Russians hoping to glean as many new scientific discoveries from the tragedy as they could before it was all destroyed. It wasn't a pleasant thought given the circumstances, but he could concede that it was immensely practical

Still, on a base that crawled with men and women in full combat suits, he felt less at ease with the man who stood in the middle in only a commander's uniform. He was barely shy of five foot ten with slicked-back graying black hair and while he was trim and fit, he was a far cry from the powerful builds they had seen around the Zoo thus far.

It was the eyes, he decided. Steely and gray with a hint of dark circles beneath, they felt like they dug into him despite the pleasant smile with which the man greeted them.

"I am happy to welcome you to the base on behalf of my Japanese counterparts," Solodkov stated and shook Sam's hand firmly. He spoke with a hint of an accent. "I apologize for the mess you see around you but we are still involved with dealing with the after-effects of the incursion I am sure you are aware of."

Elke nodded as she shook the man's hand. "I must say I am impressed with how quickly you were able to rebuild your base, especially since it was the first one to be overrun and not that long ago." Fix smirked at the very polite but open-ended statement that conspicuously avoided mention of the wall.

The Russian nodded. "I was brought in to manage that situation as it developed, although I will not speak ill of the dead. My predecessor was a decent commander in his own right and was merely a victim of the Zoo's eternal ability to surprise us."

"Of course. That is the reason why you have not yet completed the construction on your section of the wall," Chen commented. Evidently, he had yet to learn Elke's discretionary skills.

"Indeed. It was a difficult decision but we felt the base

section should be secured first, which would afford us some protection while we pushed on with work on the wall. I suppose we will need to start our construction on both sides of the base if this current situation continues. The Japanese have committed to assisting us with the portion between our two bases and so we have diverted some of our efforts to ensure that they are secured and the area cleared."

Sam couldn't help but agree on that but oddly, he still inched away from the Russian despite the fact that they held a pleasant conversation. There was something about the man that irked him and he couldn't put his finger on what it was.

"It would appear that even the most prepared base can fall," Solodkov continued. "I have a great deal of respect for Lieutenant Colonel Kimura and I wish the man a speedy recovery. If he was caught unawares, any of us can be."

As if to emphasize his point, two bombers took off from one of the airstrips in the distance, likely going for more runs over the Zoo from what was hopefully a safe distance. Thanks to Chen, he had seen a handful of vids where helicopters engaged in sweeps over the jungle were suddenly overwhelmed when the locusts and other creatures swarmed from the treetops.

He could only hope that the bombers attacked from a higher altitude than the beasts could fly. It was an unsettling thought, honestly. He already hated most regular insects that could fly and roaches in particular. He didn't see the need to also have monsters that were the size of Great Danes doing the same thing.

"We are in the process of clearing the last few sections on the Zoo side of the base while most of the effort is directed toward eradicating what remains of the New Zoo at the same time." The Russian motioned for them to follow as he moved to what looked like a medical unit, although the area was still being defended by a dozen or so men in combat suits. They wouldn't be taken by surprise by the Zoo again, which seemed to be the overall motto of the rest of the troops who were still in the area.

It looked like quite a few mercenaries were still mixed with the actual soldiers, but most of the former appeared to have already been shipped out as more of those officially affiliated to their countries were made available.

Solodkov nodded when the soldiers saluted him as they entered—yet another indication that he had no real military experience. Dozens of men and women with various injuries lay on cots, although they appeared to be walking through the area that was populated by those already in recovery and who showed no signs that their conditions were critical.

One room in particular stood out as they approached. Two Japanese men in uniform and carrying weapons stood guard outside, although they snapped a salute as Solodkov passed them and entered the room when they opened the door for him.

Sam was not surprised to see that the patient was the Japanese base commander. The young major who had assumed command in his absence was seated beside the bed, although she stood as the newcomers stepped inside.

"The retaking of the area where the incursion took

place is due to these two," Solodkov pointed out as the major approached them. "Bravery while surrounded by the Zoo in your own base is the kind of courage that all should aspire toward."

Fix couldn't help but agree as he shook the major's hand.

"The current aggression phase in the Zoo is something we will need to prepare for," Major Murakami commented and brushed a few errant strands of hair from her face. "We are thankful to see that most other bases have increased their pace in the completion of Wall Two, although all we can hope for is that it is not too late."

"Still, the work you've put in has been impressive and you're making excellent progress too," Chen commented. "We're happy to help and add to the overall productivity."

"We need all the help we can get," Solodkov agreed. "For the moment, it appears that you three will overnight here. I'll have someone escort you to where you'll stay but I thought you should meet our Japanese comrades first."

Sam nodded as they were escorted from the room. The Russian rattled off his orders to a couple of soldiers in the area, likely to escort them to where they would be bunk for the night. It seemed odd that the Japanese were willing to allow the man to issue orders with such complacency, but they had no doubt reached some kind of agreement. He wasn't sure that he would have trusted the Russian like that but decided he should look at the positive rather than focus on his instinctive dislike.

Their first night around the Zoo was a hard thing to think about. He wasn't sure he would be able to sleep but it had been a long day. Despite his misgivings—knowing you were in a location that had so recently been swallowed by the Zoo tended to leave one feeling inordinately discomforted—he was most probably ready to collapse almost anywhere.

———

Cody had recommended the deli around the corner from their ramshackle headquarters. While there were numerous things he didn't trust the man with, he knew a thing or two about locating the obscure venues for good food and the deli proved no different.

Logan had only tried the pulled pork sub they served, and it was about the best damn sandwich he'd ever spent his money on.

He took another bite as the sound of motorcycles rumbled from the street. Through the grimy window, he could see the four men he'd sent to discuss renting the strip mall as their new place of business.

Given the hard thud of their boots as they marched up the steps to the second floor of their abandoned building, he didn't need to hear the news to know that none of the group was impressed with the result of their excursion.

Cody was the first one through the door and from the looks on all four faces, he'd been right about what had waited for them at the strip mall.

"Don't tell me," Logan interjected before they could speak. "Zhang told you guys to kick rocks and eat shit and not in that order, am I right?"

His second dropped into a chair and nodded. "How did you know?"

"I could sell you some crap about being psychic, but the fact of the matter is that they always say eat shit the first time. In our business, you should already have that schedule marked off in your head. If you don't have a local rep already in place, they merely assume you're all hot air and turn you down. Once they know that kneecaps will be broken and loved ones will be kidnapped, they are a little more receptive to whatever offer you might have for them."

"It still sucks, though. Maybe we need to get on their asses immediately and make sure they know who they're fucking with."

Logan nodded. "Look into that and see what our options are, but we don't need to jump on this. Let them sweat a little before we act. Maybe it'll get them to lower their guard and make it easier for us to make our point."

His second in command nodded and moved to where the rest of the guys waited in a stiff group.

Keeping Cody busy for the moment felt like the right thing to do. Logan had a feeling that something hinky was in the works and another hidden agenda was at play. He couldn't put his finger on it exactly, but his gut told him something was off.

It was time for him to do a little research of his own. It wasn't that he didn't trust the man to get the job done, but his motives felt a little suspect and he seemed too eager to push into the violence stage. Besides, the guy had a rep for undermining the people around him out of spite, and the only reason no one had done anything about it was because of his father.

Eventually, Miles would realize that the little shit who

had sprung from his cock was bad news for the GAMC but for the moment, his presence would have to be tolerated.

It didn't mean, however, that he should be trusted, not when every instinct insisted on the opposite.

———————

It was always a good idea to get the tensions worked out. Given that they all spent so much time in such close proximity to each other, Taylor had a feeling they would be at each other's throats before too long. Aside from the basic need to train and keep at it, this was the other reason why he encouraged physical exercise in the group. It seemed sensible to get them to the gym to make sure they were all too tired to rip each other's arms off.

While the usual daily regimen served a positive purpose, a little time out in the suits felt like exactly what the doctor ordered, even if it was only in the sims. The effort it took to run around in the jungle and shoot monsters of all shapes and sizes, all while honing their skills, was bound to do someone some good, and even he felt pleasantly drained by the end of it. It wasn't to say he couldn't keep going for hours on end afterward, but with most of the day spent pretending to be in the Zoo, things certainly felt better.

"You still need to work on watching your surroundings," he noted as he saw the strip mall in the distance. "Your suit will do much of the work to correct you, but there's not much you can do if you walk into a tree. Then, you're out of position and vulnerable and leave the rest of the team at risk too."

Niki cleared her throat and took a slow sip from the coffee they'd picked up outside the facility. "Wait, are you talking to me?"

"I don't remember Vickie wandering ass-first into a tree." The hacker laughed softly in the back of the truck and he glanced at her in the rearview mirror. "What the hell are you laughing at? You tripped over your feet trying to keep up with us in the first two rounds."

"It's been a while. I needed time to get back into the groove."

"And you had problems with positioning too," Niki pointed out. "Do you remember that the pack of panthers caught us from above when you thought you could push in a little deeper to finish that crawler off? How many rounds in was that again?"

"I think that was on the fifteenth round." Taylor nodded. "The first time we managed to last long enough that they had to break one of the more challenging monsters out for us."

Niki grinned and glanced at her cousin who continued to laugh in the back seat.

"Come on, guys. I had that crawler on its back with the mine I left for it. I was only going in there to confirm the kill."

He shook his head but couldn't help a smile as they turned into the parking lot of the strip mall. "It was good training anyway. The freelancers have kept up with their training too, which means we should be hot to go if Vickie needs us to take any new work on. Do you think our alphabet friends followed us?"

The hacker nodded. "Three cars tailed us in and out. I

don't think they pulled the surveillance off the strip mall, though, so despite the apparent miracle that no one followed you to the biker bar, they probably have teams at the ready if we need to go out and buy groceries and shit. Anyway, it doesn't matter because we'll have to work much harder if we want to convince the bastards to leave us the hell alone."

He scowled but had to agree as they pulled up at the door of the strip mall and waited for the door to open so they could park in the shop. Niki's face said everything it needed to, which made any further commentary on their situation a little superfluous. He didn't particularly like it either. While he had no objections to staying there, if she wasn't happy, neither was he.

Staying at a five-star hotel with all the pampering available would have been the best and he was determined to make it up to her once their situation improved.

As they pulled in, he could immediately tell that more problems loomed on the horizon. Bobby's brow was furrowed in a way that he hadn't seen in a while, which meant something was wrong—over and above everything else that was already wrong, of course.

Taylor was the first one out of the truck. "What's up?"

"How did you—"

"Your face looks like it's about to start throwing lightning bolts. I generally assume something is off when you look like that, so will you tell me what it is or should we play twenty questions?"

Tanya entered the shop from the break room with a similar expression on her face. "We had a little trouble from one of the local criminal elements."

"Marino?" Niki asked. "I knew he would try to screw us over but I didn't think it would be while we were still here."

"Not Marino," Bobby corrected her quickly. "A new element as far as I can tell. They looked like they were newly out of South Boston—bikers, armed and sporting prison tats. The last I heard, there weren't any Southie biker gangs in the area so the assumption is that they are new players here. They likely selected a location the other organized crime groups didn't have any claim on and thought it was some kind of oversight. Four of them arrived said they were looking for a place to rent. Of course, they made it noticeably clear that they weren't asking."

"If they know the areas the other gangs are avoiding, it makes sense that they have some kind of connection with the local police department, who would have let them in on why the mafia and the other criminal elements in the city leave us alone." Taylor looked around the shop. "And if they came here, they have to know we're packing. Are they desperate?"

"They didn't seem desperate," Tanya muttered. "Maybe they think Vegas is like a prison yard and they have to get into a fight with the biggest guy to make them seem tough enough to avoid being messed with."

"I wouldn't put it past them," he responded with a snort. "More likely, though, they prefer to get into a fight with us than with Marino or the Thirteens. Desk, do you think you could give us some kind of identity on these assholes?"

"I have already put their names through the various databases—federal, local, and in Boston," the AI answered. "All four have criminal records ranging from possession with intent to assault and battery, the kind of thing you might expect from people involved in a criminal organization at the lower levels. The one who introduced himself to Bobby, on the other hand, is a little higher up. He has possession charges as well, but he was marked off for murder one. The charges were dropped when the witnesses recanted their statements so I did a little more digging into him."

"Yeah, Cody Lynch is his name." Bobby growled irascibly and scratched his cheek in irritation.

"He is the oldest son of Miles Lynch, known by Boston law enforcement as the de facto head of the Guardian Angels Motorcycle Club. They have chapters set up all over the east coast and a couple in the Great Lakes area too and have been on the FBI's radar for smuggling everything from drugs to guns and selling them on the black market."

"It looks like Papa Lynch is pushing for expansion in Vegas," Niki muttered. "How violent do you think they'll get?"

Bobby tilted his head and scowled again. "It didn't seem like they would take no for an answer. They were packing when they got here too so I imagine their plan is a little bluster and if that doesn't work, they'll take it to some kind of extreme."

"It won't need to go that far if we hit them first," Taylor suggested. "Desk, do you have anything on where they might be based?"

"All four have their known addresses still in Boston but I can keep an eye on it and will know if they decide to change that. I wasn't able to keep track of them after they left, though. My impression is that they know a thing or two about staying away from cameras and many of those in this area have been vandalized anyway."

"Keep working on that." He shook his head. "I want to hit them and nip this problem in the bud before they try to convince Bobby again."

"Yeah. That sounds good to me," the mechanic agreed.

CHAPTER SEVEN

The fucking mosquitos were all but driving him crazy.

Mashoul decided that having something itching under his suit for the whole duration of their time in the Zoo was about as nightmarish a scenario as anyone could devise. Well, unless that nightmare ended with all of them dead, but only barely. It was difficult to focus on anything other than the fact that he needed to scratch something that was utterly inaccessible.

And he could see that others in the group suffered from the same affliction. Ordinarily, he would have simply told them to suck it up and keep working, but a hint of empathy touched him and held him back from being too harsh on them.

It wasn't like they were doing a bad job, after all. A little distraction wouldn't be a problem—until it was, at which time his attitude would change.

But for the moment, they were out of the jungle and had begun to check the pelts they'd selected. They had their quota and it was a matter of cleaning and drying them and getting them ready for shipping. Preserving them in the vacuum-sealed bags was a good start but eventually, a little elbow grease would be required.

They all mounted the trucks and thankfully, left the jungle behind for the moment.

Once they were at a safe distance, Mashoul scrabbled to pull his suit off while in the front seat, out of sight from all save the driver as he freed his arms to enable him to finally scratch an itch that had plagued him for hours now.

"Fucking mosquitos," he muttered aloud and rubbed lotion over the bumps that had formed. "I thought I'd be done with the shits when I came to the desert."

The driver nodded. "Then again, the jungle is a brand-new biome. The fact that there are blood-sucking insects in there should come as no surprise. I'm only glad that no tsetse flies have moved in or we'd be looking at a whole other level of shit on top of what the Zoo has already brought."

As much as he hated to think it, the driver was right. Tsetse flies had prevented all attempts to turn any region they settled in into farmlands, which led to many calling them nature's game wardens. If sleeping sickness was somehow introduced to the Zoo, it would be a whole new level of biological warfare for the jungle to use against them.

Unlike many of the other poachers, Mashoul had long since believed that the Zoo was a sentient organism in its own right and needed to be respected as such. There were too many signs to ignore. The most convincing evidence, of course, was the fact that he was still alive while so many others had died.

In the end, the itch wasn't even that bad. Having been stuck in the suit and unable to scratch it was what made it feel so much worse.

"How long a drive?" he asked.

"We got the intel from our buyers a few minutes after you alerted them that you had the quota," the man answered. "I guess they must be desperate for them, given that the schedule was for delivery in three days."

He nodded. "I'm not surprised. They must be desperate to offer that much money for each pelt but I'm not complaining. If they want them this quickly, it means they will do all the prep work before they sell or use them, which means we don't have to. And that, my friend, means more profit for us."

The driver nodded and turned on the GPS in their vehicle for him to see where they were going.

They were only a few miles from one of the Sahara Coalition camps, where he had found most of his work over the past few months. Patrols were technically supposed to prevent this type of criminal activity, but the men who ran those made more money protecting the criminals than they did from their military coffers.

Even if there were a handful of honest men mixed in with them, there would be no one for them to report to who wasn't already taking money themselves. It was an invitation to end up with their bodies dropped off at the edge of the Zoo. Missing in action included all kinds of action, nefarious or otherwise.

Badawi was already at the location as the sun began to set and a handful of trucks awaited them as they pulled in to park.

Mashoul was the first to debark and immediately peeled the rest of his suit off and handed it to one of his men to be stored. "You got here quickly."

"As did the clients." His Algerian counterpart indicated the handful of SUVs that were parked and already waiting. "I'll admit that I have a few concerns."

"This would not stem from your experience with the rabbits you dealt with before, would it?"

The man shrugged and tugged his beard. "You cannot say that you are not a little unsettled by the prospect. We planned to sell the rabbit pelts too but it didn't even get that far before we needed to dump every last one of them. How did you know about the rabbits?"

"News travels quickly on the bush telegraph." Mashoul smirked. "You should know this already. I see no cause for concern, though. You dealt with the live creatures. These are dead, cleaned, and vacuum sealed. I've never seen anything, even from the Zoo, that can survive those kinds of conditions."

The clients approached and he gestured for his men to show them the cooler they had sealed the pelts in. One was taken out and inspected quickly before it was replaced and the container was sealed again.

When those conducting the examination nodded to confirm that no problems were noticed, a man approached with a briefcase handcuffed to his arm.

There was no direct contact between Mashoul or the client, who had sent his so-called facilitator to conduct the business on his behalf. That was the deal for the moment, but he hoped for something a little more personal with a greater degree of trust in the future. Rather than press the point in this exchange, however, he maintained a bored expression and gestured for his second in command to check to make sure all the money was there and none of the Euro bills were counterfeit before he brought the brief-case to him.

A good cash payment like this one went a long way to ease some of the resentment the standoffish exchange might have generated. The business concluded to every-one's satisfaction, the client's men dragged the cooler to their vehicle and loaded it inside before they left without so much as a word of farewell.

"The money's good," Mashoul said and patted Badawi on the shoulder, "and what happens hereafter isn't our problem. Let's get a drink."

"I do not drink."

"A cranberry juice then. We need to celebrate this kind of deal."

The Algerian smiled and nodded. "Very well. One drink and then I must return."

There were already enough problems in the city and from the sound of things, they weren't set to improve.

The first one they had to contend with was too many people dealing in the same white powder they were, which meant prices dropped when competition became fierce.

"Seriously, the cops need to stop trying to deal." Juan-Pablo growled his irritation and shook his head. "They don't have the talent for it and the only reason we can't get rid of them is because—"

"They're cops." Juan-David nodded. "But we have more problems coming from Boston. The crazy fucks decided they'll make more money if they take the middlemen out of the equation."

JP nodded, leaned back in his seat, and sipped his beer as he studied the pictures his brother had brought for him. Their parents hadn't been very creative when they named the kids. All five boys had Juan as their first name and the three girls were Maria, and the only way to tell them apart was the second name.

It was a pain in the ass but in the end, it was a part of their identity, something JP would not see taken away. He would probably end up doing the same if he had any kids. It was more distinctive than their last name.

"They're a small group," JD commented. "And while they probably have the backing of the GAMC, they're in Boston and shouldn't be an issue."

Juan-Carlos took a step forward. "We should get rid of them now. Snuff them out and drive the infestation from Vegas before they establish themselves."

The pictures did have his attention, though, and JP leaned in a little closer. "Where were these taken?"

"The local cops staking out the McFadden strip mall sent the pictures to us."

"How much did you have to pay?"

"Fifty bucks for all of them. It's not like they were doing much with them anyway."

"Do they know why these biker assholes went there?"

JC shook his head. "No word has come through on that yet, but given that they left again five minutes later, we can assume they didn't get what they were looking for."

"Or they had their conversations beforehand and this was a formal greeting or an exchange of goods." JP pushed the photos across the table to his brothers. "We can't hit them until we know whether or not they're dealing with McFadden and his cronies. I think we all know better than to fuck with those assholes. If they are, they might be doing business with Marino too—although we are supposed to have an agreement with the mob, I wouldn't put anything past them."

His two younger brothers nodded and folded their arms. He was never sure if the twins knew that they consistently mirrored each other's movements and it was a little unsettling to see them, as identical as they were, each doing what the other did without thinking.

"We'll wait," JP decided with a firm nod. "Watch and wait to see what the mick bastards are tied up in. If they're merely dealing with the parent gangs, we'll burn them out, but I don't want to deal with Cosa Nostra or the redhead giant."

Both nodded, although he couldn't tell if they were more afraid of the mafia that had practically built the city of Las Vegas or of the vet who had quickly become a legend within its limits.

"Do we know who's running the incursion?" JP asked as his brothers turned away.

"Not with certainty. The short one at the front there is Cody Lynch, but it doesn't look like he's in charge of the operation. I've heard that Logan Quinn is the one in charge since he's the one who's sold powder and guns here before."

"I've met him. He's a tough bastard. I heard he killed

three men while he was in prison but they weren't able to pin it on him."

"Who told you that?"

"Flaco was his cellmate in Souza-Baranowski while he was still working in Boston. While I can't honestly say I believe him, I know that there aren't many people who can make Flaco shit himself."

The twins chuckled and shared a look before they realized that their brother wasn't joking.

"Be careful," JP instructed. "Tell our informants to stay low and keep a close eye and ear out for any more intel coming from Boston. I'll let you know when we can move."

"You got it."

At least his family wasn't included in the list of problems he had to deal with.

Stepan smiled at the thought that there was poetic justice to all this.

He had watched his family enterprise go to shit for years now. A Jakubec had run the furrier business in the area for centuries by this point, and the biggest claim to fame they had was when his great, great, great grandfather was summoned to the Russian Czar's palace to present his wares. From the retelling of the story, he had left their farm with a full wagon and come back with it empty of the furs and full of treasures.

The guy probably would not have been so pleased if he realized that it was the highest point of the family. Maybe the curse of what happened to the Romanovs only a few years later should have been some kind of indication but since then, they had dwindled relentlessly to the point where they had to dabble and diversify and even sell leather instead of the furs they were known for. In the end, his older brother Petr had joined the military and been sent to the Zoo. That he had died there was both predictable and unfortunate, but at least he hadn't succumbed before he'd made some connections in the area for his family.

He'd discovered a small niche market for illegal Zoo-based pelts. It paid well and allowed them to pull away from the menial work of tanning leathers from the nearby cattle ranches for the growing demand for them across Europe.

It wasn't the kind of thing that many people were in favor of but thankfully, the Zoo-based inventory paid far better for less product, which increased their overall profits.

"Pavel, take five men to inspect the pelts and make sure they're usable," Stepan instructed. The man nodded and helped to carry the cooler to where they could start working on the contents as his boss approached the delivery men.

"I'll be honest, I didn't think this shipment would arrive on time." He offered the man a small glass of schnapps. "When the warning came through that Mashoul would be late, I was worried that we would have to put a delay on our orders."

"That is not required this time, at least." The man nodded and sipped the strong spirit in his glass. "But you may find that further deliveries will be delayed."

"Why?"

"They are pushing for Wall Two around the Zoo to be completed quickly, which makes it more difficult to send teams in without being seen. That will certainly drive the prices up."

"My clients don't care about the prices." Stepan scowled and shifted his glance to where the team began to remove the pelts from the vacuum-sealed bags and inspect them one by one. "They merely want to have the coats. Price has never been an object. My only concern is to deliver on time."

"All this is paranoia for the most part." The man emptied his glass and placed it on a nearby table. "The Zoo has shown aggression before and it's never remained an outright problem. We'll see the current issues disappear in a couple of months."

"Still, we might be able to squeeze a few more Euros out of the rich pricks as a result. There's no need to let our people in the Zoo be the only ones to charge high prices, right?"

The driver chuckled and nodded. "As long as you stay away from live animals, you should be fine. I'll tell you here and now, after the shitstorm they had in Germany, the demand will be all over the place from the same rich pricks. You'll need to be prepared for that."

"Hell no. I've seen what happens when you bring live creatures from the Zoo. We've been in this business long enough to know what's safe and what isn't."

Stepan narrowed his eyes when a couple of the men handling the pelts scratched their arms. If they had used a preserving agent that caused allergic reactions, he would need to wash them a little more thoroughly. Still, Pavel would know to do that.

They'd been in the business long enough that they knew all the tricks and secrets.

Cody didn't honestly have anything against Logan. The guy was a tough sonuvabitch and the type who garnered considerable respect from the GAMC but putting him in charge of an expansion was a mistake.

To do so while he had to operate as his second in command was an even bigger mistake. His dad and Logan had both explained it as a political decision but it smelled like bullshit to him. Miles never planned for failure and all this reeked of something they were doing to spare his feelings.

If he had been put in charge of the situation, he would have already begun to implement the strategies they had discussed to wrest control of Vegas from the Thirteens and the mob bastards. Instead, Logan rolled in late and yelled about playing nice with the other kids in the playground.

He shook his head in reaction to the Vegas heat that beat relentlessly on him as the other three who had been sent out with him got their bearings. Logan wanted them to look for alternative locations where they could establish their headquarters. While it sounded sensible, he was sure it was some kind of punishment.

Cody knew this kind of work was beneath him but he wouldn't go directly against the guy who was in charge. That was a good way to simply be beaten down, something he had no inclination to subject himself to. There were some things old man Lynch wouldn't tolerate, even from his son.

Besides, he was currently in the weaker position in more ways than one. Logan had strong loyalty from the people who had come with him, whereas he had managed to bring only a few of the people he knew had his back along for the ride. The strongest of his supporters were out and about with him now.

Maybe that was their leader demonstrating that he knew where everyone's loyalties lay. Or he tried to make sure that Cody worked with people he was comfortable with out of respect. The guy was a class act, make no mistake, and under any other circumstances, he might have been more amenable to learning what he could from him.

But his position meant he was taking Cody's laurels, and that wasn't something he would ever accept from anyone.

"Do you have any ideas of where we can go?" one of the men asked as they returned to their motorcycles. "We can probably find some areas that aren't covered—maybe a warehouse at the edge of the city we can start with."

"I won't run around like a chicken with its head chopped off simply because Logan Quinn fucking tells me to," he snapped.

"We could always stage a drive-by of some kind," Danny Walsh muttered. "And make it look like the mafia is responsible for offing the bastard. When that happens, your dad will need to step in with an army to correct their mistake in killing a Southie leader, with you at the head."

"It's certainly an alternative, but the last-ditch kind

should all else fail." Cody growled in annoyance and scratched his beard. He'd grown it out to counter the remarks from the people around him about his baby face and so far, it had achieved the intended result, even if it was itchy and uncomfortable in the heat. "We might be able to convince them to do it for us. If we can seed word around town that Logan ordered a hit on one of their leaders, we might draw them out to kill him for us and spare us the trouble."

"Or—"

"Liam, no one wants to hear any more about your market-level schemes," he cut in before the man could say anything and the others laughed. "I'm sure the energy drinks you've tried to sell are great but we won't peddle them for you."

"I wasn't going to suggest that," Liam retorted and nodded toward the road. "Isn't that the woman who was with Zhang at the strip mall? What was her name again?"

Cody squinted to focus as he pushed his sunglasses up on his nose. He located the woman in question in a small car that seemed to be headed to the donut shop at the corner of the street.

"Tanya...something." Her name had been on the business paperwork but he couldn't remember the last name. The woman with her was Elisa, although he couldn't remember her last name either. Both were under contract with Zhang to work at his shop.

"They might be our ace in the hole," Liam suggested and mounted his bike. "If we snatch them, it's bound to draw the wrath of the McFadden and Banks team. They'll think Logan did it, and if there's any backlash, it'll land on him."

Liam was generally a dumbass but he had a good mind for this kind of thing at least. Cody frowned in thought as the vehicle stopped at a red light and he considered the possibilities before he pulled his helmet on again.

"If we can make the snatch without attracting any attention, we'll do it," he decided as his cronies started their bikes.

"Maybe next time, you won't simply discard anything I have to say out of hand—"

"Shut the hell up, Liam. Your MLM scheme is still some dumb shit."

He pulled his bike out of the parking lot as the car began to move again with a green light and remained within the speed limit until they reached the donut shop at the end of the street. They pulled off the road and into the parking lot of the store.

It was almost too good to be true, but the area was mostly contained and certainly the kind of location where they could accost the women without raising too much attention.

Everyone deserved a lucky break, though. Cody motioned for the three coming in behind him to go into the parking lot as well.

CHAPTER EIGHT

For some unaccountable reason, Eben had the weirdest feeling that things would never be the same again. He smiled inwardly and told himself that it likely had something to do with the way his colleagues in the FBI treated him when he entered the office. Gazes settled on him immediately when he exited the elevator, and some of those present began to whisper to one another as he strode across the bullpen.

Other voices joined them although he couldn't make out any of the comments. They were accompanied by ripples of laughter which were hushed quickly whenever he looked in the direction of the source. It was unsettling to know that his reputation among his fellow agents had fallen so quickly.

Or maybe they had always had an incredibly low opinion of him to start with and they merely felt emboldened by his recent failures and thought they could get away with being so blatantly obvious about it.

In all honesty, he didn't blame them for it. People would

always be jealous of those who were more successful than they were and would inevitably be happy to see them fail. All he had to do was hold his head high, push on, and refuse to let their opinions slow him.

That said, the reaction on that particular day was a little more intense than usual. Eben paused at the break room and poured himself a cup of coffee from the machine as one of the other agents approached for some as well.

"People are in a good mood today," he noted casually as he poured coffee for his fellow agent. "Am I still the one everyone's laughing at or do they have someone else on their minds?"

She paused and looked a little surprised, and he laughed.

"I fucked shit up. There's no denying that. I'll have to work through that like anyone else and it's best to do it while I'm able to laugh at myself along with the entire office."

"Yeah, it sounds about right." Kat smirked and sipped her coffee. "And...well, yeah. Kind of, anyway. Word down the chain of command is that the IT geeks at the DOD managed to pull off what you couldn't."

He tilted his head and focused all his attention on her. "They found the AI?"

"It might as well be the holy grail, but yeah." She tucked her straight black hair behind her ear. She generally wore it much shorter, which meant she was due for a visit to the barber this week. "They picked up a standard alert in their systems and practically tripped over it."

"Shit." Eben shook his head. "Has there been confirmation on it yet?"

"If you mean that our computer guys have been told to stop looking, that would be a hard no," she answered with a soft snort. "It doesn't matter, though. The odds are that this is what we've all searched for."

"Well, it's good to know this will all be behind us."

"You have a good attitude, you know." She patted him on the shoulder. "It doesn't mean people won't still snicker at you behind your back but that'll stop if you buy them a couple of beers. Don't let it get you down."

"I'll try. Thanks, Kat."

"No problem."

It was difficult to keep his composed expression until she had left the break room but he grasped his coffee cup with both hands to avoid spilling any of the foul black liquid inside. The fact that it had been found when he was not present and everyone enjoyed rubbing his nose in the reality that he had nothing to do with it was hard to stomach, despite what he liked to say and the brave face he assumed.

Eben took a moment to sip his coffee calmly and compose himself before he moved to his office and closed the door and the blinds quickly so no one could see him.

There had to be someone he could bully into providing him with hard facts on the matter. He couldn't afford to have another black mark on his career but he could damn well get a copy of it for Shane. At least that would save him from having to repay the debt incurred for hiring the useless hacker Ghosteye.

Before he could reach for his phone, there was a soft knock at his door.

"Come in," he called without thinking and the door opened.

He looked up as one of their IT agents slipped into his office. He remembered working with her when he had the task force and although he couldn't remember her name, he was saved the embarrassment when she moved close enough for him to read the key card she wore.

"Melania, right?" Pretending he had a better memory than he did generally paid off. "Melania Hunter?"

"That's right." She smiled and approached his desk. "I have something I think you want."

She placed a USB drive on the surface before she took a step back.

"What...what are you talking about?"

"I have a friend who's working on the DOD recovery team, dredging their servers and drives. He was the one who found the AI and he owed me a favor so he sent me a copy."

His mouth went dry and Eben had to breathe deeply to control himself before he pounced on the drive on his desk. "Why would you bring this to me?"

"Because I know you're going places, despite what all the other assholes might think." She tapped her temple. "And now you owe me a favor."

He couldn't stop a smile from touching his face as he collected the drive and held it up. "If this is what you say it is, you're damn right I owe you a favor."

Melania winked and slipped out of the office.

It probably wasn't a good thing that people knew how much he wanted the damn thing and he knew better than to ever assume a debt like this one would be repaid easily.

Still, it was better to owe a fellow FBI agent something than Shane, the shithead.

"Shane," he muttered quietly. "Fuck."

It was about time he got in touch with the bastard.

"I still don't understand why you keep coming here to get the donuts."

Tanya looked up from her phone and narrowed her eyes at Elisa while they waited.

"It's tradition. We've done it since we started working at the shop. It's not the kind of thing we can simply discard for no reason."

"I'm not saying we discard it for no reason. I'm saying there are many venues in the city that would deliver better donuts and better coffee to the shop without us having to make the trip every goddammed day."

"You're not wrong but again, it's tradition. You never buy donuts for the quality anyway."

"You should."

She frowned at the woman and tried to curb her patience. Elisa had always been the type of person who needed her food to be locally sourced, grass-fed, and free of GMOs or whatever the current health scare about food was. As a result, she would never be able to understand the simple joys of eating large amounts of delicious food that came cheaply, no matter how bad it was for the body consuming it.

All things considered, they had been through enough

troubles that a few extra calories and processed foods would not be a huge concern.

"Besides, Bobby pulled an all-nighter," Tanya continued. "We've had all those urgent calls for repair coming out of the Zoo lately so he gets to be the one who decides where we get our junk food."

"Don't remind me. Why the hell don't you have a car of your own yet?"

"I do."

"So why did I have to drive you home last night?"

"Because Bobby and I carpool most days. Am I that much of a burden on you? I already paid for the fucking gas."

Elisa chuckled and shook her head. "Whatever. Do you think we should buy some for the whole team? They could all use it from the sound of things."

"What do you think I've been doing here?" Tanya showed her phone, which displayed the order that was being prepared inside.

Before too long, it pinged to alert them to their ready order, and both climbed out of the pickup and hurried into the store.

Elisa's expression indicated that she would have to admit that it had a mouthwatering smell to it—coffee and pastry, the kind of aroma no one could turn away from. Two boxes and a container with disposable cups of coffee waited for them at the counter. Tanya took the former and left the latter for her companion and they turned, exited, and began the walk toward the car.

The faint prickle of alarm was the only sign that all was not as it seemed and she paused and looked around her.

"What?" Elisa asked with a frown.

"I'm not sure but I'd bet good money that whatever it is, it's trouble."

"Do we go back inside and call Bobby?"

She glanced over her shoulder and assessed the distance between them and the store while she used the hasty scan to determine any possible sources of the strong presentiment of danger. "We're closer to the car," she said briskly. "Try to walk a little faster but don't run. If whoever is out there sees that, they'll move quickly. This way, we can hopefully get in and lock the doors before they make a move. You drive and I'll call Bobby."

"Crap," the other woman muttered and struggled to press the car fob that dangled with her keys from one finger.

The shorter distance to the vehicle seemed to take forever, a perception exaggerated by the fact that Tanya hadn't been able to see any suspicious characters lurking in their vicinity. Whoever they were, they remained carefully hidden and were therefore confident in their ability to cover the distance between them extremely quickly. That immediately told her there was more than one and they probably waited in different positions. One or two would act as distractions while the others moved in.

They reached the car and she put the donuts on the hood before she yanked the handle to open it, already half-regretting her decision to not return to the shop. When a hand settled over hers and closed the door again, she knew she'd miscalculated badly. Maybe she'd spent a little too much time fighting Zoo monsters and had forgotten that human monsters behaved with a little more street smarts.

She spun to face a group of four men. All were familiar from their visit to the shop the day before. They were dressed in flannels and leathers and sported tattoos, no doubt from the time they had spent in one prison or another.

"Can I help you?" she asked, hoping to brazen it out.

"You can." The young man with a dark beard nodded and gestured for two of his men to secure Elisa before she could do anything to alert anyone to the situation. "I hoped you would help convince Bobby Zhang to rent his place to us. I am sure the request would sound more convincing coming from you."

"Only his friends call him Bobby," she answered calmly although her heartbeat picked up when he slid his hand casually to the pistol he wore openly at his hip. "The last I heard, you and he are not friends."

"No, but again, I'm sure that's something you could change."

"I would do that as a favor to a friend. But you're not my friend, so…" She shrugged.

He looked around and the fourth man stepped forward and grasped her roughly by the shoulder. She caught hold of the offending hand and twisted until she felt a loud crack from the wrist. He uttered a string of curses and delivered a backhand to her cheek that made her yelp. She scowled at him and spat out the blood from where she'd bitten her tongue.

As he lunged at her again, she responded with what she thought of as the Soprano Squeeze. She closed her hand around his genitals and tightened her hold until he squealed in pain—and, she noted with savage satisfaction, at a considerably higher pitch than her yelp had been.

Any further efforts stopped when the cold steel of the 1911 pressed against her cheek and forced her to release him very slowly and reluctantly.

"I had hoped that would change too," he answered. "You'll come on a little ride with us so we can get better acquainted. Your friend here—"

"Elisa," the woman snapped and shoved one of the men away, but her gaze was focused on watching what was happening on the other side of the pickup rather than on her guards.

"Elisa. She can tell Bobby about your delay and the reason for it. Maybe that'll help move things along in our upcoming friendship. Come on."

He nodded his head and gestured to the motorcycles that were parked next to the building where they had been obscured from her earlier line of sight.

"What are your demands?" Tanya asked.

"Demands? We're only—"

"Cut the bullshit, Lynch." She smirked at his surprise. "Yeah, we know who you are. Besides, all this double-speak makes my stomach churn so why don't you simply tell us what you want and stop pretending that this is anything other than a kidnapping at gunpoint."

His expression turned flinty as he pressed the barrel a little harder into her. "Your boyfriend will partner with us and the price we'll pay for his loyalty is to return you unharmed. Either that or he loses you and declares war on the Guardian Angels. His choice. You hear that, Elia?"

"Elisa, you moron."

"Whatever."

Tanya didn't resist when he took her phone, crushed it beneath his boot heel, and pushed her toward the motorcycles. The men started them once she'd been forced onto one and she saw Elisa scramble into the driver's seat of her car and pull her phone out, likely to call Bobby or Taylor to tell them what was happening.

"You dumbasses have no idea of the shitstorm you brought on yourselves," she snapped as Cody climbed onto the bike with her.

"You'd be surprised," he called over the roar of the engines before he accelerated fast enough that she had to clutch his shirt to stay on.

Juan-Javier didn't drink, use or sell drugs, or gamble. He didn't screw around with girls he wasn't dating, and he didn't screw around with guys either, for that matter. That left him with only one vice—which he thought was good in the bigger scheme of things, but his parents had nagged him about it every day of every week. It was for the best that he had moved out, but he had to visit them every Sunday after church and he so still needed to steel himself for the talk that came every time.

It was like Mama didn't know that the rest of her sons were heavy drinkers, in a gang, fucking around, and doing all kinds of shady stuff when they thought no one was looking. But no, the fact that he smoked was a mighty sin that needed to be addressed at every goddammed opportunity.

The one son who wasn't in a gang and paid his way through college while working at a shitty donut shop was the real disappointment in the family.

"Hypocrites," JJ muttered quietly as he lit up behind the shop near the dumpsters. "Mama acts like she doesn't know that the goddammed fifty-inch plasma screen TV they bought for her birthday wasn't paid for with blood money."

Maybe she knew and she didn't care. It could be that she put more stock in how much money they made than in how they made it. Either way, every time he lit a smoke, the automatic jolt of guilt was immediately met by a surge of rage that reminded him of exactly how shitty his whole family was, starting with his jackass of a father who hadn't been able to hold a job for the past three decades.

And there he was, hiding behind the dumpsters to indulge in the one thing that kept his raging anxiety in check, and it was the kind of sin that would see him in hell for some reason.

He froze when he heard voices from the parking lot. The people who generally stopped at the donut shop didn't like to be reminded that the employees had lives beyond smiling and asking what coffee they wanted. His manager had told him that the breaks outside were okay as long as he kept himself out of sight.

His instinct to hide while smoking was already deeply engrained so that particular admonishment was entirely superfluous.

Juan-Javier peered cautiously around the corner and recognized the colors worn by the bikers as he'd heard his brothers discussing the new gang in town over dinner. The four men were accosting someone he was familiar with too from back when he still worked with the Thirteens.

Everyone knew to stay the hell away from the strip mall that housed the crazy redhead who had access to military-grade weapons, a short temper, and who generated one hell of an explosion when he did go off. Even the mafia stayed away from them. It looked like the Guardian Angels hadn't learned that particular lesson yet, though.

"Shit, shit, shit." He ducked even lower so they wouldn't see him. They were talking about Bobby—he recalled that being the McFadden's mechanic friend's name—and friendship when one of them grasped the woman by the shoulder. She reacted quickly and twisted his arm firmly. The gangster responded with some impressively colorful language and his backhand made her yelp. JJ expected that the blow would subdue her but grinned when she caught hold of his cahones and, judging by his squeal, squeezed hard enough to make it count. The apparent leader suddenly held a gun in his hand and aimed it at her head.

The other woman tried to move in and help but was constrained by two of the other gang members, who pushed her against the vehicle.

The ball bruiser had the look of a fighter, someone who wouldn't go easily but wouldn't be so stupid as to resist when she had a gun to her head. She came across as tough and smart, the type of person who had been around violence fairly regularly.

He grinned again in approval when she remained undaunted, snapped at the man she called Lynch, and told him to call the kidnapping what it was. It didn't look like they intended to harm her, though, as she was shoved across the parking lot and around the opposite side of the building from where he remained unnoticed. A moment later, engines exploded to life and the motorcycles roared away, leaving the other woman at her car, likely so she could deliver the ransom message.

She looked a little flustered but already had her phone out and immediately made a call. In her hurry, she abandoned the coffees and donuts they'd carried out and accelerated out of the parking lot like the hounds of hell were on her tail.

Any fantasies about intervening to help to save the woman and thus earn her eternal gratitude were immediately purged. He was only nineteen but he'd been around long enough to know that wasn't how the world worked for so many reasons.

Still, it wasn't like there was nothing he could do. JJ sucked in one more drag from his cigarette before he tossed it away, retrieved his phone, and punched in the number he already had committed to memory, although he would never risk having it on his speed dial.

"JP?" he asked when the line was answered.

"Yeah, JJ, is that you?" his brother asked. "What's the matter?"

He could vent a ton of crap about his parents being terrible people but he would never mention any of that to his siblings and especially not the eldest. JP had his problems, sure, but he had always been there to help his brothers and sisters when they needed it, no matter when or at what cost. It explained why the others were so willing to work for him in the Thirteens and it was what made him think long and hard before he'd made the decision to leave the gang.

More importantly, he had helped him with work in the gang to get the money for his tuition and got him his job at the donut shop to cover his expenses while studying. If anyone didn't deserve the litany of bad parents, it was him.

"I...I think I saw someone being kidnapped."

"It happens every day, *hermano*. Call the cops if you want to."

"This is different. It was that girl Tanya who works at the McFadden strip mall and the guys who kidnapped her...well, I'm sure they were the Guardian Angels. I thought they were still small around here."

"They are." JP's voice took on a different tone and sounded considerably more dangerous now. "Letting me know was the right thing to do, JJ."

He hung up and Juan-Javier slipped his phone into his pocket. His break was over and it was time to get back to work. A woman being kidnapped was tough but at the end of the day, it was none of his business. Besides, JP would look into it and decide what should be done about it.

CHAPTER NINE

Elke was impressed.

Sam had honestly never expected to see that particular expression on the woman's face but it was indisputably evident when she looked at the work that had taken place at the Chinese base. The wall was complete and heavily reinforced. That in itself was something they hadn't seen much of thus far aside from the Japanese base, and even more impressive was the fact that the entire personnel, including civilians and researchers, were housed inside the wall.

"Jesus fucking Christ," Chen muttered. "You'd think the people at the other bases would simply hire these guys to tell them how to make their things work."

"Their work model is not as easily accomplished on the other bases," Elke commented as she flipped through the engineering plans they had been supplied with. "For one thing, they don't have mercenaries. They have sub-contractors who are strictly controlled by the military command structure. That's not the kind of thing the other militaries around the base would do for a variety of reasons."

A group of men in uniform approached their position. They had been escorted by one of the many patrol groups that were stationed along the perimeter, and while they were allowed to go about their business, Sam had a feeling their movements would be strictly monitored while they were in the area.

The reason offered was that they were watching for any sign that the Zoo was advancing.

"There is considerable tension around the base," Chen commented after the commanders had introduced themselves. "By that I mean everyone in all sectors is tense these days. Are you still running teams into the Zoo?"

"Trips close to the perimeter only, and we attempt to keep the jungle at bay between these," the base commander answered through an interpreter. "We have suffered many casualties over the past few weeks, but keeping the men contained to the base created serious problems with morale. As a result, we have allowed them to make shallow runs into the Zoo when they escort the plasma throwers tasked with pushing the expansion of the jungle back."

"You let them go out there to get killed?" Fix asked.

"It is better for them out there doing something than pushing the limits of morale and discipline inside the base."

That explained how they were able to work so quickly to some degree, as well as how they were able to keep their troops in line. If he had to guess, there had been a couple of fights and maybe a fatality before the higher-ups cracked down and sent the troops out into the Zoo to release their tension. It was effective although he personally found it repulsive.

"We have been able to contain the Zoo and prevent it from advancing to the wall, so it is not close enough for us to test our wall-mounted guns to their full potential. I fear, however, that day will come sooner than we'd like."

"Sending troops in is a temporary measure at best," Elke commented and continued to flick through the details on the wall's construction.

"We know but we lack other options at the moment. Until more is known about this...cycle the Zoo is in, we simply do what we deem necessary. Shall we continue with the inspection?"

That sounded closer to an order than an invitation but the ENSOL team acceded willingly enough. They were there to inspect their engineering work on the walls, not question how they were running their troops through the area, after all.

"Let's get it done," Fix responded for all of them.

The vehicle pulled into the shop and Taylor could already see how the situation would go. He wished he'd been at the gate when Elisa had arrived but as luck would have it, that was exactly the moment that he decided to get a cup of coffee. It would be a long day for all of them, and Bobby had been up all night working too.

The mechanic was already on edge and when he rushed toward the car, he knew it wouldn't end well. Taylor put his cup down and jogged closer as Bungees yanked the door open and pulled her out.

"Why didn't you do something?" he roared and pinned her to the car. "How could you let something like that happen to her while you were standing right there?"

She looked almost more terrified of Bobby than she had been of the bikers who had accosted her, but before the man could get another word in, Taylor stepped forward and yanked him away by the shoulder.

"You need to calm your shit," he snapped, dragged him to the hood of the vehicle, and poked a finger firmly into his friend's chest. "I understand that you're under considerable stress now. Believe me, I get it. I haven't been the image of self-control in the past, but if you want to keep Tanya safe and secure, you need to think with the right head—and I don't mean the one you're packing in your briefs, do you understand me?"

He knew the man would point out that he hadn't been the best example of staying cool under pressure when the people he loved were on the firing line but in the end, Tanya was family for him too. If they intended to rescue her, cooler heads needed to prevail.

The mechanic nodded slowly and swallowed his rage a moment later as Taylor turned to see Elisa barely holding herself together.

"Shit," he whispered, shut the driver's door, and closed the distance between them. He wrapped his arms around her and held her close for a minute. Convulsive sobs wracked the small frame against his chest.

Bobby looked genuinely contrite as he approached and

placed a hand on her shoulder. "I... I'm sorry," he mumbled. "I don't—"

She didn't answer but grasped his hand firmly as she tried to contain herself. Niki watched the scene in silence, and while Taylor had a feeling that she hadn't liked the contact he'd had with the woman, she was adult enough to leave well alone.

Elisa finally managed to suck in a deep breath and brushed her sleeves roughly over her cheeks. "I'm sorry, I don't know... It all happened so fast and I called you as soon as I could and shit...just—fuck."

Taylor paused and let her take a step back now that she'd calmed a little. She took deep breaths and smiled when Niki offered her a box of tissues to clean up with.

"It was the bikers. They said they wanted to convince Bobby to rent to them."

"I should have known they would do something stupid like this." Taylor growled in frustration. "Well, I knew they would but I didn't think it would be this soon. Desk, do you have any idea where they went?"

"They've popped in and out of my vision for the past few minutes, but they have now disappeared and I don't think I'll locate them again. I think they might have switched their bikes or maybe the license plates, so I won't be able to track them through the traffic cam alerts. I can scan for them manually on the feeds but it might take time."

"Do what you can." He folded his arms and fought the need to unleash his anger at the situation because he knew it would be the worst thing for Tanya at the moment. "In the meantime, the rest of us need to try to find out where they're stationed. It's unlikely that they will hold her there, not if they have anything resembling a brain, but we can have some kind of leverage over them if we know where they stay when they're not kidnapping people."

"I'm already working on it," Vickie commented. "As far as I can tell, these assholes are already on the cops' radar, but it looks like they have connections in local law enforcement. From what I've been able to pick up on the FBI chatter, they've tried to pin these Guardian Angel assholes on gun-running for a while now, but they haven't been able to get any real intel on them yet. If I were to gamble—kind of a dangerous habit to pick up in Vegas, I know—I would put my money on them having run guns and drugs to the gangs in Vegas before, which is why they suddenly had the idea to open a branch in the city. If that's the case, we might be able to pick up on any places where they might have stayed in the past and start from there."

He looked at Bobby, who leaned against the car. The man barely seemed in control and his fists clenched and unclenched. His entire demeanor suggested that he was ready and willing to kill anything that moved and while there would be a time and a place for that attitude, this was not it, especially when he was surrounded by friendlies.

"How long do we have until they begin to feel the heat about holding a hostage?"

Niki looked at him and it took a few seconds to realize that Taylor was asking her.

"What?"

"You had training in hostage negotiations from your time with the FBI, right?"

"Yeah."

"What did it tell you about situations like this?"

She seemed to need time to settle into the right mindset and he could tell that she was shaken by the news. Most people wouldn't know her well enough to read the signs, but she was at the point where the wrong look would end in blood, although she made it a little less obvious than Bobby did.

"They won't wait long," she said cautiously. "To move to this step so soon after the original approach means they're desperate. They will probably have demands in place already and will be prepared to act against the hostage if we delay. My feeling is that they think they hold all the cards in this and they won't wait around for us. They'll shoot the hostage if they think it won't get them what they want."

Bobby slammed his fists onto the hood of the car before he leaned forward and covered his head with his hands.

Taylor moved close to him, placed a firm hand on his shoulder, and squeezed gently. Niki was right to lay the facts out the way she saw them, but he could still understand the man's hurt over it.

"How long do you think we have until they contact us with their demands?"

"Twelve hours," she answered after a moment of thought.

"We won't wait for them to contact us." He scowled and dragged in a deep breath. "We'll find them, fuck them up, and get Tanya back before then."

He directed the comment to Bobby but Vickie nodded and hurried to the room where most of her computer equipment was set up to begin her search to find Tanya in earnest.

"It's kind of weird," Niki pointed out.

"What?"

"That they jumped so quickly from polite overtures to crazy aggression."

"You said it yourself, they're desperate."

"Sure, but if they were desperate enough to kidnap someone, they would have been at that point from the beginning, right? Something must have changed for them to shift so quickly from one to the other."

"Or we might be dealing with an idiot who acted without sanction from their leader," he suggested and she nodded her agreement that this was possibly a reason as well. "Either way, I don't like the current outlook. We have a limited window in which to find Tanya before they get their act together, and I want to make sure we're the ones holding the guns on them when they do."

Niki nodded and turned away to join her cousin in the search. She didn't have much technical knowledge, at least not when compared to Vickie, but her experience while dealing with criminals and her time in the FBI did give her some good insights that might help to shortcut the process.

Taylor turned to Bobby and hugged him despite the fact that he could feel that the mechanic was maybe not so comfortable with the affection. He didn't push away, though, but drew back after a few seconds.

"I appreciate your control, Bungees," he whispered. "We'll get Tanya back alive and safe, no matter what."

The mechanic nodded, his teeth gritted. "And I plan to rip a couple of heads off when it happens."

"You're damn right."

During the short drive to his base, Badawi considered the possible consequences of his little venture.

They were looking at a solid gain. Split down the middle, the profits were around three million Euros, about half of what their little base earned most years. He wasn't stupid enough to think he could hide that kind of profit margin from Khaled, not when he knew that most of his men were more loyal to their overseer than they were to him as team leader.

But it would be a solid bonus to all of them for a job well done and they would then have to find another way to hide the money they made. Khaled would not approve of any deals made without him so he would have to ensure that the men received most of the money when it was divided so they didn't take umbrage and see to it that he was summarily replaced.

He had expected Mashoul to cheat him on the payout and while maybe ten grand was missing from the split they had agreed to, he was happy to note that what he'd been paid was more than enough to justify the venture.

"You'll all have a lot of money to send home today," he commented when they arrived and the rest of the team gathered in front of him. "We knew there was money coming in but this is from your work."

They all cheered as Badawi handed the briefcase with the money to the man responsible for distributing the payouts. He was sure the bean counter would take a considerable bonus for himself before the night was out, but they all knew better than to cut their boss out of the profits, no matter whether he had been involved in the deal itself or not.

His eyes narrowed when he saw a few of those sent on the mission scratching their arms and shoulders. He recalled Mashoul showing similar discomfort when they had shared a drink, but he hadn't thought much of it. Still, if it had affected the rest of the men, there was always the possibility that something had gone wrong.

He approached one of them when he scratched his arm vigorously again. "Is something the matter?"

"We pulled our suits off to get the pelts and there were insects all over the place, biting and being a nuisance. It wasn't any different than the rest of our trips in, but you kind of forget that there is a horde of smaller creatures out there when you have the massive locusts to deal with."

Badawi nodded. He did remember reading about some of the latest discoveries, and more than a few of the researchers had said that there was a large number of the smaller creatures in the Zoo that weren't being studied given that the larger ones received most of the attention.

Still, it wouldn't be wise to simply shrug this aside. He wondered if he was simply being a little paranoid, but the memory of what happened with the rabbits was still very clear in his mind.

"I'll work up a poultice for you and all those who need it," he responded brusquely. "It'll help with the itching and hopefully prevent any further irritation or rash from developing."

The men inspected their arms and nodded in agreement. A few were already showing signs of both irritation and a rash, and he wanted to make sure there were no health problems that would force him to explain anything to Khaled.

He headed to the building that doubled as their clinic. None of them were doctors but a few had some training as army medics, nurses, and the like. It was better than nothing, especially since the actual doctors could make far more money and be much safer for it on any of the established bases.

While he'd never practiced any medicine himself, he did know of a handful of concoctions that would help with the kind of thing they suffered from. Not that he knew how or why it helped, but he didn't need to know why medications helped either, only that they did.

The first of the men filtered in as he finished putting the ingredients for it together.

"You know a little medicine, then?" the man asked as he sat and presented his arms for treatment.

"My mother was raised in the forests to the southwest of our current position," he responded. "She had to deal with all kinds of insects and their various means of being a pain in human asses and she taught me how to administer her treatments for when she wasn't in the mood to do so herself. I've kept them as a family secret for many years now."

"They can't be that useful around the desert, I would imagine."

The camp leader grinned and wrapped the first arm deftly. "No, but still, it is always a good idea to have such knowledge on hand should you need it. This will help with the itching and the irritation should be gone by the morning. If it isn't, come back to me for another application."

"It feels better already. Thanks."

The next man came in for his turn and Badawi's grin faded. If his suspicions were wrong, there would be no need for them to return for another dose in the morning. If they still had issues, however, he had a feeling they would be up a particular shit creek again as Americans liked to say.

And there was no paddle big enough to help them this time.

CHAPTER TEN

Of course they would keep her in a dump. She'd had no great expectations but even the remaining faint hope had been disappointed by the reality.

Tanya looked around and tried to make out exactly where they had brought her. She didn't know Vegas well enough to make any real assumptions and they had blindfolded her along the route after they'd made a couple of stops to cover their tracks.

They knew what they were doing, she had to give them that. Or maybe they were used to having to stay out of sight and merely went about this the way they usually did.

It wouldn't make much of a difference to know where she was but it was something to keep her mind occupied. She didn't particularly want to focus on the fact that she was currently kidnapped and waiting for word on what would happen to her.

They had been infuriatingly vague about what exactly they wanted from Bobby to secure her release, but she had a feeling that negotiations were not on the table. That said, whatever these guys thought they were doing, they had no idea of the amount of trouble they could expect, especially if something were to happen to her.

Something already had, of course. She had put up a fight when they dragged her into the building and even though she was blindfolded, Tanya was sure she'd broken someone's nose during the skirmish.

They'd given her a thick lip and a black eye for her trouble, but fuck if it wasn't worth it.

Now, unfortunately, all she could do was sit and listen to what sounded like a debate about what to do with her, which raised the question of why they had gone out of their way to piss Taylor and Bobby off if they didn't already have a plan in place for the situation.

"Are you kidding me?"

The voice drew her attention to the speaker, a tall man with blond hair and a short beard who advanced on the shorter, stockier one who had kidnapped her. The way the other man retreated from him revealed a clear distinction of power between the two of them.

"I showed some initiative in getting us a decent location to set up in," Cody snapped in an attempt to not lose any face in front of his men. "Something you should have done, quite frankly."

If this was where they were based, it was no wonder that they were desperate for other premises. Tanya couldn't help but wonder if she could catch tetanus by inhaling all the rust that was in the air.

"Do you think we need trouble with the police at this point?" the blond demanded, shook his head, and looked at the other men. "If anyone caught sight of you and they report it, do you think we'll be able to conceal that we're living here? Or if the Thirteens find out that you're snatching people in their territory, we'll be at war with them before we're ready."

Tanya tilted her head and tried to think of a name that was missing from that list. Having spent so much time around McFadden made it easy to forget that the man was something of a primal force, yet most of the criminals in the city had learned the lesson that messing with him would draw rapid and severe retaliation.

Thanks to Vickie and Desk keeping track of what was being said online by the organized crime in the city, she knew for a fact that they were well aware of the man's ability to fuck over anyone who raised a hand against him.

They all knew that he and Bobby had held Marino's money trucks up. Most knew that he had gone to Italy and unleashed a swarm of cryptids on the mafia boss who tried to bring him to heel.

That confirmed that these guys were new to the area. They hadn't heard of his reputation and would no doubt have a personal lesson on it sooner rather than later. It was something to look forward to.

Another point of interest was that Cody Lynch—who appeared to be second in command—did know what Taylor was capable of but his superior did not.

"We need to move out of here," the blond decided and shook his head. "Clear out in case someone saw you and find another place to set up, even if it's outside the city."

"What will we do with the bitch?" The pinched voice suggested that it was the one she'd injured when they dragged her up the steps, but she wasn't sure.

"We should kill her and move on," another suggested.

"We could have a little fun with her before we do," the one with the broken nose suggested. "Break the bitch before we send her off to pasture, wouldn't you say?"

"How the hell does that make sense?" The leader stopped in front of this man.

"You know—"

"A bitch is a dog. They don't go to pasture."

"I mean—"

"Shut the fuck up."

The man shrugged. "My point remains. We need a little fun after the boring shit we've been doing here. We might as well find out what Zhang thinks is so special about her before we have to kill her, right?"

Tanya's blood ran cold. It wasn't the kind of conversation she wanted to hear from her captors. Them talking about killing her was bad enough and she shuddered to think what the dumbasses thought of as fun.

The leader appeared to consider the suggestion for a moment, but even in the dull light of their surroundings, she caught sight of a karambit that he drew slowly from the back of his belt and she could tell from his body language that it was not intended for her.

The man moved quickly and buried the blade to the hilt in the man's stomach. She knew a thing or two about where to put a knife and knew it had gone directly into his liver to add to his growing list of injuries.

He groaned softly and his whole body suddenly lost all power it might have had before he sank to the floor.

It was not the kind of reaction she expected from criminals, and from the looks of the other bikers, they hadn't expected it either. All of them inched away slowly as the man cleaned his blade calmly before he sheathed it while he watched the injured man writhe on the floor in agony, still unable to do anything other than groan.

"You dumbasses went and did the only thing I told you not to do," the leader snapped, grasped Lynch by the neck, and shoved him against one of the nearby walls. His tone, however, was cold and emotionless. "Your dad is the only reason why you're not the one bleeding out right now. Until I say so, you and the two who were with you do not leave this building, do you understand?"

Cory nodded slowly and tried to pry the vice-like fingers away before he was finally released. He dropped to his knees and sucked in a deep breath while the other two approached.

"We need to call an ambulance for Danny," one of them said and backed away quickly like he expected to be the next one to feel the blade.

"You'll do no such thing." The blond shook his head. "He'll be dead in a little while, after which we'll find a nice little unmarked grave to bury him in. You two will clean up whatever mess is left behind. Call that the first stages of your punishment."

He shook his head as he moved away and left his men with little else to do but watch as their comrade continued to groan in agony. Tanya had been punched in the liver before and it had left her curled in pain for about fifteen minutes. She could only imagine the degree of suffering that stabbing it caused, and from the amount of blood coming from the wound, it looked like he had been cut deep and the blade had found numerous blood vessels.

Try as she might, though, she found it difficult to summon any kind of sympathy for the asshole who had suggested raping her not too long before.

Still, she thought she understood what was going through the leader's mind as he shook his head and crossed the room to get some water. He was between a rock and a hard place—he could either look weak in front of his gang or face retribution of the worst kind, although it didn't seem like he was aware of how bad things could get.

Either scenario would push him to kill her and cut his losses, and she could only hope that the team found her first. Bobby had to be going through hell too and would no doubt need to be talked down before he burned Vegas to the ground to find her.

Taylor seemed like the guy who would get the job done in that regard. Between him and Niki, they could make sure that his rage was unleashed on the right people.

JP paced the length of his office area, his scowl enough evidence of his displeasure that his brothers chose to simply wait until he'd cooled his temper to the point where he could act rather than react. The fact that he'd called them in before he'd reached this point was significant. It told them very clearly that something had happened to push all the wrong buttons, and they braced themselves for what could only be a serious wave in their relatively calm pond.

Finally, he spun on his heel to stride to his chair and sit with a grunt of displeasure. Juan-Carlos leaned forward expectantly while JD chose to lean back and regard them both warily. It was sometimes wiser to let the two of them thrash things out between them and then add his opinion if he had one.

Juan-Pablo thumped his fist on the table that doubled as his desk and his scowl deepened. "Those fucking Southies are either as nutty as squirrel shit or they have a master plan."

"Or both," JC conceded but his light tone was belied by his sudden frown. "What have they done?"

His older brother rested his elbows on the table. "They kidnapped Zhang's girlfriend."

"What in God's name possessed them to do something that stupid?" JD asked, his preference to remain neutral as long as possible suddenly forgotten. "Don't they know who they're dealing with? There's a goddammed good reason why we, the mob, and the cops steer clear of the strip mall."

"Either they don't know and have simply blundered into a very deep shithole—which I don't believe for one minute—or they know and have done it deliberately."

"But why?" Juan-Carlos asked. "What could they hope to gain by fucking with crazy McFadden and his team?"

"The way I see it, there is only one possibility. They want to take over Vegas."

"Well, yeah." JD shrugged, the gesture a silent expression of the "duh" he left unspoken. "But I don't see how leaving themselves open to retribution from Zhang and McFadden can help them accomplish that."

"It won't. They have a small presence here, which is why I chose to watch and wait. But Miles Lynch is no idiot, even though his son might not be the brightest bulb in the chandelier. My guess is this is a set-up—an excuse for the old man to send massive reinforcements in. I've been suspicious from the get-go, but this confirms it. They've deliberately antagonized the strongest player, even though they have no hope against him on their own. To survive, they need Miles to move his soldiers in. Once they've dealt with McFadden and Zhang, they will be perfectly positioned to move into a turf war."

"And we don't stand a chance against the full might of the GAMC forces," Juan-Carlos finished grimly and his brothers both nodded.

"No, we don't," JP agreed. "First prize is that they're simply assholes who have bitten the tail of the beast without realizing the shitstorm about to be unleashed on them. McFadden and his team sweep in and clear the decks and in so doing, remove the Southies before they become a problem for us."

"But we can't take the chance," Juan-David muttered. "We need to be prepared for the worst, which is Miles Lynch's cavalry riding in to rescue his asshat of a son as a pretext to wipe the rest of us off the map."

"Which means we need intel." JC pushed to his feet. "I'll get the street sweepers out—those with the natural ability to absorb snippets of information from unlikely sources and recognize what's important. We don't want to be caught with our pants down."

"Yeah." JP stood as well, his expression grim. "And have our soldiers watch these asshats closely too. I don't believe their farce of being this inept chapter struggling to make a place for itself. Miles Lynch is too savvy for that and does nothing without a master plan. It's a ploy. He wouldn't send his precious son into anything doomed to failure and the fact that Logan Quinn is heading up the local team speaks volumes.

"Even if they did miscalculate with this damn fool kidnapping, you can bet your bottom dollar that they'll milk the situation for all its worth. One way or another, the Southies are up to something and the Thirteens will be ready. Let them learn the hard way that they can't muscle in and take this town from us. Fuck them and Miles Lynch too."

CHAPTER ELEVEN

Logan ran his fingers through his beard and fought to control his emotions and think clearly. Containing his rage had been an effort and he hoped his actions would show them exactly what would happen if they tried to defy him again.

The fact was that he was at a loss as to what to do. Killing Danny had been the right move, he didn't doubt that for a second, but that was only because he wasn't sure if the real culprit was someone he could punish. Miles doted on his son, which made it difficult to judge what could be done to him without consulting the head of their organization.

Which, he decided after a moment, was exactly what he had to do before he considered further action. He shook his head before he took the burner phone from his pocket and dialed the number he was told to memorize before he'd left for Vegas. The phone rang three times before he hung up, crushed the device, and tossed the pieces into a nearby toilet. He made sure they flushed completely before he turned away.

With a few of the gang present in the communal area, he moved to the room he'd designated for his sole use only because it allowed him a modicum of privacy away from the eyes and ears of the rest of the men. In a few moments, his computer pinged with a message directing him to a private server that had been set up by their IT experts. Miles had grown increasingly wary of the FBI investigations surrounding the MC and now put every effort in to make sure the feds didn't listen to their conversations.

The video chat opened to reveal a man with a thick black beard and long hair, both starting to gray noticeably as he moved into his late fifties.

"Logan, it's nice to hear from you again." Miles growled his greeting in the kind of voice that told of a relationship with cigarettes that spanned decades.

"I'm sorry to make a connection like this so soon but a problem arose."

"The kind of problem you need my help with? I already told you to deal with the Thirteens the way you see fit. I trust your judgment."

"It's not about the local gangs. As far as I know, they are still in the dark about us and we've been careful to keep it like that until we're established and ready to implement the plan. My problem is with your son."

The older man sighed deeply and shook his head. "What the hell did Cody do this time?"

"We have had a real challenge to find a location to work from. He suggested one that's not owned by any of the local gangs, and it seems like they stay away from it. I send him in to have a talk with the owner—some guy named Bobby Zhang—and he refused point-blank. While I was thinking about ways to change his mind, Cody jumped in and kidnapped the guy's girlfriend."

"It sounds like a standard move," Miles commented and stroked his beard. "I get that he moved without your orders but it's something you should have done first."

Logan bristled at the admonishment but maintained his calm demeanor. "I would have, but the talk is that Zhang and his silent partner have connections with the Italian mob around here. I wanted to make sure there were no problems with them before I committed to a course of action."

"Wait. This silent partner—do you have a name?"

"Uh...yeah, give me a sec." He minimized the call and looked in the files they'd put together on the strip mall. "The dude's name is Taylor McFadden."

"Oh."

The grunt that followed sounded a little odd, and he opened the call again but hesitated when he saw something that was entirely out of character in the other man.

Miles Lynch looked concerned. Possibly even afraid given the way he fumbled for the pack of cigarettes he always carried inside his coat pocket.

"Oh?"

"I know a thing or two about Taylor McFadden and the team they run. The people in the city don't avoid them because of any connections to the mafia. It's because he's stone-cold crazy."

"We've dealt with crazy before."

"Not crazy with access to military-grade hardware and

connections in the Pentagon, and certainly not the kind of crazy that's been in and out of the Zoo more than eighty times."

"Shit. How many times?"

"You heard me. The biggest point is that Cody knows about the guy too. I talked to him about his situation in Vegas a few times before he left."

Logan's eyes narrowed as he considered what Miles was telling him. "It sounds almost like he is trying to involve me in a shit storm—intentionally."

"He might be. I love my son but he's a devious little prick. If I were you, I would keep my eye on him."

"I…might have already laid hands on him."

The older man leaned forward for a moment and looked like he was processing the news, but he nodded slowly. "There's a reason why I put you in charge of our Vegas venture, Logan, and not Cody. Do what you think is right and I'll support you for it."

"I don't think Nora will feel the same if she found out."

"She understands how we do business. Although she might put a beating on you for it, but it's for you to decide if it's worth it or not."

"What if I have to kill him?"

Miles scowled like he hadn't finished processing the idea himself. "Then Nora will probably beat you up at the funeral."

"I appreciate your confidence in me, Miles. I'll do everything to make sure that the worst doesn't happen."

"Don't worry about sparing my feelings about Cody. You have a crazy redhead who will descend on you any minute now and you need to decide what to do about it."

"Will do."

He cut the connection and the chat room was immediately shut down before anyone could pick up that it was in use. Logan took a deep breath before he stood, moved away from his computer, and left his "office" to join the rest of the men who had begun preparations for dinner.

It was takeout—surprise, surprise—but he doubted he would ever get tired of good Chinese food.

"Where are Brian and Kyle?" Logan asked and sat casually, his expression neutral to hide the conflict within.

"Danny died," one of the others muttered. "They're finding a place to bury him out in the desert."

He nodded. "From what I hear about this city, any number of bodies are dumped out there. Do you think they'll finally find Jimmy Hoffa?"

The other bikers chuckled but he noted that Cody was surprisingly silent and simply stared at the food, his jaw clenched. He knew the look well and it rarely boded well. Miles had told him to do what he needed to, and if the young man had earned the gang the ire of someone even his father feared, he would have to make sure he learned a proper lesson in authority—far from where his dad could save him.

People knew Miles Lynch didn't like hearing bad news. The idea was that if they knew that truth, they would be able to find the solution themselves so that by the time he was involved, they only had good news to share.

It was the kind of thing that inspired his people to be

creative and to take charge while still holding a healthy fear and respect for him. The only real downside was that they would sometimes encounter a problem that needed his attention and it would take a while before word of it reached him.

This time, Logan was right to involve him as soon as he did, even though the reason for his involvement was Cody.

In all honesty, he never much liked the kid, even if he was his son, but there were responsibilities that called to a man like him. Nora, doted on him, of course, and spoiled him rotten. Unfortunately, she had passed her devious mind on to him as well.

While it had undoubtedly served the kid well, Miles had always assumed that it would get him killed. It was possible that Logan would transform the presentiment into actual prophecy.

"Mark, get Colin and Sean in here. We need to have a chat."

His lieutenants looked up from the TV and he knew what they were thinking, although they were careful to hide it. It felt like a mortal sin to interrupt them while the Bruins were on the ice but sometimes, business had to interrupt sports. They could catch the highlights later.

All four moved into his office. Sean was the last one in and he made sure the hallway was empty before he closed the door behind him.

"Is there a problem?" Mark asked.

Miles nodded.

"Vegas?"

"Yeah."

"Fuck."

Mark had always discarded unnecessary words in conversation. The fat bastard was efficient to a fault sometimes.

"What problem has Logan gotten into this time?" Sean asked and folded his massive arms.

"Not so much gotten into as much as dropped in his lap. He's...inadvertently at odds with the group we know as McFadden and Banks."

His three lieutenants shared a quick look that told him he didn't need to explain how bad the situation was.

"How did he get into a situation with those crazy motherfuckers?" Colin asked and narrowed his eyes.

Miles hated to do it but it had to be done. As much as it hurt his reputation for it to be known that his son was a dumbass, it would hurt it even more if it looked like he was covering for the little bastard.

"I think Cody's trying to usurp Logan's position while he's there. He's not particularly smart but he's a slippery little shit, and he might have brought the storm down in an effort to take his place. But, as usual, he hasn't thought of what will happen to the rest of the organization if McFadden decides to take his problems up with the manager, so to speak."

He pointed at himself as if the point weren't already clear enough.

They nodded and exchanged glances.

"Okay, yeah, it is kind of funny that they managed to step in the shit five minutes after they touched down in Vegas," Colin commented with a soft chuckle. "You'd think they would know better than that—Logan especially. That dude has a knack for staying out of trouble.

Aside from that...uh, you know, situation with the garden hose."

That was a memory Miles didn't need to revisit and he shuddered and reached instinctively for his groin before he yanked his hand away.

"Either McFadden and his group will step in to clear the decks," he continued, anxious to change the subject, "or we'll have to send them reinforcements long before the planned timeline. If we do that, though, we'll officially side with the bastards and there will be no chance of plausible deniability. If we merely let them do their thing and McFadden and Banks come for us, we can claim they were starting their own gang—away from us and contrary to my orders."

It was a slimy thing to do but Miles would have been lying if he said that it was the worst thing he'd ever done to his fellow GAMC members. The whole point was that he knew they were more than willing to do the same to him if it ever came down to it. A dog-eat-dog world was the best way to describe the Guardian Angels, and the only way he'd reached the top was to claw and scratch up the food chain.

"I think we should wait on that for now." Mark growled belligerently and scratched the gray stubble on his cheek. "We should enlist some of our informants in the area and get a better idea of where our people in Vegas stand. For now, we hold off on making any commitments one way or the other."

The guy didn't say much, but Miles had learned to trust in his advice. He was one of the friends he had brought up with him. They'd been in kindergarten together, for shit's sake, and the man had plenty of opportunities during the past to fuck him over and take the top-dog position.

He hadn't, for some reason. Some people thought he was an idiot, but he knew his friend was content with his place. That said, the man didn't have the energy to be at the top where he would have to fight off every dumbass who wanted to take his place.

"Okay, that sounds like a good idea," the leader agreed. "Sean, you still have eyes on the streets in Vegas, right?" The man nodded. "It's time for them to earn their paycheck. See if they can provide the intel we need before the shit hits the fan."

"Will do, boss."

Sean and Colin both left the office but Mark remained and grunted softly while he opened the minifridge in the corner of the room. He retrieved two beer bottles and handed one to his boss before he twisted the cap off the one he held.

"Do you honestly feel right about this? It means you'll leave your kid hanging high and dry if that's what's needed."

"My wife has coddled the little shit for his entire life. If he wants to break out for himself, this is the time for him to show it. He's thrown himself into the deep end now and it's time to sink or swim."

There was a time when Vickie regularly worked all-nighters but she'd fallen out of the habit since joining

Taylor's team. Still, she could generally pull it off although it required considerably more coffee these days.

Having to do it when it was work, though, was a little more tiresome and when someone she considered part of their little family was in danger, it was even worse.

She lifted the cup of lukewarm coffee on her desk, took a quick sip, and winced at the acidity of it before she swallowed and returned her attention to the screen. Focus was a little difficult so she rubbed her eyes gently until the fuzziness cleared and she got to work again.

She and Desk had worked nonstop, combing through traffic lights and records of any kind to find out where the motorcycles went. Given that they had to do it manually, it took far longer than she wanted.

Taylor had set his freelancers the task of trying to find Tanya the old-fashioned way, and they coordinated their efforts to try to find any locations that had local security systems and cameras facing the road. When they saw anything that might work, they alerted Desk to them so she could hopefully find more eyes that would help with the tracking.

"Slooooooow," the hacker moaned as she spun her chair. "How many cameras does this city have?"

"Is that a rhetorical question or do you genuinely want to know?" Desk countered.

"Wait, do you know how many cameras are in the city?"

"I do not have a specific number as to how many cameras there are, given that there are so many going in and out of use at any given time from people's phones to security measures—"

"No, no. I meant how many traffic cameras there are."

"Thirteen thousand seven hundred and forty-three traffic cameras are currently functioning at this time," the AI responded. "The number currently in operation inside the zone where we estimated Tanya would be in is closer to two thousand."

Vickie rubbed her eyes again and leaned a little closer to her screen as she switched across each of the feeds and entered the code to search for the motorcycles the bikers were using.

"Is Bobby still in the strip mall?" she asked, not because she was curious but because she needed something for her brain to do while she went through the relatively mindless task in progress.

"He is but he is ready to jump down the throat of anyone we point him toward, so if you have a conscience, you might want to consider it."

"Do you have a conscience?"

The AI paused before answering. "I believe so, although whether it equates to what humans describe as their conscience is up for debate. I do not have a cricket on my shoulder telling me right from wrong."

"It would be weird if you did."

"It might interest you to know that the dummy AI has been discovered on the DOD's servers," Desk commented as they resumed their efforts.

"It took them long enough. Should we monitor that?"

"I do have measures in place to cover the developments but the search for Tanya has priority usage of my processing power."

That was good to know. She had many balls in the air, what with avoiding detection as well as monitoring the dummy AI situation. Still, it was reassuring that their little ploy appeared to be working.

Vickie made a mental note to check how much processing power she had at her disposal another time.

She almost didn't realize her phone was ringing before she pressed the answer and speaker button at the same time.

"What do you have me for me, Chezza? And please don't say another drive-through camera. Those things are crushing my will to live."

"I think I have something," the freelancer answered after a pause as if to decide what Vickie was talking about. "I had a quick chat with someone at an all-night convenience store in Huntridge. He's a motorcycle enthusiast, so he made sure the cameras were pointed at the street when they passed so he could see them."

"I'm already on it," Desk interjected and immediately called up the footage from around the time their search was focused on.

"That might be a problem. This was about a half-hour ago and there were only two bikes."

"We're looking for four."

"Sure, but if they're wearing Guardian Angel colors, we might be able to focus our search area to Huntridge since it could be where they're based."

The AI made a good point and Vickie called up the image from the timeline Chezza suggested.

Sure enough, two motorcycles passed the store and one of them carried a suspiciously shaped bag on the back. It also rode a little lower than the other one.

Her immediate assumption was that they had already

killed Tanya and were disposing of the body but she pushed it down savagely. She wouldn't lean toward that particular brand of despair yet.

"See if you and Jiro can track them," Desk suggested. "I am following them right now. They aren't as careful as the other team was so I'll be able to get you a map."

"What do you want us to do when we find the bastards?" Chezza asked. "What—oh, yeah, Jiro says we should drive them off the road and tune them up a little."

"Not yet," Vickie disagreed quickly. "If you find them, follow them but don't do anything else and make sure you aren't noticed. We don't need any itchy trigger fingers to panic and do something stupid."

"Noted. We'll be in touch."

The line cut and she took a sip of the coffee and made another face as she made herself swallow it.

"Why do you force yourself to drink it if you hate it?" Desk asked.

"Because, while I need the coffee, getting a fresh pot made takes a few minutes that are better spent helping Tanya. I'll drink decent coffee when she is safe—or when this shit that tastes like bile runs out."

CHAPTER TWELVE

He would bet good money that some kind of preservative had been used on the pelts.

Pavel rubbed his arms gently and sighed at the temporary relief it provided him. Unfortunately, he knew only too well that it would return like it had over the past two hours while they had processed them. It brought little comfort to know that the other five who had worked alongside him suffered the same effects, although to varying degrees.

They'd used gloves too, which meant that whatever was affecting them was probably in powder form or something. It reminded him of how everyone had laughed when he suggested they start working with masks whenever they applied the processing chemicals to the furs. It was like the dumb assholes wanted to die or something.

"We should wear full hazmat suits with these," one of the other workers commented. He was a new guy who hadn't been around when the rest of the crew had been so rudely amused by his suggestion to use masks.

"Agreed." Pavel grunted and pushed the third to last pelt into the storage container they used to keep them cool. "We're skilled workers. If Stepan wants to work us like this, he needs to provide proper gear. He should know that there aren't many people qualified for this kind of work."

"Why are you complaining?" Tomas paused to look at him and shook his head. "These pelts make him so much money that he pays us ten times the going rate we would usually earn. If you think you can make better money elsewhere, I know of at least fifteen assholes who would be willing to take your place and with less than half the complaining. Buy your own security wear if you're so concerned about what we're touching here."

Pavel raised his hands to display the gloves he wore and gestured at his mask. "Both bought at my own expense. But no, you keep talking about how much money you're making while you inhale who the hell knows what they used on these pelts. I'm sure your wife will appreciate your bonuses while she's sucking Matej's cock at your funeral."

"Fuck you."

Matej smirked at the comment but none of them had anything else to say about it while they worked. The last few pelts were processed quickly and stored, and Pavel was the first to move away from them. He scratched his arms and growled softly as the rest of the team changed out of their work clothes.

It certainly was more convenient to stay at the processing plant during the long work week, and while they had to spend the nights in the barracks when they were on shift, they would be able to return home for the weekend and spend time with their families.

He'd been away for too long, he thought morosely. Ada would prepare something warm and homemade for him when he arrived and he would take her shopping as a reward for having the full responsibility of the kids while he'd been away. Tomas was not wrong about the bonuses they would make from working on the goddammed pelts, after all, and they would have a healthy surplus of spending money for the next six months or so.

"Damn it," Pavel whispered and attacked his arm again. He shook his head as he pulled his gloves and mask off and tossed them into a nearby refuse bin. At this rate, he would have to invest in gloves that went all the way up his arms. They were a little more expensive but if they had to deal with the shit that came out of the Zoo, it would always be better to be safe than sorry.

They exited the factory and locked the door behind them before they crossed the grassy area between the workspace and the barracks where he could already smell food being prepared for them by the staff inside. It wasn't quite as good as what waited for him at home but he wouldn't turn his nose up at a meal prepared by other people.

A small thicket of trees offered some shade to the living areas. It was a low-cost area that didn't require much work or maintenance when it came to landscaping and had no fancy beds or hedges or anything like that. Still, it was a decent enough space where they could enjoy their lunch break or downtime when the weather was good and the buildings were a little too hot.

The perimeter fence, although distant, was visible all around and the guardhouse at the gate was considerably farther away at the end of the long driveway from the entrance to the factory buildings. The access point was manned but not weaponized. It was a civilian establishment that had never needed to fight off anything more than a couple of errant poachers from time to time. A few shots into the air were generally enough to remind any criminals that they were on private property.

A couple of his colleagues continued to scratch their arms and from what he could see, a rash had developed in places.

"Take a shower," Pavel suggested as they approached the barracks. "I think there's ointment in the first aid kit in the kitchen that you can use too if it's still a problem."

They nodded and gestured for him to enter the kitchen from where the smell of food already made his mouth water even before they stepped inside.

He would have to have a chat to Stepan about what was being put on the pelts these days. Maybe the guy would do his job and protect the people working for him from whatever caustic shit they'd used in the fucking barbaric lands in the Sahara.

It was like the wild west out there, and he could only imagine the kind of mindset people would have to dive head-first into an alien jungle for money. It made for interesting fiction but the reality was a little too horrifying to contemplate for too long.

Pavel drew a deep breath and shook his head when he realized he needed to scratch his arms again. Maybe it was time for him to take his own advice. A hot shower and the application of ointment would probably be a wise choice for what to do before dinner.

It truly had begun to feel like a wild goose chase. As much as they had managed to narrow down the search area for Vickie and Desk to keep looking, the idea of following the bikers who transported a suspiciously human-looking package had grown old fairly quickly.

Chezza shook her head and rubbed her temples as the bikers pulled into a nearby convenience store parking lot. It was an hour until sunrise and their quarry had driven around aimlessly for hours. The thought that they were carrying a body had been full of promise before but at this point, all she wanted was for the endless driving to end.

"Any minute now," Jiro whispered as they pulled into the parking lot as well but kept their distance while the bikers left their vehicles outside and went in for refreshments.

"Any minute now what?" she asked.

"Vickie will call and tell us they found where Tanya is and we can corner these asshats and beat the living shit out of them."

"Taylor might want us to join the team to get Tanya out."

"Sure, but I don't think he would mind us tuning the shitheads up a little first to get some information out of them about the place we'll attack."

"Information? And satisfaction?"

"That too. We don't have to enjoy our work but it's always a plus, right?"

Chezza scowled at him. "You're a sadistic bastard, aren't you?"

"It's a good thing I'm in such good company, eh?"

She shrugged. While she would never have described herself as outright sadistic, there certainly was a streak to her that was more than happy to inflict fifteen different kinds of pain on anyone who hurt the people she cared about.

As much as she hated to admit it, the McFadden and Banks team had inched themselves into that category. Maybe she was connecting to them too much and it was time to back off. She did care for Trick and Jiro, though. That was unavoidable given that they had worked together for so long.

Well, longer than she had worked with most other people, even when she was in the military.

"Heads up."

Chezza looked up from her phone, hoping and waiting for some kind of call to come through. Jiro was too much of a professional to point and he even looked away, which allowed her to see what was happening without being noticed.

Another car had pulled up at the convenience store. Bright decals, pulsing lights, and music playing way too loudly indicated that these were the Thirteens, a large local Mexican gang that had a tenuous alliance with La Cosa Nostra in the city. Although from what she heard, such alliances were not guaranteed and had resulted in all-out wars in the Midwest not very long before.

Four occupants scrambled out and they saw the motor-cycles almost immediately. Jiro leaned forward and his eyes narrowed as he watched the group kick the tires of the bikes. It looked like their appearance in the area wasn't by chance. They had been called in, maybe to deal with the unwanted gang members and kick them out of territory controlled by the Thirteens.

It wasn't long before the two bikers inside heard the noise and moved out quickly to see what was being done to their bikes. The Thirteens confronted them immediately. Chezza couldn't hear what was said but it was absolutely clear that an altercation was about to break out between the two groups.

She punched Vickie's number in and the hacker answered after the first ring.

"Vickie, do you see this?"

"See what?"

The girl sounded buzzed like she had reached the height brought on by her third cup of coffee and wouldn't come down anytime soon.

"We're parked out in front of a convenience store on..." Chezza craned her neck and tried to catch sight of the street name.

"I have you on camera now," Desk interjected before she could finish. "It looks like our bikers ran into some trouble."

"Or some trouble ran into them," Jiro corrected. "I would say they were alerted to the presence of bikers in the area and came to try to drive them off. Do you think we can listen in on what is being said?"

"I'll get on that. Give me a sec." Vickie paused for a few moments and tapped her keyboard until voices could be heard in the background. "When will these dumbasses learn to tape the mics on the phones? How haven't they been caught by the FBI yet?"

"I think it has something to do with a reasonable right to privacy," the AI suggested.

"Since when has that ever stopped those assholes in the triple-letter agencies?"

The hacker made a good point. All they were capable of, as amazing as it was, had to do with the kind of intrusions that had been put into effect in the early double aughts. Chezza knew more than a few of the paranoid types and as much as she liked Vickie, she only showed exactly how right they were to be paranoid.

"What the hell are you doing here?" one of the Thirteens asked the bikers. "Have you lost your way? You might want to look into installing proper GPS on these toys of yours."

The gang members were blocking the bikers from their vehicles, which meant that this wouldn't be a pleasant or civilized discussion about property ownership.

"Let us get out of here before anything gets blown out of proportion," one of the bikers responded sharply.

"So you can run back to your little friends and they can get on their bikes and come to help you? Not likely. A lesson needs to be taught. There's no room for you mick shits to barge in here. This'll show the rest of you assholes that you're better off peddling whatever you can in that cold, dark shithole you call Boston."

"So we should leave this city to you beaner assholes and your guinea fuckbuddies?" The biker took a step forward and spat on the ground. "Go suck a bag of Italian dicks."

That last insult seemed to touch on a nerve that hit harder than any of the others. All four of the Thirteens drew the knives they carried. The bikers did the same and it wasn't long before it devolved into a melee that prompted the owner of the convenience store to call the police. Or maybe he had alerted the Thirteens to the bikers and he now called to say he'd never intended for things to get that bad on his doorstep.

It was over almost as quickly as it began. The bikers were heavily outnumbered and while one of the Thirteens fell heavily and clutched a knife wound that cut deeply into his jugular, the others pounced immediately and it wasn't long until both of their rivals lay in a pool of blood.

"See, that should have been us," Jiro pointed out and flipped a butterfly blade he owned open and closed while he watched idly as the violence unfolded.

The gang members froze for a moment when they heard the low, distant wail of sirens but they recovered their wits and rushed away. They made no effort to retrieve their fallen man before they dived into their car, still blasting music, and drove away to the sound of squealing tires.

"We should probably get out of here too," Chezza suggested. "It's possible the cops will decide to question everyone in the area about what happened here."

Jiro nodded, slapped his knife shut again, and started the engine. He pulled out of the parking lot mere moments before the flickering red, white and blue lights approached the scene.

"Another dead end," he muttered as they pulled away and turned to take the shortest route to the shop. "And it started with so much promise too."

"And we didn't even get to look in the bag," Chezza agreed and her expression revealed the direction her thoughts had taken. While she didn't want to say it out loud, her greatest fear was that the suspicious package held Tanya's body.

"It's not her," Jiro said as if reading her thoughts. She looked at him, ready to argue, but he simply shrugged. "Whoever was in there—and yes, I agree that it could only have been a body—was considerably bigger than her. At best, we might have got the identity of some dead gangster, which might also explain that altercation earlier, but it wouldn't have brought much in the way of a clue as to where she is right now."

During the short drive to the workshop, Chezza rubbed her eyes as the effects of having been up all night doing a whole bunch of nothing crept in. Her partner's assurance had eased her concerns somewhat but it was still immensely frustrating to be so exhausted with nothing to show for it.

Even worse, it looked like Trick had enjoyed a good night's sleep.

"How was your hunting?" he asked as the two climbed out of the car.

"We are left with a grand total of nada in our hands having been out there all night," Jiro answered. All she had the energy to do was flip the man the bird when he offered them a cup of coffee as the sun began to rise.

In all honesty, Jennie had expected them to make an appearance much sooner than this.

She had waited for two whole damn days for them to

find the fucking dummy and come to her about it and now, they waited for her in her office—with her boss, she noted, as if his presence would lend weight to their demands.

A laugh almost escaped her and she took a hasty sip of her coffee and used the cup like a mask to give herself time to wipe the smug grin from her lips. It was important to react realistically in the situation for their ploy to work.

And realistic, in these circumstances, meant that she would be enraged, and being approached about it before she was given the chance to enjoy her morning coffee was that much more insulting.

Enraged had a good ring to it. She could pull that off. As she lowered the coffee cup, she tensed her facial muscles to show how annoyed she was at seeing people in her space before she'd reached it herself.

"What in the name of the true and unmitigated hell is going on here, Hammond?" she demanded as she barged into the office and made the agents jump from the seats they'd taken the liberty of occupying.

"These are agents with the DOD, Banks," Hammond answered and ran his clammy hands nervously over his balding head. "They're here to...well, they want you to..."

"We need you to confirm that what is on this USB drive is your work," one agent interrupted before her boss could complete his stuttered explanation. "I'm Agent Marvin and these are Agents Marvin and Edwards. No relation."

Given that the other Agent Marvin was African American and the first was very clearly of Welsh descent, that assumption was easy to make.

"What's on it?" Jennie asked and took the device with

sufficient impatience to signal that she didn't already know exactly what she was looking at.

"That is need to know and you do not need to know, Miss Banks."

Jennie growled in annoyance as she sat behind her desk and plugged the drive firmly into her computer on the first attempt as it was booting up. There was no time to contemplate exactly how impressive the feat was, and she opened a coding program to check what was on the drive.

"Well?"

Marvin looked a little too smug for her liking, and as much as all this was part of the plan, she had to fight the impulse to knock him down a peg or two for the time being.

"Motherfucker," she muttered, hoping to try to drag it out a little more while the agents waited for her.

"Is it your work or not?"

She looked up from her screen, an eyebrow raised. "Do you seriously need me to answer that? You wouldn't be here asking me about it if you didn't already know."

"Answer the fu—answer the question, please."

"Yeah, that's my code work." It was both weird and ironic how that wasn't even a lie.

"Is that an admission, then?"

"An admission of what? It's my coding, yes, but I don't know why you brought it to me. Some dumbass corrupted it almost to the point where I can't recognize it."

"What?" Marvin circled the desk to see what she was looking at.

"Yeah. Look at these simulations. If I were to plug that

into a functioning program, it would shut it down almost immediately."

"Can you repair it?"

She looked at the man and sighed heavily. "Of course, if I had three weeks and nothing else to do with my time. As it is, I have considerable work—the kind I'm paid to do. Don't you assholes have IT specialists of your own who could do the same?"

The agent opened his mouth and turned to Hammond, who looked like he tried not to laugh.

"Don't look at me," her manager said with a chuckle. "She's not wrong about that. If you want her to work for you, it has to be done the way it was before—through the proper channels that bring the company money. The fact that she was willing to look at it at all is a favor she does not owe you."

"Now, if you assholes are done wasting my time by asking questions to which you already know the answers, I have actual work to get back to." Jennie turned her attention to her computer screen, pulled the USB drive out of the computer, and tossed it to the other Marvin. "In case you need lessons in subtext, that was me telling you fuck off."

The last two words made Hammond hurry to the door to hold it open for the agents while he motioned for them to leave as quickly as possible.

She kept her expression as annoyed as she could until they had all left and reached the elevator. Satisfied that they were safely out of earshot, she closed the blinds quickly and ran a quick sweep through the office to make sure the agents hadn't left any listening devices behind before she connected to the secure network she used to stay in touch with Desk.

"Did you catch that?" she asked as the AI joined the connection after making sure they weren't being listened to.

"I did and I will keep track of the results."

CHAPTER THIRTEEN

Logan had dated a yoga instructor before he'd spent time in prison, a crazy woman who knew how to bend around him whenever she could—a predilection that hadn't encouraged any kind of future together. Despite this, the one thing he took from the relationship was that she taught him to control his nerves, his anger, and his anxiety. It was a simple process of taking deep breaths while he let his mind go to a quiet place.

He doubted that she meant him to use it while helping to push for a criminal enterprise's expansion. She probably hadn't intended for him to use her instruction to help himself stay calm in combat situations either—the kind he'd had to endure while behind bars—and yet he had.

She'd broken up with him when he was in prison but her lessons remained fixed in his mind.

Deep breaths, calming thoughts, and a quiet place—one where he beat the absolute shit out of Cody and the men he'd brought with him—were what he needed right now. He had hoped that letting the kid have people he trusted around him would settle his mindless ambitions, but all he'd done was embolden them.

It was entirely his fault for not seeing how that would play out.

Now, both of the kid's remaining supporters had wandered into another gang's territory with predictable results, the kind he had expressly told them to avoid by not leaving the base. Worse, they hadn't disposed of Danny's body—ostensibly the reason for their absence—and that left a grand total of three corpses, enough to ensure the committed attention of local law enforcement.

"Fucking shits!"

Logan stared ahead, surprised as the bottle of beer that had been in his hand careened across the room into the wall. If anything, he was improving the overall look of the dump but it was a waste of good beer. Still, he felt a little better having something physical to vent his anger on, even if it was only a bottle.

The idiots were dead, although that would probably prove to be a good thing given how stupid they were.

And, of course, he had other problems. A little research had revealed the kind of legend McFadden had become in the area. It seemed the real reason people avoided the strip mall was because they were afraid that if he chose not to fuck them up royally himself, he would unleash a horde of cryptid monsters on them in their sleep.

He ran his fingers through his beard and looked across the room to where the other men slept on their cots, undisturbed by his outburst. They could sleep through a hurricane.

Maybe if he returned Tanya to the strip mall, he would

be able to mitigate the fallout. He didn't need the McFadden and Banks team breathing down his neck while he stared down the barrel of a turf war. Their numbers were already low and now, he was down three more.

These first few months were critical to their overall plan—one they'd dissected, discussed, and thrashed out until it had been honed to the sharp edge of a military campaign. They would move in with low numbers, establish themselves in a small territory that presented a non-threatening façade, and when the time was right, Lynch would mobilize his forces. When they descended en masse, the GAMC Vegas chapter would unleash a concerted attack against both the Thirteens and their mob cronies and with their greater numbers, would sweep the opposition from the board.

The people in Boston would not be impressed by the current setbacks, and this was his one chance to prove himself to be more than merely a foot soldier in the GAMC.

The worst part was that he knew his men well enough to realize that when they found out about what happened with the Thirteens, they would be riled to the point of violence. They would want someone to pay and Tanya was there, an easy target.

He was not quite established as the leader with the men yet and despite his efforts, he still needed to do something to assert his authority. Killing her was one option. Roughing her up badly if he did choose to return her was another, except that would also antagonize McFadden and Banks.

Or he could kill another couple of idiots who seemed to

lean toward loyalty to Cody to let them know who was in control. He'd already pushed the kid into revealing himself to be nothing more than a cut-throat thug whose own father had no real love for him. The fact that he was still determined to undermine him showed what a bad idea it was to give him any kind of authority.

Logan drew another deep breath, closed his eyes, and pulled another beer from his cooler. He needed to sleep. It was pointless trying to tackle all these issues when exhausted.

Surprisingly, the base run by the French, Israelis, and Indians was somehow the most cosmopolitan of them all.

Sam could see it was where most of the independent merc groups had established themselves, and this made it the one place that seemed less like a military base and more like a small city that burgeoned with work and bustled continuously with activity.

"It looks like they see considerable business," Chen commented as they drove through the streets.

"Most of the mercs received a good chunk of money for helping to reclaim the Japanese base from what I heard," Elke noted and studied her tablet. "People who live in these conditions generally don't save too much of their money, not when their next day at work could leave them unable to spend any of it."

It was an unfortunate reality that under all the shine and veneer of the people around them, they were looking at men who committed themselves to the Zoo on a daily basis. Most of the higher quality mercs were based in the US base, though, which meant that these guys were generally those outfitted with weapons and armor of lower quality. This made their fears that much more real.

There were also several independent businesses in the area that profited from the mercs as well as the French Foreign legion and the small forces supplied by their Israeli and Indian allies.

"Why don't they commit more troops to the base?" Sam asked.

"My guess is that they only put in the barest minimum to claim a place here," Chen suggested. "It leaves them an opening should politicians or profits drive them to expand their presence."

The kid was right, of course. The merc village, with all the informal housing set up for the enterprising individuals, would easily make way if they wanted a proper force on the base. For the moment, though, what they lacked in official numbers was easily made up for by the freelancers who filled their ranks when they were needed.

"From what I can see here, they have facilitators who post jobs from outside the Zoo and so help the mercs find clients. It makes it the best location to find work that isn't from the local militaries," Sam added.

"And it doesn't look like their work on the wall has suffered from it," Chen commented.

"We'll see about that," Elke muttered. "One thing you can't trust freelancers to do is report everything with precision. They'll twist and bend data to suit whatever gets them paid the most."

"Says the freelancer," Fix muttered and covered his words with a cough.

"Fuck you."

He grinned and looked up as they approached the area where it looked like the people in charge of the base were waiting for them.

Uniforms from all three militaries were present, and it appeared that there was no separation like there was between the Japanese and the Russians. All shared the same base, although they had their individual sections.

"Your base is alive with activity," Elke commented as the commander of the French Foreign Legion greeted them. "It's like nothing else in the area."

"You are not wrong," the man replied with a heavy French accent. "They all got paid for their work at the Japanese base and are trying to reinvest it in the businesses here. It is a welcome change."

"Change?" Sam asked.

"Limited Zoo excursions meant an economic slow-down. It impacts everyone and drives those who are more desperate to take the more dangerous jobs. It's an ever-present threat and too real for us to be foolish about it. Which, I suppose is the reason for you being here. Come, we will see to what you need to know about the construction of the wall."

"That's why we're here," Sam muttered and tried to ignore the terse stares directed at the ENSOL group as they were guided into a nearby building.

"Miles? How can I help you?"

It was early morning in Vegas and Logan didn't look like he'd had much sleep. Still, Miles had a feeling that he would be more than pleased to hear what he had to say.

"I'm sorry. It looks like I dragged you away from sleep."

"I only had a couple of hours," Logan muttered and rubbed his eyes. "It's been an eventful evening and morning so far."

"It's about to get more eventful. We spoke to our ears on the street and it looks like our position in Vegas is under some threat."

"Are the Dopplers being recalled to Boston?"

"The opposite. We've decided to send you much-needed reinforcements to deal with the problems you're facing. Some of our more battle-hardened veterans are already on their bikes and headed to Vegas. They're coming armed and ready to do battle under your command."

Logan studied the screen incredulously like he wasn't sure what to say to that.

"You're putting considerable trust in me."

"I already put trust in you to lead our Vegas venture. All I'm doing now is making sure you have the men and weapons you need to win."

"How many?"

"I've called the chapters and issued a call for the men who have the experience necessary and a determination to see our enemies eliminated. I've had word that a dozen are already on their way toward you and more are coming. You'll have some real tough shits, ready to deal with the mafia, the gangs and...other problems you might have."

The younger man lowered his head. Miles had seen

many of his men jump at the opportunity to tell him about what they had planned or even make boasts about what they could achieve, but Logan was quiet for a moment as he considered the news he'd received.

Or maybe he was simply too exhausted to react with enthusiasm.

"I know you've put considerable trust in me," the Vegas leader said finally, his expression grim and dour. "I'll make sure you see a return on your investment—all your investments."

"I'm sure you will, you crazy bastard." Miles chuckled and shook his head. "Now, get a little more rest. You have people rolling in from Phoenix in four hours or so and I want you rested and ready to show them the ropes."

"Will do."

Miles killed the connection and went through the motions of erasing everything. While he believed the assertion that nothing was ever truly erased on the Internet, his IT people had assured him that they had put his business beyond the skill of the dumbasses employed by the FBI.

After all, if they were any good, they would be plying their wares on the free market, not forced to work for the feds.

Mark looked like he hadn't slept much either. He stood in the corner of the office, his arms folded in front of his chest.

"Starting a war like this is never a decision that should be made lightly."

He wasn't wrong about that.

"It wasn't made lightly. We know almost everything there is to know about the situation in Vegas and our long-term plans were to move in force. This simply means we've been pushed into a possibly prolonged turf war rather than the quick strike and destroy tactic we'd prefer. All options that would allow us to keep the peace and our original time frame would mean we lose the kind of face that would result in us losing considerably more than that in the coming weeks. We have to make a show of force now."

"You're not wrong about that," Mark muttered. "And Logan's a tough bastard. He knows how to manipulate the gangs in the area. My real concern—"

"Is McFadden. You watched the fight, didn't you?"

"I made some money on it too. Betting on the giant redhead got me my new wheels if you'll recall."

"Right. But we're sending an army to support Logan. Even McFadden won't be able to stand against that."

CHAPTER FOURTEEN

There were worse places to be imprisoned in. Tanya knew that on a practical level although not many came to mind, but the bathroom was at least a little more private than being tied to a chair in public where the men were. A twin mattress had been provided for her and they had managed to hook up the water in the room that allowed her access to the sink and the toilet.

While these were small luxuries—the kind she usually took for granted—she was relieved that her captors had provided a way to preserve at least some of her dignity. The alternative truly didn't bear thinking about.

They'd even untied her on the assumption that the lock on the door was enough to prevent her from escaping—a serious underestimation they would hopefully soon regret. She smirked when she considered that their mistake could have been avoided if they had kept the one man alive who had personally experienced what she was capable of.

Still, she had no phone or smartwatch on her to reach Bobby or that would enable Vickie and Desk to track her location. She could hear them talking outside, and while most of the words were muffled beyond recognition, the tone was easily understood. They were in trouble and they didn't know what to do about it.

It seemed that was what happened when people knew Taylor was coming for them. It was an odd thing to be on the opposite end of the situation but it was instructive— not only to hear them planning but also to be away from where her team was so she had to guess what the crazy giant would do next.

She hadn't been there long but already had some idea about their patterns, their situation, and what they were most likely to do at what point in the day. This meant that when more motorcycles pulled up outside, it broke the tentative pattern she'd established and drew her to perch on the narrow sill of the tiny window so she could peer out.

From what she could tell, the bikers had received reinforcements. Given that the two factions she'd identified were already turning on one another, she could only question whether having more people mixed in the current mess would be better or worse.

Still, the routine seemed unaltered. From the shadows outside, it looked like the morning was almost at its end, which meant someone had been sent out to purchase lunch. If what she could see of the packages being brought up was any indication, it included a good supply of beer to celebrate the newcomers.

If there was ever a time to break out, it would be now. She drew a deep breath, steadied herself, and peeked out through a narrow crack in the door. Not that she could see much. Logan—she'd picked up the name of the leader from their conversations—had ordered her to be confined in the bathroom to keep her away from the men, but she wouldn't make the mistake of assuming it had been out of the goodness of his heart.

Tanya reminded herself that she owed the assholes absolutely nothing, and that included zero cooperation on her part. From inside her little cell, she could hear the distinctive sounds of beers being cracked and what she assumed was some type of sports event on the television they'd installed. She assumed the new group was from Boston and that the sports team was from there as well but gave it little thought.

They made an infernal racket, shouting some kind of chant loudly in a good rhythm to tell their team to do and hit something.

As irritating as the cacophony was, it gave her the opportunity she had hoped for.

She shifted slightly so she could push her hand into a small hole in the drywall beside the door. It had taken forever to scrape and cut as best she could with a small sliver of broken tile she'd found to widen the aperture enough to push the rest of her arm through.

Most of the work to replicate the hole in the outer side had already been completed, but she'd been hesitant to push through completely without some kind of distraction. The last thing she wanted was for her escape efforts to be noticed, and this seemed like her first and only opportunity to make the final push through so she could feel the opposite side of the door. She set to work and had to consciously release the breath she'd held inadvertently more than once.

Finally, the last of the wall crumbled and she managed to use the piece of tile to stop it from falling outward. Cautiously, she peered through into the open area beyond and nodded with satisfaction. The bikers were all faced away from her, their attention fixed on the screen.

It might not be the most effective way of doing things and could easily come to nothing but at this point, she counted on their general idiocy to play in her favor. If this didn't work, she'd have to look at ways to safely exit via the third-floor window or dig a hole through the drywall big enough for her to squeeze through. Neither option had much appeal given the time constraints.

"Please, please, please—yes!"

They'd left the key in the door, the dumb idiots, and all she had to do was twist it carefully and not pull the goddammed thing out. Working blind was tricky, especially since she didn't have anything like a mat or a blanket to slide under the door so she could push the key out, let it drop, and pull it through.

A part of her wanted to simply kick the flimsy barrier down and fight her way out. That had always been an option to attempt if the situation became desperate, mainly because she had no control over whether these assholes would decide to cut their losses and run, leaving her dead or mangled, although she would certainly enjoy it.

Unfortunately, the new arrivals rendered the odds of her success even more remote than they had been previously and it was now relegated to an absolute last resort.

She twisted the lock when a loud cheer erupted from

the next room to provide her with all the noise she needed to pull the door open slowly. Her heart racing, she tried to stay as low as possible and not in direct sight until she was sure that no guards had been positioned close to her improvised cell.

Either they weren't too experienced at this whole holding someone hostage business or they simply underestimated her. It was faintly insulting that they didn't think she was trouble enough to require watching, although the sensible part of her brain reminded her that it was something to be grateful for. She could be offended later when she was out and safe.

Tanya peeked through the opening to make sure her captors were still focused on the screen before she darted out, slipped under the rotting railing, and lowered herself carefully to the first floor of the building. Although she moved as silently as she could, the racket they made provided more than enough noise to mask her escape. She knew they always made someone watch the bikes parked out in the back but they hadn't seemed concerned that the front door wasn't covered.

Moments later, she bolted out of the house and sprinted up the street with as much power as she could summon. The first prize would be to locate someone who would be able to help her, but the area didn't look like it saw much traffic, even in the middle of the day. The rundown buildings gave the distinct impression of an area where she could not expect to find the kind of good Samaritan who would allow her access to a phone.

Still, not all hope was lost. She noticed a small parking lot not too far away, although the midday heat made it difficult to focus and to continue her pace. They hadn't spared much in the way of food or water for her, and she'd had no idea how much rust would come out in the water of the sink in the bathroom they'd locked her in.

As a result, she'd been hesitant to trust that it wouldn't kill her before it accomplished anything close to hydration.

"Oh…shit," Tanya whispered when a sudden onset of dizziness slowed her as she reached the parking lot. She staggered toward the door of what looked like a convenience store where an older gentleman with tanned skin and a receding hairline watched the television in the corner of the store.

Someone like him wouldn't be alone like this without some protection—the kind she might find useful.

After a deep, slow breath, she pushed the door open and winced when a soft electronic ping alerted the owner of her arrival and startled her a little. He turned with a practiced smile that faded quickly when he saw the condition she was in.

"Call…call the police," she whispered.

"Do you seriously think the police come here, lady?" the owner asked with genuine disbelief.

"Fine." She approached the counter he now half-cowered behind. "I need to use your phone to call the people who will come here to help me."

"I don't want to get involved in whatever gang violence bullshit you're a part of. You have to leave."

"I need your phone."

She knew what he was reaching for the moment he moved his hands and reacted instinctively. Fortunately, her body was still able to access memory that years of combat had ingrained in her and she grasped the barrel of the shotgun as soon as it appeared from where it had been hidden on the other side of the counter.

The man was relatively small, thank God, and she was able to drag him and the weapon over the surface before he could bring it to bear. With little effort, she yanked it from his hands.

"I won't ask you again," Tanya snapped. "And unlock it."

"There's money in the register," the man pleaded.

"I'm not here to rob you, dumbass. I only need to call for help."

He handed her the unlocked phone and she pressed the numbers quickly. Even though most of her calls were made from her phone's directory, she'd needed to call Elisa more than a few times and press the digits herself, something that had irritated her at the time but was now a godsend since they were committed to memory.

The device started dialing but it had barely rung once when the thunderous rumble of motorcycles outside told her that this wasn't quite the victory she had hoped it would be.

When she looked up, she realized immediately that the two bikers had recognized her as soon as they pulled up in front. Whether they had noticed her disappearance and had come looking or not didn't matter.

"Hello?"

"Elisa, it's me," Tanya shouted into the phone and lifted the shotgun to aim at the door as both men entered.

"Tanya? Where the hell are you?"

"At the 702 Mart—I'm not sure where, but still in Vegas," she yelled as the men entered, their hands already on their weapons although they hurried toward cover as she pulled the trigger.

The click of an empty magazine was almost as loud as if the gun had fired.

"I'm sorry," the owner whispered from the ground where he'd fallen prone in anticipation of gunfire from the new arrivals. "I'm not allowed to keep the weapon loaded."

"Motherfucker." She growled in frustration when she saw realization enter the bikers' eyes too as they began to advance on her.

"Tanya, are you there?"

This would have to do. It was close enough to the biker gang HQ to help the team and if Vickie and Desk were on the call, they would be able to track the location even if her directions were less than helpful.

She did the only thing she could think to do and tossed the phone into the back of the shop where some pillowy bags of chips would hopefully break the fall and keep the phone active to give them more time to trace it.

"Put the gun down," one man ordered.

It wasn't like she was unarmed, although she couldn't use the shotgun conventionally and they both had pistols trained on her. Even so, they had seen someone killed for disobeying Logan's instructions and she thought she could rely on them to at least not try to kill her.

And she had the stupid shotgun. It could be used as a club or something like that.

Inaction would only put her back in the bathroom or worse. Having made it this far, she had no intention to risk it.

There was nothing quite like giving depositions in court. Months after Eben had handed an investigation off to the appropriate individuals, he was called by a lawyer to come and answer more questions about it. Like, he thought caustically, he didn't have fifteen other investigations on his plate.

And he needed to act as if cases weren't a dime a dozen, which meant he had to go back to the files and read through them like he didn't have a growing pile of other matters to deal with in the present.

Still, he'd always thought he was better at it than most other agents. He could look into a file and remember almost everything that had gone through his head during his investigation and even recall the emotions and feelings that had long since passed.

It was the little things like this that had helped him rise so quickly through the ranks. The fact that many federal prosecutors liked to work with him, even though most of his fellow agents did not, ensured that there would always be a place for someone who could sway juries and present the facts of a matter in a way that brought the desired results.

A full day of deposing in front of bored-looking judges and slimy lawyers was not the kind of law-enforcement work most people thought of when they joined but it was a necessary evil. Eben stepped out of the building with the distinct feeling that he'd been utterly eviscerated and had spent the past eight hours or so having his guts examined by disinterested assholes. As if that wasn't bad enough, it accomplished nothing to change his current situation in the slightest.

At least it meant people would go to jail. Not for long, admittedly, since it looked like they would make deals that would see other people jailed until they jumped on the deals wagon as well. The process would continue until it was clear that no one would spend more than a few months in a minimum-security prison for the kind of crimes that would see those with worse lawyers in prison for the rest of their lives.

It didn't seem right but he realized that he was friends with more than a handful of those who would probably make those deals in the future.

The truth of that hammered home when his phone vibrated to tell him that Shane wanted to have a word.

Eben sighed and tried to quell the annoyance that had built in his chest for the past few hours. He needed to be in the man's good graces to make sure he didn't think he was still owed something. It had taken a fair amount of work to get the USB to him so quickly.

"Shane, how's it going?"

"Cut the crap, we're on a secured line," the man snapped. "I've talked to some of my experts about what you sent me."

"Is there a problem with the AI?"

"A problem?" He sounded about as stressed as Eben felt. "I should say so. The AI you sent me is corrupted almost beyond recognition. My people say it might take months to restore it if they even can."

"But it's there. And it's years ahead of anything your competitors have."

"Did you hear the part where they might not even be able to put it together?" Shane almost shouted into the phone. "Do you have any idea what will happen to me if I present this broken shit to my board and tell them this is the future of our company?"

"What do you want me to do about it, Shane?" he retorted as he climbed into his car. "That's what I was able to get—by the skin of my teeth, I might add—when the DOD discovered it."

"I need you to do better, Eben. I don't know how and frankly, I don't care. Maybe not with an AI, though. At this point, I'm willing to simply call it a loss and move on. But for this relationship to work between us, you have to do better."

The "or else" part of that sentence was barely hidden and unmistakable. It was implied as firmly as it could have been without being explicitly stated. He wasn't sure what Shane could do to him or his career, but the point was that he could do something and possibly even derail it entirely, and it wasn't above him to simply do so out of spite.

There was no real friendship between them, Eben realized. Whatever there had been was severed the moment when the man took his current job and chose to put impressing his board above all else. At this point, the asshole was probably willing to throw even his own family under the bus if it got him ahead.

And there was a long list he could throw them under the bus for from what he knew about the bastards.

"Understood," he answered after a moment and made the effort to ensure that his voice didn't contain a modicum of emotion. "I'll see what I can do."

"I appreciate that, Eben. I'll talk to you later."

He stared at his phone as the line cut. "Eat a bag of dicks, you useless, inbred asswipe."

Saying it after the call was over felt like a pussy move, but it was about the best he could do at this point. Even if Shane managed to wrangle something out of the drive he'd sent, it was utterly clear that a debt was still owed. Even worse, he now owed that IT bitch something too.

"I was very sure it wasn't possible to be up two separate shit creeks at the same time and lack a paddle for both of them," Eben muttered as he started his car. "I guess things have changed."

It was a whole new world.

Fix wasn't sure how it was possible, but there was an immediate difference in the construction of the wall as they passed into the Sahara Coalition sector surrounding the Zoo. The quality of the wall didn't appear to have suffered, although whole sections remained unbuilt and construction seemed to have ceased on those that had been started.

Not only that, it appeared that different engineering specs had been applied to each section, no doubt the result of the collective nature of the coalition and the various parties involved each doing their own thing.

"Holy shit," Elke muttered and shook her head.

The woman probably already had a headache merely from looking at the structures and trying to decide how so much had been allowed to progress so differently for so long.

"It gets worse," Chen commented as their Nigerien escort team fell back and was replaced by the Algerians. "The Libyans are not happy with other people telling them how to build their section of the wall, which means they've chosen to boycott the project entirely."

"So we won't be able to look at a whole section of wall because they aren't here to escort us?" Sam asked in disbelief.

"Something like that."

"That makes it the most critical sector," he commented with a scowl. "From what these people are saying, the Zoo has a tendency to attack the wall where it is at its weakest as hard as possible. And don't ask me how the hell it knows. No one seems to have the answer to that, but the general consensus is that it does and it's good enough for me."

"Politics," Elke muttered belligerently.

Given her expression as she frowned over the engineering plans she was looking at, her headache would quite probably endure for a week. A glance at Chen confirmed that he shared the impression, which meant they needed to be prepared for it. The Elke monster was respectful when well-plied with coffee and chocolate treats. Experience had taught them that it was even better when the chocolate treats were in the coffee which made them coffee-and-chocolate treats.

A quick trip to the Belgian chocolate shop two blocks down from their offices would do the trick when they got home. They merely had to survive until they could do so.

"They have a token base—which is essentially little more than an informal camp—with a minimum number of troops," the woman continued and flipped through the pages on her tablet. "The last time they sent a team into the Zoo was six months ago and that was only three people to support a shallow run."

"It might have something to do with the smuggler's paradise that's developed in their area," Fix commented. "I talked to some people at the French base and they said that most of the smugglers working out of the Zoo were all based in this sector because the people in the region turn more than a blind eye. Libya is in a prime position to facilitate the illegal trade and doesn't need to access the jungle to make money off it."

"What?" Elke leaned closer to see his notes.

"From what they told me, they sell an official stamp to anyone who moves products out of this sector that would even allow them to ship shit directly out of Libyan ports. They have the best of both worlds."

Chen nodded. "Not only that, but any outbreak that might affect the Sahara Coalition side won't be their problem since they're tucked safely behind the stronger bases on the opposite side. They're protected by the US, the Middle East, and the Russian-Japanese sector and can simply milk the opportunity to plunder anything and everything they want from the Zoo without having to worry about defending themselves."

Fix shook his head and tried to curb his frustration. Despite very clear statements to the contrary, their inspection and the comprehensive report they'd undertaken to deliver were somehow compromised by all the petty political bullshit that ran rampant across the whole of the jungle.

They pulled to a halt when their escort allowed a group of Hammerheads heading to the wall to pass them before they drove on into the Algerian base.

It didn't look like too many people there were happy to see them but at least they were allowed onto the base, where a small contingent of officers waited for them.

Elke was the first one out, and she seemed ready to give the men present a piece of her mind.

"You thought coffee and chocolates too, right?" Chen asked when he and Fix were the only ones still in the Hammerhead.

"Yeah. Something from the Belgian place. I doubt we'll find anything to meet her standards around here."

"What do we do until we get there?"

"We'll...uh, have to tolerate the monster for a little while."

The young man shook his head, clearly dreading the prospect, but it wasn't like they had a choice in the matter.

By the time they reached their colleague, she was already in a heated discussion with the senior officer of the group.

"I have told you already," the man said with a heavy accent, "we do not have access to the Libyan base—which I'm sure you know is more of a somewhat informal camp rather than a base per se—and even if we did, we would not be allowed entry with you accompanying us."

"I don't care what political and criminal bullshit they're trying to cover up on their base," the German woman snapped in response. "If there were a place where the Zoo would attack, it would be this sector. We need to run an inspection on every section of the wall. You can tell them that we're not here to report anything to anyone about whatever might be coming or going to or from their base. Our job is to make sure that the wall is secured, especially after the whole rabbit shit debacle."

The officers exchanged a quick look before they nodded. "We will see what we can negotiate but we make no promises."

It did raise an odd question, however. It seemed like the Zoo had made no effort to take advantage of the unprotected "path to freedom." Fix already entertained the fact that the Zoo was probably a sentient entity in its own right, which meant there was some reason for everything it did or didn't do. Maybe with the new, aggressive trend of the jungle, it did not want attention drawn to the area.

He was being paranoid but he was willing to lay blame for that on the fact that he'd dreamed of cryptid monsters ever since they'd touched down in this goddammed place. They had not been restful dreams and a few ended with him dead. Most involved endless fighting until he woke up, but it was in a pool of his sweat every time.

"But you have to understand that any foreign interference in the area will not be well-received," another officer pointed out who spoke considerably better English.

"We're well aware of that," Chen interjected. "As long as you understand that we're not foreign interference. We're merely here to make sure there are no more incursions like the one that happened at the Japanese base."

"They will not see much difference," the first officer muttered.

CHAPTER FIFTEEN

Juan-Carlos took the stairs two at a time and burst into his brother's office, breathless and with an expression that suggested bad news.

"What now?" JP asked and leaned back in his chair with a scowl. "You look like your pet rat died."

"Rat? I don't even qualify for a dog?" The attempt at levity fell flat and he dropped into the closest chair. "Okay, yeah, not the time or the place. I get it." He dragged a breath in and straightened his posture. "You were right, JP. The shit is about to hit the fan. The Southies have brought reinforcements in—only a handful for now, about ten—but there are bound to be more on the way."

"Bastards. I knew they were up to something. The question, though, is how this will play out."

"McFadden and Zhang are bound to launch a retaliatory strike to rescue the woman. I'm surprised they haven't already."

"They have their reasons, I assume. My concern is that by the time they act, the GAMC will have bolstered their numbers to the point where even McFadden won't be able to win against them. If they go down, there's nothing between the Southie bastards and the Thirteens. I'd hoped that maybe they could clear them out for us, but that looks much less likely by the minute."

"Sooo…do you want me to call the guys in?"

Juan-Pablo nodded without hesitation. "Yeah. It's time. We need to get in there and strike before their full numbers arrive. It'll be suicide to wait for them to strengthen their position, deal with the crazies, then turn on us."

"And what about McFadden?" his brother asked and leaned forward with a frown. "I've heard he doesn't like others to mess with his business. If he decides it's time to pick the bone, we don't want to be in his way."

"We won't be. He has the first call and we can hang back and see how it plays out. If nothing else, we'll be on hand for backup if the battle doesn't go their way."

JC nodded. "I'll let our Italian friends know. They'll be very interested to hear that these assholes are gearing up for a major offensive which will probably include them as well."

"Do that, but make sure to fill them in about McFadden and Zhang. We don't need them to do anything to upset them at this point. Honestly, there's already been way too much stupidity that has done nothing more than stir up a major shitstorm for all of us. For now, we bring all the boys in, arm them, and move them into position for a preemptive strike if it's needed. We can move in and finish the job once the McFadden team pulls out."

"And the mob can then play as much as they like." Juan-

Carlos grinned. "You know, this could put us in a stronger position than ever if the crazies think we're willing to back them up."

JP smirked. "I know. And it's shitloads better to be on their good side and have an understanding with them instead of simply giving them a wide berth. If we play this right, we can be much better off and get rid of these mbastards who are trying to muscle in on our turf."

It was like the whole team was an arrow and the moment that confirmation came through on where Tanya was, they were suddenly launched with all the speed that was expected from this kind of situation.

The fact that they didn't have her exact location didn't seem to matter. They'd already raced out the gates from the moment when the call came in and Vickie directed them as they headed toward the convenience store she'd pinpointed—one that had cameras but only on the outside. If there were cameras inside, they weren't connected to any network Desk could access.

"I've picked up two motorcycles outside in the parking lot," the hacker alerted them. "But there might be a back exit. If Tanya managed to get away, I think that's the exit she would have used."

Taylor pressed his foot on the gas when a light turned red as he approached and a cacophony of horns sounded as he passed them. He ignored them and focused on the road. Hell, if a ticket was all they got for their troubles, it would be worth it.

"Chezza, are you on the call?" he asked once they weren't in danger of being involved in a traffic collision.

"I'm here," she announced.

"Circle to the back and see if you can find any sign of Tanya or anyone else trying to get out that way. We'll take care of the front and the bikers."

"Copy that."

When the convenience store was in sight, Taylor accelerated again and the truck lurched as they careened over the sidewalk between the road and the parking lot. He winced as they hit something that made the whole vehicle shudder and shake. Shortcuts were necessary in certain situations but that didn't make them pleasant.

As he braked sharply to bring the vehicle to a halt, they heard the sound of a gunshot from inside.

"Bungees!"

His call was too late. The man was already out the door and now raced toward the store without so much as waiting for the vehicle to stop fully.

It wasn't exactly safe but no one could fault him for it as Tanya was hopefully still inside. A glance confirmed that the freelancers were pulling up to the back of the store.

Taylor paused only to collect his sidearm before he slid out and sprinted to the door that Bobby barreled through without hesitation. Niki jumped out of the back, already armed, and checked her weapon before she joined him.

"Shit," was all he could say as they reached the entrance.

He was greeted by a blast of cool air from inside and the sight of a man already on the floor not far from the door. His attire was easily recognizable as belonging to the biker gang and from the looks of it, he was still alive.

A smaller man crouched behind the counter and whispered in a language Taylor couldn't understand. Tanya leaned against the same counter and looked winded and a little the worse for wear with a few bruises, a black eye, and a split lip.

She was alive, however. That was far better than anything they might have expected before they heard from her.

Bobby didn't look up when the door opened and instead, tackled the second of the bikers and the two fell together with a magazine rack that was upended by the momentum.

"You shit-eating, goat-fucking asswipe!" He punctuated each syllable with his fists that battered the head of the biker who he had pinned beneath his weight. Blood spattered across the polished tile floor, the walls, and some of the shelves too as the mechanic seemed determined to inflict as much damage as he could in the shortest possible time.

Tanya clutched the counter and swayed a little like she had difficulty staying on her feet. She checked the shotgun she held almost absently like it was habit rather than a conscious act.

"Are you good?" Niki asked and eased the weapon carefully from her hands.

The woman smirked. "It's not loaded. This would have been one hell of a short fight if it were. As it stands, I managed to knock that asshole out with the butt and then got tangled with the other."

Taylor looked around and finally realized that the slug from the pistol had gone into the ceiling. "When we heard the shot..." He shrugged rather than complete the thought.

"Yeah. Bobby was on him before I could do anything fancy. I had him all set up to flip him over the counter when Bungees came in like a fucking edge-rusher."

"Shit." Taylor was suddenly reminded of the sound of fists beating flesh. "Bobby, try not to kill the bastard."

The mechanic stopped for a second and looked over his shoulder. "Why the hell should I?"

"Well, for one thing, I'm sure Tanya here would appreciate a hug," he responded. Breaking out the logic of what they were doing at this point wouldn't do much to pull his friend from his bloodlust, but hopefully reminding him of the reason why he was in the mood for blood in the first place would do the trick.

After a second, Bobby pushed to his feet and stood over the fallen biker as he turned to look at Tanya. His entire look was fierce and furious with blood spattered on his face and every muscle in his body rippling as if aching to continue the violence.

"Sorry," he muttered and approached her slowly. "I was...it... Shit, Tanya, I was worried that—"

She closed the distance between them quickly, wound her arms around his neck, and held him close. He tried to contain his sobs as he clutched her as tightly as he could and Taylor turned away, a little uncomfortable about intruding on what felt like an incredibly personal moment.

Instead, he circled to where the mechanic had left the biker. It looked like Bobby had every intention of murdering the absolute shit out of him and good progress had been made on that front, but a soft cough and a groan of pain indicated that more work was needed.

He pressed a finger to the man's pulse to make sure that he was still alive and kicking—unnecessary, perhaps, but it seemed like the right thing to do—before he grasped him by the collar and dragged him to his unconscious comrade.

"You probably have one hell of a concussion there, bubba," he muttered. "If you know what's good for you, stay down, though—merely a hint of advice you might want to take seriously."

Neither biker looked like they were in the mood for a fight and he looked up as Tanya kissed Bobby gently after she wiped the blood carefully off his face.

"This was stupid of you," the mechanic whispered and pressed his head into her neck. "You should have stayed where you were and let us come and get you. That's the smart thing to do and you know it."

"I ain't no damsel in distress and you know that," she responded with a weak laugh. "I saw an opportunity to escape and I took it, no question."

"Still, though."

Taylor turned away again, reluctant to intrude as the freelancers entered through the back door. They held their weapons at the ready and looked surprised that none were required for the moment.

"Are we late for the party?" Chezza asked as she holstered her pistol.

"On the contrary," he answered. "Your timing is perfect. Get Bobby and Tanya to the shop."

"Maybe the hospital first?"

He shrugged. "You're the medic so I'll leave that call up to you."

She paused and studied the two bikers at his feet. "It seems like my medical expertise might be needed more around here."

"These guys?" He laughed and patted the man Bobby had been beating on the cheek. "They're the picture of health. Niki and I will have a little talk with them about where they like to spend their time."

"I'll take your word for it, boss."

She motioned to Jiro and Trick to usher Bobby and Tanya to the back door. The couple made no effort to release each other and Taylor couldn't find any fault with that. If Niki had been the one kidnapped, he would have acted in exactly the same way.

The only difference was that he would have murdered whoever he had his hands on.

For now, though, a conversation would suffice.

"What are you thinking?" Niki asked and crouched next to the two bikers.

"We'll have a little talk to them. If Tanya can't tell us where the gang is holed up, they will."

"Like hell," one of the men muttered.

"Shush," she whispered. "You'll have a nice long while to understand how useless your bravado is in a second. The adults are talking now."

Taylor turned as the man he assumed was the owner of the store looked up slowly from behind the counter.

"I trust we can count on you to not let the cops or anyone else who might be interested know about what happened here, right?" he asked and walked closer to the man.

"Well, I'll have to clean and..."

His voice trailed off as Taylor put two hundred-dollar bills on the counter and picked up a small pack of gum.

"Keep the change."

"Right."

He wasn't sure how far he could trust the proprietor to keep his mouth shut if the cops or the biker gang arrived, but he had a certain amount of faith. People were oddly reliable when it came to bribery.

"Let's get these dickwads out of here," he ordered, took hold of one, and dragged him to the door as he retrieved his ringing phone and held it to his ear with his shoulder. The owner scrambled to start cleaning. "Vickie, what are the possibilities of erasing any sign of us being here on the nearby electronics?"

"Already done," she confirmed. "Is Tanya okay?"

"She needs a little TLC but Bobby's already on that. And probably a couple of aspirins."

"I bet you Bobby's on that shit too."

Taylor pushed the gang member onto his bike and Niki did the same with the other one. Both men appeared to slip in and out of consciousness, but he and Niki exchanged a glance before they retreated out of earshot.

"We'll have to deal with these assholes," she whispered and shook her head. "I know we got Tanya back and that was the priority but now, we have to consider the fact that if we move to Italy, we'll leave Bobby, Tanya, and Elisa to handle this mess while we set up elsewhere."

"That won't happen."

"My point exactly. Do you have a plan?"

Taylor tilted his head and scratched his beard while he studied the bikers. "Plan is...uh, a strong word."

"So no plan?"

"More of an idea—a concept you could say."

"How strong are the words 'idea' and 'concept?'"

"Borderline."

She sighed. "Okay, tell me what you have."

A shower and a liberal application of ointment had sounded like a good idea at the time. Hell, it was a sound concept. Cleaning off any allergens that might have collected on their skin from the pelts was a good idea and something to treat the damage already done was merely taking precautions.

But there didn't appear to be any change in the men. Pavel shook his head as he noted that they all still scratched their arms around the dinner table but acted like it was nothing.

All he could hope for was that they would take a page from his book and see a doctor before anything got infected. No amount of money was worth setting himself up to die of some kind of plague because one of his coworkers had a phobia of hospitals.

The meal was surprisingly good despite his discomfort. It didn't quite meet the standards he could expect at home but it was certainly better than most local workers could expect in the area.

He was the first one to finish and stood quickly and

smoothly and stepped out of the barracks into the crisp evening air.

It was quite a spectacle to watch the sun starting to set and as he usually did, he tapped a cigarette from the pack he carried in his pocket.

Pavel paused in lighting it as Tomas exited the building as well for the same reason.

Neither man said much as they lit up and took the first few drags in blessed silence, broken only by the swelling drone of cicadas all around them.

"Shit," Tomas whispered and rubbed his arm.

He shook his head and tried not to deliver the curt response that sprang to mind.

"You were right, you know."

Pavel almost dropped his cigarette. "What?"

"We give you shit but you are right about getting some proper equipment for dealing with whatever comes out of the Zoo."

"Sure. But who will listen?"

"No one important. But when do they ever care about the safety of workers over profit margins? If we were to suggest that they start supplying us with proper equipment, we would find ourselves replaced very quickly. I cannot risk that with a kid going to university in England. It's expensive."

"Holy shit." Pavel coughed softly and patted the man on the shoulder. "Congratulations. It could not have been easy."

They paused the conversation momentarily as their four colleagues who shared their shift joined them and lit up. The small group moved away from the building to where there was a little more space under the trees before Tomas continued.

"I think it was a little too easy for Adriana. She was a know-it-all even when she was a child and marched around the house like she was smarter than everyone before she could even talk right. It turns out she wasn't wrong about that and is on her way to being an honor student."

"That's amazing. You must be so proud."

"I am—and maybe a little jealous—but I'm giving her what my father never thought to give me."

Pavel nodded. "I hope to see my children enjoy a better future too. Maybe they're not smart enough to go to an English school but perhaps one in Germany. Or France."

"Germany, please. French universities are shit."

He chuckled, dropped the butt of his cigarette into the gravel, and ground it out with his heel. Focused on the conversation, he failed to notice that something small and barely visible to the human eye slipped out from the rash on his arm.

It was quickly followed by another and others began to crawl out from under the skin of all the men present in rapid succession. They dropped quickly to the leaf-strewn earth and burrowed into the soil while the men continued to talk without realizing that the itching in their arms slowly faded to nothing.

After a while, their cigarettes finished and extinguished, the group returned to the barracks. None of them would know that the mite-like creatures burrowed deeper into the rich earth, nor would they have been able to see them split in two before each half grew into a whole new creature and repeated the process.

It was impossible for any of them to know that they had just seeded their deaths and those of their colleagues. Neither would they know that they were responsible for the Zoo having found a new Ground Zero in the middle of Eastern Europe.

If anyone even registered the connection with the strange itching and irritation, it would be way too late to warn the world of this new and insidious threat.

CHAPTER SIXTEEN

"I'm seriously starting to regret this."

Sam wasn't sure why he said that but assumed it was prompted by a sickening feeling in his stomach as they looked at the destruction of what had once been a very promising project.

The fact that the work had been completely unrelated to the Zoo merely added to the tragedy, yet he had still asked their escort if they could take a few hours to see what remained of the now-infamous Sustainagrow site.

"I know what you mean," Chen whispered as he settled into a crouch and aimed his phone's camera at the scene before them. "There's something…wrong about this place. It's like we're treading on sacred ground."

"Or cursed ground," Elke responded quietly and shook her head.

The desolate slag before them had once been desert sand and more recently, a struggling yet vibrant project that had been intended to benefit the whole region.

It provided sobering insight into the reality of what the Zoo was capable of when people weren't careful enough.

"Why the hell are you filming this?" Fix asked when the other man moved a little closer with his phone's camera still trained on the area in front of them.

"I'm making a quick PSA for people who think they can mess around with the Zoo and get away with it."

It was an honorable notion but Sam knew it was the kid's full intention to share that PSA with his channel, which would certainly make waves and bring him more viewers and more people who would want to sponsor his efforts. Maybe the motive was a little insensitive but he would make it look like a lesson, which would make everything all right.

"What are those pipes coming up from the ground?" Elke asked.

One of the Algerian guards stepped forward, his expression somber. "Those were the tunnels they set up to draw water from the mountains to sustain their project. All of them had to be unearthed and blocked up to make sure that none of the contamination that destroyed the project spread anywhere."

Fix lowered his head. The reports told of dozens of deaths and an international effort to make sure there was no spread from the location. A careful watch was still maintained, albeit from a good few miles away, to make sure there was no attempt by the Zoo to spread.

He could have called the people involved paranoid but in the end, if they had been a little more paranoid from the beginning, none of this would have happened. It was a real testimony to how all the hard work, investment, and planning of mankind could be overwhelmed and destroyed overnight.

"Do we have any more meetings for the day?" he asked quietly and turned away from the sight before them.

"No, we'll camp for the night," the sergeant who headed their escort responded. "There's a good site nearby where it should be safe."

"We should go now," Elke whispered and Chen tucked his phone away in agreement.

As much as they hated the blistering heat from overhead during the day, the cold that crept in at night was enough to kill those who were caught outside in it. Oddly enough, though, Sam had heard from some of the men who went into the Zoo that the humidity inside made it difficult to ever feel cold again.

It was an adventure of a lifetime to be in that part of the world but he didn't want to think about ever returning to the Zoo again if he could help it. Of course, he'd do what the job demanded but a part of him wanted to make sure he wasn't one of those who would undertake or oversee the actual work. Merely seeing the green sea out in the distance was enough to make him feel sick to the stomach.

"We go?" the sergeant asked.

"Let's get out of here," he whispered and scrambled into the Hammerhead.

It was certainly easier to keep a firm hand on the reins now that Logan had real professionals on his side. Even so, it wouldn't take them long to lose what semblance of control they still had when they discovered that the Thirteens had delivered the first strike in a war without them knowing about it.

Already, the arrival of the reinforcements had prompted the men to discuss the probability of aggressive action while they gathered and checked their weapons. One of the newcomers sat beside him and took a sip of what looked like a protein shake.

"Haven't you told them?" he asked and raised an eyebrow.

He shook his head. "I should have but it's been a long day. I've only had two hours of sleep in the past forty-eight and it looks like we'll have to deal with far more in the coming days."

"True. But the assholes attacked us first and our boys will want payback. You'd better be ready for that and ready to deliver. No one wants to feel like we're simply letting them get away with killing our people."

"True. But I think most of this anxiety is because our prisoner escaped."

The man paused to stare at him in silence while he digested this information. "How long has it been since she got away?"

"I'm not sure. We sent someone with food for her and she was gone. It's not like we could have done much with her but they aren't happy that she escaped. Something needs to be done about that too. How long until Max and Trevor come back?"

"Why did you send them out?"

"We're out of beer. It's what happens when the Sox put Diego in on the mound. That dude sucks at pitching, which means bottles get thrown at the TV much more than usual."

"Does that mean that you have to get a new TV too?"

"Nah, I was prepared for that. I got one of those that has the additional protection they usually sell to the bars where they have a problem with people throwing shit around."

"Yeah, that sounds like a smart move. You'll save a ton of money on broken TVs that way."

"Not so much on beers."

"So do you plan to send someone out to find your missing prisoner?"

Logan scratched his beard. "I already have bikers combing the area but I haven't heard from them. Still, I expected people would be more up in arms about the Thir-teens than an escaped prisoner."

"Given that all this is happening at the same time, you might want to consider doing something a little more effective. As of right now, there are too many whispers about putting a war party together to raid them."

Logan looked up and sipped his beer. "You heard that?"

A simple nod was all the answer he needed.

"It might not look like I'm doing much, but that's my way to stop the trigger-happy lunkheads from acting before we're ready. I have other informants on the street these boys don't know about—those connected to our Boston chapter—and they are working overtime to find the information we need. The last thing I want is to rush out there without knowing the facts that will make the difference between success and failure."

He sighed and swallowed the last of his beer. "When we

go out, it will be in force with a clear target and a plan that guarantees a win. But you're right that it's time to do more. The first step is to prioritize and defense takes precedence. Our escapee will have to wait. If we're lucky, she'll find her way to the strip mall and the McFadden team will turn their attention elsewhere."

"You think we can't take them on?"

"Sure we can if that was all we were focused on. The guy is well-armed and well-connected, but he's no army. He has a team of mercenaries with him who we might be able to pay off to do the work for us if it comes to that. At the moment, though, we have to focus on not losing our foothold in the city and making sure the Thirteens aren't able to cause us any more casualties. It will be far more beneficial to have the kidnapping simply resolve itself when the bitch turns up, although we can't count on that. Still, I sure as hell don't want to have to engage both McFadden's group and the Thirteens."

The man chuckled. "You have a good mind for this, you know. Were you ever in the military?"

"No, but I play Call of Duty as often as I can. Why do you ask?"

"It seems like you're talking about leading an army as though you've done it before."

"I was there when Miles landed in that little kerfuffle with the Camorra over their attempt to push their business interests in South Boston. I'm merely following his example."

"It sounds like a good way to do things."

"For the moment, go ahead and tell the guys to get their weapons ready and to improve the security around the building. It'll give them something to do until we have a concrete target. Besides, a live threat is a little more urgent than a possible one and my gut says the Thirteens are the biggest threat right now. They will want to finish what they started and we need to be ready for that. Once we're done with the bastards, we can face McFadden if he decides to retaliate rather than be grateful the woman is back and simply leave well alone."

"Right. I'll spread the word, boss."

Logan wasn't sure if there was mockery in the man's voice. It made little difference in the bigger scheme of things but it sounded more like he was getting used to the term himself.

The guys from Arizona had some experience dealing with the Mexican gangs already, and that would certainly be an advantage. This was always the frustrating time—waiting for the intel to come in so they could plan the campaign. Despite his pretense at calm and the impression he gave that he was unconcerned and not doing anything, he was well aware that there was currently no way to tell how much time they had. Every second counted but as long as everyone was ready and worked together to improve the defenses, it would be a step in the right direction.

Once he was satisfied that the men were fully engaged in the new orders, Logan pushed out of his seat and placed his beer bottle on the table before he headed to his room.

Trust in his people would always be preferable but at this point, he wouldn't put Cody above intentionally guiding any potential assassins directly to his door.

He slipped inside, locked the door, and checked to

make sure it wouldn't open if someone pushed hard enough—the kind of thing they needed to be worried about with most of the doors in the building—before he moved to the back of the room and shoved his desk to the side.

In the past, he would never have considered being anywhere but at the front lines with the rest of the guns, but he'd been around long enough to know that even in a gang like the Guardian Angels, there was no honor among thieves.

Having a bolt hole that would enable him to make a hasty escape felt like a solid insurance plan if and when shit hit the fan. He checked that it was still secure before he concealed it again.

If things went poorly, he could slide out and into the pile that had been created when the dumb bastards still thought they could renovate the building. He had no qualms about leaving the gang to face a clusterfuck of their own making.

They were idiotic enough to trigger a battle before they were ready, and Logan knew for a fact that he would have no regrets about walking away from their stupidity to start again somewhere else.

Peter Tellisman pushed aside his resistance to having to endure another video call. He wished he could somehow compel the Overwatch team to meet in person one of these days, but they were all active members in their individual fields of study. It was therefore highly unlikely that all of them would have the time to travel to a single location in the world that would allow them to meet face to face.

But a man could dream as long as he reminded himself that it wasn't likely to ever be a reality.

For now, all they could manage was a video call and even that took a monumental amount of planning and negotiation. All those who attended understood that what they were doing was possibly one of the most important missions of their collective lives, which meant it was worth putting everything on hold once in a while to consider and discuss what was probably the greatest threat mankind would ever face.

He thought so, at least, which made his abhorrence for video calls a little easier to ignore.

The familiar faces began to appear on his computer screen and it was a good sign that they were all present despite a foreboding expression on each and every one. It affected his mood as well. He dragged his long, spindly fingers through his thinning hair and adjusted his glasses on his nose before he pulled himself a little closer to the screen.

"I appreciate the effort everyone has made to be present for this meeting," Peter commented as the last of his team made an appearance. "I know you're all incredibly busy but you know I would not have called for it if there weren't signs for concern."

Even Dr. Lidgton—generally a source of some levity at such meetings—looked like she'd bitten into something incredibly sour and still tried to process it.

"We can cut the formalities here, Dr. Tellisman," she muttered and rubbed her temple pensively. "I think we are all only too aware of the dangers we face as the Zoo enters what can only be described as a more...uh, let's call it an active phase in its growth."

"Indeed," Noami Katz responded and made a quick note on a pad in front of her before she returned her attention to the call. "Dr. Kondo was kind enough to share the reports sent to him on what happened to the Japanese base. The question remains, of course, what this more active phase entails and what it means for the rest of humanity. We might not be on the front lines of the fight to contain the Zoo but we might find ourselves in such a position if they fail."

The woman had a way to state the obvious in such a manner that led everyone to address it effectively, a skill Peter had never possessed. Even so, now that the preliminary points were out of the way, they all needed to consider what to do about it.

Uwe Schafer was the next one to speak. "I would say our efforts to expand our intelligence network has thus far provided more than enough fruit to justify our commitment in that regard. With that said, I have to put considerable work into verifying the intelligence sent along those channels, which makes it a slow process. We don't want to be caught with our proverbial trousers down when the time comes to present our reports."

"It's necessary," Peter insisted. "We need to be ruthless and ensure that we cut any speculation and exaggeration out. Our credibility as a group relies on every detail—no matter how small—being as accurate and verifiable as is humanly possible."

There was a general murmur of agreement to this statement. As concerned as they were about the need to ensure that the world didn't meet its end as a result of the Zoo, they all had sufficient academic ambition to not want to see their careers go down the drain over the matter. Even Peter was willing to admit that he wasn't above such considerations.

"We need an accurate view from people on the ground," Kondo agreed, his voice a little more subdued than usual. "You spoke of one Dr. Jacobs who is in a unique position to assist us in our intelligence gathering. Have you been able to contact him yet?"

"No," Peter admitted. "But I will. Even so, I have my doubts that he will want to come on board as a full member of our little organization. He is generally against working with governments, corporations, or committees. If nothing else, however, he might be able to alert us to things when they happen as opposed to after the fact. If that is the case, it might be possible to arrange to monitor the situation ourselves using other people on the ground in the affected areas."

"He is a freelancer." Madge tilted her head and shrugged. "Which means he is running a business. If we can offer him agreeable profits on this venture, we should be able to count him as our ally."

She made a good point although he sincerely hoped he could appeal to the young doctor's sense of community before he promised anything like payment for his services.

"I'll contact him immediately," he promised with a firm nod. "I know we don't all see eye-to-eye on everything but to my mind, that's exactly what we need. A healthy debate is probably what we're all best at by this point."

"But what we can all agree on is that humanity is running out of time," Kondo said quietly. "Even if the majority of the populace does not want to think about it or even consider the facts. They're making too much money to realize that everything currently being built is about to crumble around their ears."

The man was right. They could all agree on that, as evidenced by the lack of argument among the group of peers. While they all liked to enter into lively debates about the details, the bottom line was the point that none of them could contest.

"Very well. You all have your assignments," Peter said briskly, ran his fingers nervously over his head, and adjusted his glasses again in the same nervous tick he'd had all his life. "As I do as well. I think we all hope to hear some good news when we meet again."

They offered their farewells before they signed off and left him alone in his office. Almost reflexively, he stretched his hand to a bottle of bourbon that had been given to him as a birthday present by the folks at the university.

He had never drunk much aside from when he was at social events but in this moment, there seemed to be no other alternative that could ease the tension he lived with on a daily basis.

His hands shook as he poured the drink but his nerves didn't settle when he took a sip. Good news was what they wanted to hear, but none of them honestly expected it. There was no way to counter the feeling that they were putting a fan up to resist an oncoming hurricane.

CHAPTER SEVENTEEN

"I hate to be the grownup in this situation but we do have a plan, right?"

Vickie knew she undermined her statement about being a grownup by chewing on a mouthful of gummy bears while she spoke but decided to simply ignore it. Jennie was snacky for sugary treats when she was working too. Desk didn't do much eating, of course, but she was an AI so it didn't matter.

Word had come in that Tanya was fine, alive, and on her way to the workshop with the freelancers. That encouraging news meant she wouldn't feel guilty about turning her attention elsewhere, even if she was running on coffee fumes and a sugar high.

"Nearti will be an issue," Desk pointed out. "Given that she is on your original server. We don't want anyone to decide to search it before we go."

"We're fine to move the vanilla server the investigators have finally returned since everyone's aware of its existence."

"We do have a problem with moving the real servers, though," Jennie pointed out and looked about as tired as her young cousin felt. "Hell, even if we download Nessie into a suit, people will be suspicious."

"So we need to conjure up a way to smuggle the server out without anyone knowing," the hacker muttered. She was tired enough that somehow stating the obvious was necessary. It would provide her with a solid focus on what they needed instead of dancing around it.

"I should not be an issue," Desk continued. "I would be able to remain as I am and download myself into the new server location at the earliest opportunity. Nearti, however, is too young and inexperienced to be parked unsupervised on a foreign server."

"Couldn't we move her to one of your company servers while we work on relocating everything?" she asked Jennie.

"It would be a good idea if the DOD weren't on my ass, trying to get me to repair the dummy AI for them." The other woman shook her head. "It looks like they're trying to pressure my boss to make me work for them on my time but so far, he's run a decent amount of interference for me. Unfortunately, I'm not sure it'll be enough. The company servers are off-limits, though."

"Too many people have too much access anyway," Desk noted. "Jennie's successes and hard-nosed attitude mean she's not particularly popular among her coworkers. If someone were to discover Nearti, they might see it as an opportunity for payback."

"Wait, who says I'm not popular with my coworkers?" Jennie asked and tilted her head in a slight challenge.

"Most of their inter-office emails. I performed a search

while I had processing downtime. They are all jealous of how quickly you've risen in the company and none of them are huge fans. All are too terrified of you to make any of that public, though."

"Two-faced bitches." Jennie leaned back in her seat again. "And I can't even address them about it directly because this is how I found out about it."

Vickie shook her head. As much as she wanted to discuss the office gossip with her cousin, all she could think about was taking a nap before Taylor returned and immediately set everyone to work. She couldn't hold it against him, of course, and everyone else had also been up all night looking for Tanya so they probably needed rest as much as she did.

Empathy was in short supply, though, and she realized she was running out quickly.

"On another note," Desk interjected, "I have managed to get a trace on a vehicle used by the bikers."

The hacker leaned forward. "I thought they didn't like having GPS on their bikes."

"They do not. They appear to have stolen a car and are using it to collect a few things around the city."

"How did you know it was them?"

"One of the cameras I've monitored has identified one of the bikers using facial recognition. I was able to work from there to where they are moving and what vehicles they're using. I would also say that more of them are coming into town with every passing hour."

"Shit." Vickie tapped her speed dial to call Taylor.

"Yeah?"

He sounded a little breathless but she had a feeling that

he wouldn't mind if she interrupted whatever he was doing with better news.

"We've picked up the movements of the bikers and it looks like we'll confirm their HQ location before too long," she announced. "So if you guys are torturing the intel out of those you caught, I guess you can cut that shit out right now."

"It sounds good to me." Taylor grunted. "Have the free-lancers arrived yet? Tanya should hopefully be able to confirm anything you find, although she left here very shaken and disoriented."

"No."

"Get them to the workshop to suit up. I don't want us to risk any injury while we deal with the assholes. Not only that, but I'd like a message to be sent to all the gangs involved—the kind that will make it very clear that the strip mall is a no-go zone."

"I'll contact them as soon as we're finished." Vickie cleared her throat and looked around quickly when she heard the gate open. "There is something you should know, though. From what Desk was able to pick up, it sounds like our biker friends have reinforcements arriving from out of town. We're not sure how many but certainly enough to keep in mind."

"Agreed, but it doesn't change what we have to do. I'll call you about it again soon."

"Talk to you then."

It sounded like Bobby, Tanya, and the freelancers were back. Tanya wouldn't join them in the fight—probably, although one could never be sure with the team—but Vickie had a feeling that Bungees had made his mind up to put his fist through more of them and the freelancers would too.

"A nap," she whispered. "My kingdom for a fucking nap."

The location didn't look like much. Then again, it was a mansion compared to the hovel his family lived in after they'd crossed the border. It was before JP had been born and he only spent the first five and half years of his life there but despite this, the one-roomed home was firmly etched in his memories.

A three-story house with numerous rooms was three or four steps up from it, even if it looked like it was destined for demolition in the coming weeks.

He settled a little deeper into his seat. Expensive cars in the area would certainly draw too much attention, which meant he'd had to use a piece of shit they had languishing in their garage. He grinned when he decided it was looking for an end that was remarkably similar to the one that would face the house in a short while.

It was hot and uncomfortable, but he remained where he was and watched the target premises like a hawk. They'd had spies on the house for the past few days to report the comings and goings. The bikers had initially done little than look around for better real estate, but that had now changed dramatically. Reinforcements arrived in small groups, probably from different GAMC chapters, and all were well-armed and had the look of fighters.

That confirmed his assumption that the Southie shits had begun to prepare for war and JP knew that if there was ever a time to strike, it was now. Previously, the Thirteens had held the advantage through the sheer weight of numbers. If the bikers switched those odds in their favor with these new imports, things would be very different.

They had to act swiftly and decisively, which was why he now watched the house like a goddammed foot soldier. It wasn't something he usually did but these were exceptional circumstances and he wanted to see for himself to determine if he needed to make adjustments to their strategy and tactics.

The other gang members had responded swiftly to the call and had begun to position themselves unobtrusively around the perimeter in preparation. When he gave the word, they would strike quickly with superior firepower to annihilate the newcomers or drive them out of town. There would be no protracted war on the streets that drew the attention of every fed in a hundred-mile radius. One swift and decisive assault should sweep the Southies off the board and no amount of reinforcements would make any difference thereafter.

He lifted the radio and hunkered as low as he could in the car seat while JC, who had taken on the role of driver, toyed with the sub-machine gun he'd brought for the occasion.

Of course, he couldn't disregard the possibility that his spies had been identified, which meant that any attempt to surprise their target would fail. It was why he'd not incorporated it too deeply into the overall plan.

"Ping when you're in position," he muttered curtly into the device. He'd issued strict orders to avoid unnecessary chatter in case the bikers were listening in on the channels, but something had to be said. JP had tremendous respect for the men he worked with but combat veterans they were not.

Well, except Juan-Carlos, who had been in the navy for a few years.

A soft ping confirmed that the first group was in position, quickly followed by a second. JP was with the third, which meant that everything and everyone was ready.

He relished the thrill of adrenaline that coursed through his veins as they all ran one last check on their weapons, but when he looked at his hand, it was utterly and completely steady. He'd been in this situation before. Coming out alive could never be guaranteed, of course, but worrying about that got more people killed than ridiculous bravado in his opinion.

"Are we good to go?"

"I...I don't think so."

It wasn't like JC to be uncertain. He was the brother who had advocated for them to inflict serious violence on the bikers the most. In general, it was difficult to stop him from being a savage little shit and JP suspected that he was the one responsible for killing the two bikers the night before.

Now, however, he shifted in the driver's seat and stared into his rearview mirror, his expression wary. An old paneled van had pulled up and parked almost a full block away from where they were. A moment later, a battered pickup stopped behind it. Seven figures climbed out and began to don what appeared to be full combat suits, which suggested very clearly that they were ready for a fight.

They appeared to be calm and unhurried and in no rush

to complete their preparations despite the fact that they were out in the open.

The apparent leader disengaged from the group and approached their vehicle while he strapped on a pair of bracers and connected a few wires from them to the chest piece with assured, practiced motions. Even without the suit, the man was a giant, a mountain of muscle topped by long red hair and a thick red beard.

That explained JC's hesitation, at least. They'd all heard tales about the massive redhead and the kind of punishment he could mete out even without a combat suit.

JP smirked as his brother tilted away when the giant sidled up next to the car and leaned against it with enough weight to make it shift slightly before he tapped on the window.

It was a carefully gentle tap, fortunately, as he wore his suit's gauntlets already. They could easily break through the glass if he'd wanted to do so.

Like he had waited for it, JC was already rolling the window down and the man peered in.

"Afternoon." His deep voice rumbled through the car and he studied all four occupants. "License and registration?"

None of them knew how to answer that, which drew a laugh from McFadden.

"Yeah, that's what I thought. Which one of you guys is leading this little attack of yours?"

After a second of consideration, JP raised a hand.

"Come on out. Let's have a chat."

It didn't feel like he had much of a choice and he climbed out and circled the vehicle to stand in front of

McFadden. He reminded himself that it was important to not appear weak in front of his men.

"Your little assault plan is good but predictable," McFadden noted as he checked one bracer and focused on the other. "My guess is that you have two more teams positioned all around the building. Your tactic would be to use the element of shock to put the bikers in their place before more reinforcements arrive, am I right?"

JP could only bring himself to nod because he didn't want the man to hear any quiver in his voice.

"Yeah, well, I need you and your buddies to back the fuck off that plan of yours if you don't mind. Me and my people have what some might call dibs on the bikers inside. See, they kidnapped and roughed up a member of our team and someone has to pay for that shit. I assume you don't want that someone to be you?"

A simple shake of the head was all the answer the giant needed.

"Great. And if we don't do so well, you're more than welcome to do whatever you planned to before we arrived, with the added benefit of knowing that we eliminated a handful or two of the bastards—thinned the herd, as it were. Are we on the same wavelength here? You haven't said a word."

He paused and glanced at the others in his team who moved toward them. They all projected a grim demeanor and appeared ready for a fight. JP had no doubt that they would not have a problem fighting the Thirteens first if he didn't accede to their request.

McFadden still waited for a response so he tugged his goatee and cleared his throat—the only chance he had to look a little more in control—before he nodded. "All right. It's your show."

"Fantastic. Tell your buddies to sit back and enjoy it."

A very light clap on his shoulder left him feeling like maybe a visit to the doctor was in order before he hurried to the passenger side of the car.

This was something of a godsend, all things considered. The man certainly looked like he'd come for blood and if there was any truth to the legends that surrounded him, he was more than able to rush in and clear the whole building without breaking a sweat.

Hell, if JP played it right, it would even help his rep. He would be able to tell people that he'd worked with the crazy giant and ensure that the Italians weren't the only ones who could claim that.

He climbed into the car and glanced at the group in combat suits that advanced with an air of purpose before he retrieved the radio.

"Stand down," he ordered in a tone that everyone would recognize as not negotiable. "We have some friends who want a chance to deal with the Southie shits first."

"What the hell?"

Anton couldn't help but agree with the exclamation, although sheer shock blocked any attempt to speak and he could only grasp his rifle a little tighter to his chest.

They'd come in to relieve the night shift and had arrived a little early in hopes of partaking of the breakfast that would no doubt be served to the workers inside.

Instead, they were greeted with a sight that could only be described as impossible and which left all the guards gaping in disbelief.

"I've heard stories of the Zoo," one of the other men muttered. Anton hadn't been a part of the morning shift long enough to learn all their names but it didn't look like he would have time to do so.

"Shut the fuck up," he snapped and checked to make sure his rifle was loaded and the safety was off. "That's not the Zoo. No one knows what it is."

"Do you have any other ideas?" Lukas asked as he stepped forward. "We were hired to deal with poachers and thieves and maybe the occasional idiot who tries to grow pot on the distant corners of the property. Not...not this."

The man had a point. Instead of a boring day of making sure none of the factory workers tried to sneak some of the products from the line, they stared at what could only be described as a jungle.

At the same time, however, it was not like any jungle Anton had ever seen. He'd spent enough time in South America working in the very lucrative pelt industry before he decided that he was too old to go hunting for other peoples' treasures.

Although he'd made enough money to retire on, he chose to continue working—it kept him occupied and made sure that no one at the tax office was alerted to the money that stacked up rapidly in Ireland. Once everything was settled there, he would move into a nice house and make sure he didn't work another day in his life.

The growth in front of him wasn't like anything he'd encountered in his fairly extensive travels. Although the trees looked vaguely familiar, they were oddly twisted and their leaves caught the light, which made them gleam with a blueish hue despite the fact that they were bright green. Each trailed a variety of vines that also had bright green leaves that made the underbrush look tighter and more confined than it would have been otherwise.

The vegetation would have needed about three or four years to reach the stage of growth they were in now, from the bushes to the vines and the trees that shivered and shuddered in the wind that sliced through the property.

None of them had been present the day before. Anton remembered looking onto the open lawn between the barracks and the factory where the workers enjoyed a meal under the shade of the motley copse of trees that grew between them. He'd felt a trace of annoyance and anger that he felt jealous of their camaraderie. Most of his comrades and friends were dead or rotting in some third-world prison or another, which made it difficult to take any new friendships seriously.

Those that had been forged in battle seemed like they would last but in the peaceful life he now lived he had been alone, on the outside looking in on the bastards.

The lawn was gone now and so were the scrawny trees that had provided shade. Or maybe they weren't gone and were merely hidden by the rest of the flora that had sprung up overnight.

He scowled and narrowed his eyes to confirm what he thought he saw. Young growth pushed from the soil and the trees continued to grow, even as he watched. A handful more trees thrust through the gravel and kicked the pebbles away as the leaves caught the light for the first time. They emerged so fast and grew so rapidly that it looked like they'd been there for weeks already.

It was not his imagination and a couple of the men began to inch away as if to confirm the awful realization. The jungle grew, expanded, and took shape in front of them.

"The barracks are already surrounded," Lukas commented as they retreated behind the gates. "Do you think any of the men inside are still alive?"

"Even if they are, who among us will head in and escort them out?" Anton asked and looked at his colleagues. There were four of them, all told, and he had no doubt that none of them would pass through the main gate again now that it was closed behind them. Not even, he thought grimly, to try to rescue the workers who were probably still inside, alive or dead.

Lukas was right in the end. They were paid to deal with human, earthly threats. What they were looking at was considerably more alien.

"Call Stepan," Anton snapped. "Make sure he knows about what's happening on his property. Maybe this is something intentional."

It was a fool's dream but he wasn't ready to commit his certainty to what would probably mean their death. One of the guards already had his phone out and he dialed their boss hurriedly and told him what they were looking at. Stepan would have serious doubts but the man would not be able to deny the evidence of his own eyes.

"Weed farmers?" he asked and hefted his rifle.

Lukas turned to look at him. "What?"

"You said you caught weed farmers."

"Right. Only once, though—some idiots from Prague who thought we were simple idiots who wouldn't notice that they were growing weed in the far corners of the property. We saw them and scared them off and they left everything behind."

"Everything?"

The man smirked. "Yes. I sold their weapons and they had a good product so I sold that too. All in all, I made a hefty profit from that little business."

"I bet you the idiots from Prague haven't tried it again."

"Damn right."

Lukas thought he meant how he had been intimidating enough that the city boys had run away with tales of the tough guards in the area but quickly realized that he stared with wide eyes at the jungle that pushed relentlessly forward toward the gate and swallowed all in its path.

"Oh, right."

Anton nodded but focused on the other guard, who had already hung up and looked a little confused.

"Stepan does not believe that a jungle has sprouted on his property during the night."

"Who can blame him?" he whispered. "But I assume he's at least curious enough to come and find out that it's true and decide what happens next."

It was a reliable expectation, given his boss' insistence that he be kept in the loop of even the smallest detail of his business. Better yet, it would hopefully result in definite orders and a good idea of what they were supposed to do about the problem.

The group waited in silence until the crisp morning air

carried the sound of a car engine, one that hurtled the vehicle up the dirt road at an impressive pace.

Stepan had something of an obsession with American-made pickup trucks and Anton couldn't understand the concept given that those made in Japan or even Korea were considerably more reliable and less expensive to import.

Still, the sight of a massive Chevy pickup was a clear indicator that the man had chosen to come in person and hadn't sent a proxy to find out what was happening. It would save them all considerable time arguing over what was possible and what wasn't.

Anton raised his weapon again and aimed at the jungle when he thought he caught movement, but all he could see was a handful of new trees that pushed through the soil. He watched them closely, however, as they made it difficult to tell if anything moved in the trees or if it was merely them growing.

It wasn't until Stepan jumped out of his vehicle and jogged to the gate that he seemed to accept that the guards were not trying to avoid a day's work through outlandish lies—an understandable suspicion given the alternative. He grasped the bars of the gate and stared aghast while his property was slowly and inexorably being swallowed by the jungle.

"What the hell?" he whispered and leaned a little closer.

"Our exact words," Anton said quietly as he approached and held his weapon at the ready. "From the rate that it appears to be growing, I would say the rest of your property will be lost to the jungle in a matter of hours."

There seemed to be no expression on his boss' face for a moment and he wondered exactly what could be going through the man's mind as he gaped at the factory. Maybe the fact that the pelts he'd paid so much for were still inside the building while one of the trees seemed to press against one of the walls.

"Seal the gate," Stepan whispered and inched away from it with a haunted look on his face.

"What will that do, precisely?" one of the guards asked.

"Don't question me. Seal the gate!" Their boss appeared to be hanging on by a single thread and wouldn't tolerate anyone second-guessing him. None of them would argue, of course, and they immediately closed the chains around the gates and locked them afterward.

"What do we do next?" Anton asked. He still felt like something watched him from the jungle, but there was no sign of anything that might move out against them—which essentially meant no sign of the monsters the Zoo was overly famous for. Unfortunately, this brought little comfort as he had a feeling that if the trees grew so quickly, the monsters would make an appearance before too long.

"We need to alert the authorities," Stepan commented finally. "No mention of how the Zoo might have arrived here, only that it did. If the police cannot do anything, they might put out the word to those who can."

"What about the rest of the staff?" Anton asked.

"I already have a bus on the way to collect them and drive them away from here," his boss answered and seemed to be telling the truth from what he could tell. "I'm afraid it might already be too late for the staff in the barracks, which are completely surrounded. I will not risk anyone else approaching that jungle, not even to save the lives of others—at least not without proper weapons and armor."

Containing the outbreak would be the first priority of any authorities informed about the growing Zoo incursion and hopefully, by the time it was contained and burned to embers, no one would think to question how the Zoo had mysteriously appeared in the Czech Republic in the first place.

CHAPTER EIGHTEEN

Telling Tanya to stay behind hadn't worked out the way Taylor had hoped. When he'd seen the woman looking like she was about to fall over, it made him think she would want to rest and recover her strength. Surprisingly, she had bounced back after a hasty meal and a gallon of coffee.

It might have had something to do with her harsh statement that she had a bone to pick with the bastards—a powerful incentive that he could identify with, although he said nothing. Her tone indicated very clearly that if he tried to stand in her way, he would face a similar fate.

He realized that it was best to step back and let her do what she wanted.

"Do you think the Thirteens will simply let you guys stroll in?" Vickie, working as overwatch for the team, asked somewhat disbelievingly.

"I have spoken to their leader and have a feeling they're all too happy to let us do the dirty work," Taylor responded as he adjusted his helmet more comfortably and attached it to his armor. It felt a little odd to be back in his old suit, but he'd decided not to use the multi-limbed one, which honestly seemed like overkill against mere humans.

They'd already wasted too much time trying to locate the bikers and he wouldn't risk anyone in the city thinking McFadden and Banks could be fucked with, even while they were in Italy. It was time to deliver the unforgettable message—with extreme prejudice.

"So, what's the plan here, guys?" the hacker asked as they approached the building. "I assume it won't be of the 'here to chew bubblegum and kick ass, and you're all out of bubblegum' variety?"

"Why the hell not?" Niki countered. "Brute force might bring the whole goddamn building down on their heads and it would be some serious good riddance. It would get rid of not only this new biker gang but also the public health hazard this dump poses."

"I agree with that," Bobby interjected. "I don't care so much about the house but brute force does seem to be the way to go."

"Charging into an area we're not familiar with against a whole shitload of assholes armed to the teeth?" Taylor knew that pointing out the obvious to two veterans like Bobby and Niki would feel a little like disrespect, but he couldn't be the only one who thought about the dangers of simply strapping their ears back and charging in blind. Desk had already alerted them to the fact that she had no eyes inside, which meant that any attack they initiated would commit to an area they couldn't see into.

Walking them into a trap didn't feel like the best way to get things done and the beginnings of an idea began to form in the back of his head. Despite this, the only certainty was that he would set his team up for a fight they might not win.

None of the freelancers had offered much of an argument one way or the other. All three appeared to realize that they were involved in a situation that was a little bigger than only the assault on the building. The fact that Tanya still hadn't voiced any opinion was interesting. If anyone would make the call of how they should treat the assholes, it was her but she hadn't said much since she'd strapped into her suit.

Maybe she was already in the killer mindset. It wasn't the kind of thing that allowed for small talk, not when she was focused on how she could best accomplish the massacre of anyone who crossed her path.

"I have an idea," Taylor stated finally. "I'll approach them at the front of the building and distract them. You guys go in from the back and find a way to get in while I keep them busy."

"Do you think one of us should hang back with you in case?" Trick asked. "Or will you be out here on your own doing the hero shit while we do all the actual work?"

"Yeah, something like that. I'll take all the credit that way."

"Oh, cool. As long as we're clear."

Taylor nodded and gestured for the team to move to the back using the surrounding buildings as cover. He waited only a moment before he advanced on the front of the building and made as much noise as he could to hold the attention of the occupants so the others could get into position.

He wasn't averse to a full-scale battle to eliminate them

but with the move to Italy so close, it would be better to let others do the wholesale killing. They were still on the radar of all the law enforcement agencies that would be extremely interested to learn that a group in full combat suits was part of a massacre involving local criminals.

Although the watchers, thankfully, were none the wiser. Elisa had taken the "packed for shipment" suits to the courier company and left them there. The team had left earlier and parked Trick's very noticeable vehicle beside Liz out front of the building that housed the sims. They'd simply walked straight through the building and exited through the back door, where the "borrowed" vehicles waited for them.

They collected the suits from the courier en route to the gang's HQ. As far as they knew, their watchers were none the wiser, but that would change soon.

"We're in position," Niki confirmed. "So what's the plan? Will you break out some dance moves and challenge them to a competition or something?"

"Or something," Taylor muttered.

"McFadden, you'd better have a plan or we'll circle back and charge in with you."

"I thought I'd given them a chance to hand over the people who kidnapped Tanya for us to deal with and let the others take care of the rest. We have the FBI on our asses at the moment so if word comes out that we launched an all-out attack, we'll probably be on the receiving end of a slew of subpoenas."

"They're all responsible for what happened to Tanya." Niki's voice went cold suddenly, the kind of tone he knew better than to argue against.

"If they're all perps, we might as well let the Thirteens deal with them. Besides, this is a moot point if they decide to be less than helpful."

She had no argument for that and he continued his advance toward the entrance. Before he could knock, the dilapidated door opened and three men stood in the aperture with their sub-machine guns aimed directly at him.

Taylor switched his comms to the speakers in his suit to address them.

"Afternoon, gents. I'll cut right to the chase. You dumbasses did some harm to someone I care about. I'll give the rest of you the chance to walk away from this with egos and bodies intact if you hand over those responsible for the heinous act. If you don't, I'll do the city a favor and demolish this eyesore with you leather fetishists inside."

"I have a better idea," one of the men retorted. "Go fuck yourself and have a nice day."

"You might want to give the people in charge the chance to hear my terms before using that kind of language, little one."

"I don't need to ask. I know what they'll say. Like I said, go fuck yourself."

His eyes narrowed and he studied the biker who'd spoken. He should have recognized him immediately. The dark hair, thick beard, and short stature indicated that he was the one who had called at the strip mall and kidnapped Tanya.

"As long as we're clear." Taylor tilted his head and smiled as the door closed again. He wasn't sure what kind of barrier they thought it would be but in the end, it didn't matter. He was merely the distraction.

"Well, that plan's gone to shit," Chezza commented. "At least you gave them the chance."

"It's not a chance they deserved, but okay," Niki interjected. "What do you think we should do next?"

"You're all in position, right?"

"Yes, but—"

Taylor drew the assault rifle from his back and made sure the magazine was full. He flicked it to full auto before he leveled it at the door and waited for a moment for the software in his HUD to set the reticle up. The sensors activated to confirm where the men stood behind the door.

He smiled, adjusted his weapon slightly, and pulled the trigger.

The assault rifle kicked hard against the suit's power and drove him back a step, but the suit's automated functions kept the aim steady as the bullets ripped through the flimsy barrier.

By the time the magazine clicked empty, there wasn't much left except splintered remains and the sight of two men sprawled on the floor.

It looked like Lynch had run before he opened fire. Taylor scowled and let his suit reload the assault rifle automatically while he drew his sidearm and trained it on the doorway as he stepped forward.

"I guess that's our signal." Niki hissed her irritation. "Let's go!"

He pushed inside as well, certain that the gang would race to the front door to deal with him and thus allow the rest of the team to attack from behind. All he needed to do was remain alive until they were in.

As he took the final step across the threshold, a piece of

the doorframe fell and slid over his armor. He ignored it and kept both weapons trained on the hallway ahead of him.

It led to what had once been a common room that was left open to the second floor with access from an indoor balcony. Five men waited on the upper level with their assault rifles already aimed down. Before he could react, a handful of rounds hammered hard into his armor. The only saving grace was that they weren't armor-piercing.

Hollow points still carried sufficient punch to make him stagger back and a couple of alarms blared in his suit. Nothing was broken yet but something would be if he caught another dozen or so bullets. The bikers peppered the area around him with gunfire, which made it difficult to plot a way forward.

Rather than waste time trying to move ahead, Taylor slid behind the cover provided by the corner where the hallway met the room, slapped a grenade into the launcher under his rifle's barrel, and aimed it around the corner. He was surprised that the walls were still in any shape to provide cover but he couldn't feel any more rounds.

The grenade whoomphed from the barrel and exploded when it impacted the ceiling above the second level. It showered them with concrete and tile as it gouged a massive hole.

He didn't wait for them to recover but dived forward immediately, flicked his rifle to three-round bursts, and fired on the men above him. Two of them dropped immediately. One more was already down, buried under the fallen ceiling, although he couldn't tell if he was dead or not.

The last two beat a hasty retreat into the second-floor space. More gunfire came from deeper inside. The rest of the M and B team had now engaged the gang and they realized that what was happening at the front was only a distraction.

Taylor wouldn't have thought they would react to the bigger threat so quickly, even if it did mean he was a little safer.

After a quick check, he adjusted the magnetic coils in his legs and launched himself to the second floor. The structure shifted as the weight of his suit landed on it—not enough to bring it down but it was an indication that the structure met only the bare minimum of what buildings were expected to do. There were problems in the engineering that ran much deeper than simply the poor condition of the paint.

He pulled another grenade from his belt and determined the location of the rest of the team to ensure that none of them were anywhere near him before he launched the ordnance into the next room. The thud as it detonated shook the entire building.

"Okay, maybe no more grenades," he whispered. Collapsing the whole building on their heads was a bad idea. Cautiously, he circled and hesitated when he caught sight of one of the men who had retreated from the balcony, who now had a massive chunk of shrapnel buried in his chest.

It was a fatal wound and the biker was bleeding out rapidly and maybe already dead.

Taylor settled himself and made sure to remain close to the edges of the room as he began to close in on the combat. It sounded like the gang was putting up one hell of a fight and they packed considerable firepower. Most gangs in the area had to settle for pistols, shotguns, and hopefully, the occasional sub-machine gun. These guys had assault rifles and displayed the kind of organization that told him that they were experienced fighters.

Experienced in fighting other gangs, he corrected, not a largely military-trained team in full combat suits.

Without so much as a thought, Taylor pushed in from behind and took care that he didn't step into the line of fire as he focused on those who still tried to remain in cover.

"Motherfuckers!"

He had no idea why he shouted that almost like a battle cry. The gang was being pushed back to where he had positioned himself to attack them.

Three were dead almost before they realized he was there. Either they'd completely forgotten about him or they thought their seven men could keep him pinned down while the rest dealt with the other six. Whatever their situation was, he didn't care and immediately felled the three who looked like they had grenades on their pouches.

Once that was done, he dove behind cover when a hail of gunfire battered the walls around him. More alerts blared to warn him that there were problems with the magnetic coils but they were quickly corrected by the suit's redundancy systems, which allowed him to circle and pick off two of the bikers. His team rushed forward now that they were no longer being fired at.

It was interesting to watch them attacking. Tanya was the first one there and she hurled one of the men through the wall behind their cover and brought down more of the ceiling as the entire wall crumbled with the impact. Taylor paused and looked around to make sure the building wasn't in danger of collapse before he aimed his weapon at the remaining bikers. They dropped their rifles and glowered belligerently at the invaders.

Only six of them were left out of the two and a half dozen or so who had used the condemned building as a base, and the M and B hadn't sustained a single fatality or even any wounded. That the GAMC were good was a given but they were far from good enough.

"Which one of you is the leader?" Niki asked and gestured for all six to drop to their knees. They seemed to know what the procedure was and put their hands on their heads.

"He's not here," Tanya commented.

"Logan went into his office when we noticed the Thirteens starting to close in," one of the bikers explained. "He said he would talk to GAMC leadership about what to do next."

Jiro was the first to respond, approached the office the man gestured to, and kicked the locked door in.

"The room's empty," he said after a quick search. "It looks like Quinn bugged out but quick."

Taylor scowled when he noticed a small section of the wall had been cut open to allow them to send bits and pieces from the second floor to a handful of containers. It was a good place to escape from and one that Quinn probably hadn't chanced upon at the last minute.

"We didn't have anything to do with this," a biker shouted and looked somewhat desperately at the impassive suits around him. "This was all about some stupid rivalry between Lynch and Quinn. Cody was trying to undermine Logan for being put in charge or some bullshit like that. We're merely the pawns in all this."

"That's some big talk from the assholes who planned to start a war in this city," Niki snapped and pressed her sidearm to his temple. "I don't remember any of you trying to help our friend escape so to our minds, you're all equally guilty, got it? Maybe this will make you think twice before you join another biker gang."

"What the hell do you think will happen to us after this?" another pointed out. "The Thirteens are still out there and when you leave, they'll simply kill us anyway."

The man made a good point and it was reinforced by three men who hurried up the stairs and approached them.

All were from the Thirteens and their guns were drawn and ready to fire.

"Lower your weapons now," Taylor instructed and stepped forward when he saw the leader among the group. "Or we'll have a problem."

The leader—Juan-Pablo from what Desk was able to tell him—motioned for the other two to lower their shotguns while he did the same with his Uzi.

"We did not know if the fighting was over or which way it had gone," he offered by way of apology. "I must say, the legend of McFadden had not been exaggerated."

"I have a team that does most of the work while I take all the credit," Taylor commented. "We're not in the business of executing prisoners, but if you guys are game, have at them."

"Do you have the leaders?"

"It looks like they ran before the fighting started. I don't suppose your people caught sight of them before they disappeared?"

"Sadly, no."

"Well, our business with these assholes is done. If you want to stop the leaders from returning, you'll have to find them yourselves." Taylor looked at their prisoners. "I would prefer to have these assholes run back to whatever holes they crawled out of to make sure people around the country know that you do not fuck with McFadden and Banks. I hope your men need no reminding of that?"

JP and his men backed away when they realized that all seven combat suits had their weapons aimed at them.

"Of course not," the Thirteens leader whispered and rubbed his goatee. "But being reminded of it is always something we can benefit from."

"Cool beans." Taylor approached the man. "And keep it in mind. Europe is a quick plane ride away and part of the team will be here, ready to put these combat suits to deadly use if they are needed to fight cryptids or any other threats. If anyone fucks with my family, you know what to expect. And next time, we won't be inclined to leave survivors, regardless of what colors they wear."

The speech was intended for the bikers too, although he couldn't be sure if they would survive the night. Still, it looked like the Thirteens weren't in the mood for executions either. They would likely direct their efforts toward finding Quinn and Lynch instead.

Tanya was the first to move away. She struck one of the bikers as she passed before she walked around the gang members and continued silently to the ground floor, likely heading to the van.

No one could blame her. They could all stand to gain from a good meal and a good night's rest before they returned to the business of getting the core M and B team the hell out of Vegas.

It would never be a good idea to put Germans and Englishmen together in close quarters. Aside from the French, the Germans had the longest tradition of strife with the Brits—the kind of thing that would always be difficult to set aside, no matter what their common goals might be.

Despite this, Sam was relieved to see the efficient way the responsibility for the Zoo base was shared between the two. According to the records they had, it had originally been administrated by the Brits, while the military oversight fell to the Germans. If he'd had to guess, he would have said it was the other way around.

For a long time, neither country was happy with the situation as it stood and it created far too many points of dissension. As a result, they now had two bases built directly beside each other and had divided the sector into two sections which were administered independently but with close cooperation. For practical purposes, this meant two separate situations for the ENSOL team to look at when it came to the wall.

Ordinarily, it wouldn't have been an issue. The two nations appeared to work together amenably enough and whatever historical blowback might take place, it hadn't manifested in any of the reports.

The problem was that their visit to the Sustainagrow site continued to haunt their little team. He hadn't had much sleep the night before and he could tell that neither Chen nor Elke had either. The young man hadn't touched his phone and stared blankly out of one of their windows, and she hadn't so much as touched her tablet as they drove up to the bases.

Fix raised an eyebrow when she noticed him looking at her and she smiled tiredly. "I can't move past the feeling that we're stepping into a parallel universe," she explained. "One that's bound to be fraught with resentment and aggression that I can fully understand after what we saw yesterday."

"How did you—"

"Don't ask because you already know the answer. I couldn't sleep last night so all I did was read through reports. These bases are essentially the antithesis of anything and everything in the Sahara Coalition sector. They will use our investigation to vent their disapproval and frustration at having to live and function next door to what is probably the most vulnerable stretch of the Zoo perimeter."

He nodded. There was no need to respond as all of them knew she wasn't wrong about that.

Officers from both bases waiting for them and the politeness in their demeanor barely masked the sentiment Elke had so accurately predicted.

"Get ready for fifteen tons of dick measuring," she whispered as they approached the group, none of whom appeared to be particularly happy to see the ENSOL team.

"As if they have anything to measure against," Chen

muttered. "It's like a whale lined up with a sardine. Honestly, though, this will be a hard visit. After what we saw at the Sustainagrow site, I'm not sure I have the patience for the civilized posturing from wealthy nations that haven't had to face anything like that firsthand. They go out into the Zoo, sure, but I think every goddammed soldier or administrator needs to visit that ghost site to gain real perspective."

"All the more reason why we need the footage put out there as part of our report," Fix pointed out and shrugged as the younger man fell into step beside him and they hurried to catch up to their colleague, who had already reached the delegation from the two bases. With the mood she was in, they might both have to step in to avoid an outright confrontation.

"We're only here to do a quick inspection on the wall defenses you've put up," she said immediately and spoke in English although she was German.

"I'm not sure why you're here," the British commander snapped, her eyes narrowed. "We've shared a border with the Sahara Coalition for long enough to know that they've half-assed this whole endeavor. What that means is that we have to work twice as hard because they cannot be bothered."

They'd heard similar complaints from most of the bases they had visited—each one was very quick to point out the perceived shortcomings of their neighbors—but the reality was that everyone needed to improve in one area or another, some more than others.

"We've visited all the different bases and will compile as comprehensive a report as possible," Sam asserted, his tone firm but—he hoped—understanding. He wanted nothing more than to complete their circuit and get the hell out of there, and if making nice accomplished that, he could smooth their ruffled feathers and soothe Elke's belligerence. "Be assured that our intention is not to point fingers but to present the facts from an independent perspective as a basis from which the Zoo Containment Protocol group can work to rectify issues in all sectors."

None of them looked happy about his intention to remain neutral, but the fact remained that ENSOL wasn't there to negotiate world peace. They were merely there to get a job done.

CHAPTER NINETEEN

They'd heard stories about the Zoo. By this time, everyone had. It was a matter of public record by this point, and Pavel was willing to admit that he and his kids had spent hours on end watching the vids from ZooTube, mostly to be a part of what was happening, no matter how small.

But the goddammed jungle had materialized in their safe reality. His team had worked through the night and been warned by the gate guards—on a line that shrieked with static—to get out before it was too late. They'd responded with alacrity but had wasted possibly valuable time frozen at the factory entrance while they simply stared at was undoubtedly an alien landscape that had somehow appeared overnight.

Tomas tapped his phone and waved it around to try to find signal.

"The Zoo interferes with devices," Pavel told him curtly as he settled into a crouch and studied their surroundings. "Everyone knows that."

His colleague snorted. "I suppose you think you're a goddammed expert on the subject."

"I can't claim to be an expert but I clearly know more about it than you do." He shrugged. "My kids and I watch the vids about the Zoo."

"It's not the fucking Zoo!"

The two men turned to look at one of their comrades. The man had his hands clamped over his ears and rocked rhythmically like he tried to comfort himself with the assurance that nothing was wrong.

"It is." Pavel drew a deep breath. "We need to come to terms with the fact and move on. The only important thing right now is to get out of here as quickly as possible."

He could understand the reaction, though, and while he tried to present a calm exterior, he knew he was one crazy step away from losing his goddammed mind. They were simple country folk, far removed from the horrors that ravaged the Sahara at the moment.

"We need to move to the gate," he said in a low, reassuring tone. "It's a long walk so we might as well get moving, right?"

"You first?" Tomas looked a little calmer than the others but even he displayed the jittery movements that betrayed genuine borderline panic.

At least so far, they didn't have to deal with any of the monsters the Zoo was famous for. Not that he thought they wouldn't appear soon, but they had an opening now where they only had to deal with trees and plants. If they could reach the gate without delay, they would hopefully encounter nothing that attacked them directly.

"Very well."

Pavel retrieved one of the shotguns that were kept in the factory and handed the other to Vincence, the game-keeper who was with them purely by chance. The man had chosen the worst time possible to try to learn the pelt trade, which was why he'd been with them through the night when the supervisors wouldn't question why the workers were sharing their knowledge informally.

The weapons were used for hunting, of course, but also when the guards were told to fire them from time to time to remind the locals that people on Stepan's property were armed and not afraid to open fire on any intruders. They were probably not as effective as the rifles most of the guards were armed with but would have to do.

He made a quick headcount of the dozen workers in total who needed to get out. Some of the men had armed themselves with a variety of cutlery from the mini-kitchen in the main building. While hopelessly inadequate when compared to the combat suits used in the Zoo, it was certainly better than nothing although not by much.

Two guns and a collection of kitchen knives. They had to pray that nothing alive, angry, and hungry emerged from the goddammed jungle.

"Come on, then."

It looked like he'd been delegated the responsibility to lead the group, but it was only because they lacked any kind of alternative at the moment. Still, someone had to do it so he urged them forward and away from the door. He knew they felt there would be some measure of protection provided by the building, but he had noticed that the walls had already started to crumble.

Any security or safety they might have had provided

would be gone in a matter of hours. Their only real chance at survival was to get out as soon as they could.

He was not sure what to expect from a Zoo that had taken root where it shouldn't be. Nothing in the vids had ever prepared him for this and seeing the jungle in the middle of Eastern Europe made his breath catch in his lungs.

His response was echoed by others as they all stepped into the underbrush and huddled close together while they tried to ready themselves for anything, given the unknowns. Even the man who had panicked seemed to have calmed and clutched a butcher's knife like it was a lifeline and he was in the ocean.

"Go, go, go!" Pavel kept his voice down and gestured for the group to start moving. The jungle made it difficult to tell where the gate was at this point but hopefully, the familiar route he had in his head would be confirmed by the traces of the road that peeped out from beneath the vegetation. If they hurried, they might push through to where the long driveway had yet to be swallowed by the growth and would have a clear sprint from there to safety.

It seemed impossible but as they moved, the jungle seemed to grow before their very eyes. He had no idea why he was surprised by this given that it had grown overnight, but it was still incredible to watch in real-time as they climbed through the steadily thickening plant life.

"How...how far is the gate again?"

He turned to where Tomas leaned against one of the trees and tried to look around it. Most of the trunks were already taller than the men and the foliage had thickened to the point that they couldn't see much of anything past ten meters in any direction.

"Above you!"

"What?"

His colleague looked up to where he was pointing and froze when he saw a handful of small tendril-like vines that reached down from the branches above them. When he snatched his hand away, they retracted.

"Do not touch the trees, then," the man whispered and adjusted his hold on the chef's knife he carried.

Pavel's attention had already been drawn elsewhere and he leaned a little closer to one of the bushes nearby. Ordinarily, he would not have been able to identify even normal plants, never mind Zoo ones. His daughter was the one who enjoyed learning about flora and flowers especially, but most of it had gone in one ear and out the other when she had told him about them.

Despite this, he thought he knew what he was looking at. The low-growing bush seemed to thrive under the trees even with the lack of sunlight and its bright red-and-blue flowers almost seemed to glow.

It was a Pita plant, he was sure of it. He'd seen them before in the vids and although those had been only blue, the structure and shape were identical. Those he'd seen were worth a great deal of money and he wondered if this version was equally as valuable—or perhaps even more so given its possible rarity. If he could take only one flower, maybe he might get lucky and come away from all of this considerably richer.

He paused as his fingers touched the petals and his gaze

jerked to the underbrush as a low squeal echoed through the jungle.

"Is that..." The speaker trailed off as if afraid to voice the full question

The gamekeeper responded as he checked his double-barreled shotgun. "A boar? Those are terrifying enough already." He snapped the shotgun closed. "There's no need to add anything like the Zoo to the mixture."

Pavel agreed but before he could voice it, he realized that the sound moved closer and more importantly, even more approached from different directions.

"A sounder of the bastards," Tomas whispered.

"Singular," Vincenc corrected.

"No, there is more than one—either that or I can hear it coming from different directions at the same time."

"No, a group of wild boars is called a singular. It is only when dealing with swine that they are called a sounder."

"That—" Pavel shook his head. It sounded dubious despite the fact that it came from the expert on the topic among them, but he snapped his mouth shut because they did not have the time to debate it. Whatever the creatures were, they moved closer and from what he knew about wild boars, they would not be pleasant to fight.

The rest of the group appeared to get the same message and they increased their pace away from the boars and hopefully in the direction of the gate, although he couldn't be sure since he could no longer stop to check for the tell-tale traces of the road beneath the dense foliage. The jungle around them felt like it shifted and twisted continuously to intentionally make it impossible for them to tell where they were going.

Like it worked hard to prevent their escape, he thought in sudden panic.

He pushed the thought aside together with the rising horror that threatened to steal his breath. They were only plants. As dangerous as they might be, there was no way that a group of trees would intentionally try to see them dead.

"I forgot," Vincenc whispered and paused as he almost tripped over a root. He held onto a nearby tree for balance, although he snatched his hand away like it had been stung within seconds. "Sounder or singular—both can be used."

"Now is…it's not the time," Pavel whispered when another shriek issued from behind them. As they moved closer, the sounds became increasingly alien. He wasn't sure how that was possible or how he could tell merely from the sound of them, but something deeper and disquietingly wrong in the resonation told him that whatever these beasts were, they were something new.

He grasped his shotgun more firmly and set his jaw. All they had to do was reach the gate. People were there waiting for them already and the sounds of a heavy vehicle approaching confirmed that they were moving in the right direction. "We only need to get to the gate."

Not much in the world made him feel worse than leaving his people behind to be massacred. Still, there was the simple truth that they were dealing with more than merely a gang, something he was both willing and able to face. Military equipment and military training were what set the

McFadden group above and beyond anything the local gangs could deal with.

And from the sound of the fighting in the building and how quickly it died down, their reputation was not based on empty boasts.

He'd managed to leave a few minutes before the attack, slide out via the escape hatch, and reach the neighboring building before the sound of gunfire even started. Now, he huddled in the empty building and listened to his men be massacred.

Although he wasn't alone, Logan realized when he noticed Lynch sneak away from their HQ and climb through one of the windows of the same building he was in. It looked like his second in command was as willing to let their people die as he was. He wasn't sure he liked this particular comparison, which seemed to put him on the same level as the idiot who'd caused the problems.

He drew his revolver and eased stealthily to where Cody leaned against the wall and looked relieved that he'd managed to escape the battle.

"Is this what you wanted?"

The man's eyes snapped open but Logan moved faster than he could react to press the barrel to the kid's head. He snatched the Glock his second carried in his belt like an amateur.

"Wha—"

"Don't even start with me, you piece of shit. I know you've tried to undermine me and done your level best to take what I've earned away. And for what? The only thing special about you is that your dad has covered your ass for your entire life. Do you think that means you've earned anything? You haven't worked for a goddammed thing and yet I have to kowtow to a traitor."

Cody shook his head. "No, I never—"

"Never what?" He moved in closer as Lynch sank to his knees and tears trickled from his eyes. "Never thought this would have consequences for you too? Well surprise, surprise, asshole! Our people are dying and it's all your fault."

"I'm sorry…"

"Why are they dying? No, I have a better question—why aren't you in there dying with them?"

He almost didn't realize that he had pulled the trigger until it was over but watching the kid fall and his brains splatter across the walls felt right. It was like he'd meant to do this his entire goddammed life. If Cody hadn't swaggered around behind big Daddy Lynch's protection, he would have killed him a long time ago.

There was no point in dwelling on the fact that the question applied to him as well. Why wasn't he in there with them? They were his people, like it or not. He knew the honor rules only ever applied to the foot soldiers in the motorcycle club but it still felt wrong to know that he was alive while they died in a battle some other idiot had initiated.

And yet, as he stood there and accepted that the gunshot would have been loud enough to attract attention, he knew he could never return to the GAMC.

He'd failed, which was bad enough on its own, but he'd also killed the boss' son. There was no way that this wouldn't end with his throat cut—and that was if he was lucky. Miles' wife would want him to suffer for a while, and the gang leader was an indulgent enough prick when it came to what she wanted.

Footsteps approached and yanked him from his maudlin thoughts. Before he could lift the weapons in his hands, seven Thirteens surrounded him. They all carried shotguns or pistols, likely provided by the GAMC when they were still in business.

"So this is how it will end," Logan whispered and looked squarely at his rivals.

"Drop your guns," one of the Thirteens ordered as he approached and held a shotgun with a sawn-off barrel in his face.

"Or what? You'll kill me?" He smirked and glanced at the others. "I'm a dead man anyway. If the McFadden team doesn't do it, your bosses will. And even if they don't, my bosses will. So go ahead, *pendejo*. Tell me why I should put my guns down?"

It was a hell of a thing when a man had nothing left to lose and Logan had never fully understood that before. His heart beat faster and his whole body surged with adrenaline. He'd never felt this free or this powerful.

Ironically, it was when he stared down the barrels of seven different guns with only a couple available for his use. He would go out in a blaze of glory. That was what people would say about him rather than that he ran from the fight like a coward.

Logan raised both his weapons and tried to select two targets for him to take with him. He had no real reason to be choosy. All seven were likely the kind of gangbangers who engaged in criminal wars all around the country. Hell, all around the world, exactly like he had been at one point in his life.

The seven Thirteens weren't the brightest among their ranks, he decided with a smirk. They stared at him in confusion as if his response to them was mere bravado and they didn't believe he would follow through. In all probability, they'd been sent to bring him in and expected him to simply comply—something most men would have done under the circumstances. They hadn't reckoned with a man who had nothing left to lose, however, and weren't quite sure how to deal with him.

It was a ridiculously dumbass reaction and wouldn't last long, but it did afford him a small window of opportunity and he made the most of it.

The Glock pulled a little to the left and the shot went wide, but the revolver hammered a round directly between the eyes of the man who stood in front of him. The shock seemed to jolt them from their inept stupor and a thunderous roar of gunfire erupted all around him.

It was weird how it didn't hurt. He fell almost before he realized what was happening and squinted to focus on his chest.

Blood had already pooled around him. Logan laughed softly but winced when his chest was wracked by a cough that suddenly ushered in a wave of pain. He doubled over instinctively but smiled when he realized that his prone position would hide his next action.

The Thirteens loomed over him as he raised his revolver to his head and tried to laugh in defiance. They had won, technically, but he would have the last say. He'd taken one of them with him and would go out on his terms.

His smile was bloody as he pressed the revolver barrel to the bottom of his jaw—exactly like the poem, he thought absently. Who was the author again? Some British motherfucker.

He gave up trying to think of him. All that mattered was that he'd caught his rivals off-guard and it was too late for them to try to stop him. He closed his eyes and pulled the trigger.

CHAPTER TWENTY

The small group was immersed in a living, ever-expanding nightmare. Pavel couldn't understand what went through the minds of those who intentionally put themselves into the jungle where it was at its most intense, simply to make money.

Of course, they were generally sent in with military-grade weapons and armor so it wasn't quite the same, but none of that had relevance to the twelve civilians who now seemed to blunder ever deeper into a never-ending jungle of horrors.

"Look out!" the gamekeeper yelled and shoved him aside. He caught his breath as he made impact with a tree trunk with a girth that defied logic or reason given how long it had been growing there. His rescuer swung his hatchet but missed the fat vine that slithered back into the cover of the foliage.

"It...it had a mouth," Pavel whispered hoarsely and wiped the sheen of sweat from his forehead with his sleeve. "The thing had a big-ass mouth."

"And teeth," Tomas agreed and shuddered at the thought. "This is the third one I've seen like that."

"And they're fast," Matej interjected with a scowl that seemed to have become a fixture. "The goddammed bastards hide in the canopy and snake out when they know you're not looking."

"They are vines," Pavel retorted but his narrow escape had left him shaken and he needed a moment to regain his composure.

"Vines with—" Vincenc's response was cut short by a scream from one of the group. The four men turned as one to where Havel, the youngest of their group, curled on the jungle floor and clutched his thigh.

Edvard crouched beside him and shrugged, his eyes wide with terror. He gestured wildly at a nearby shrub. "That bush," he told them in disbelief. "It shoots needles—quills, maybe, I don't know—and Havel got too close."

"Dammit." Pavel hurried forward with the gamekeeper on his heels. Both men knelt beside their wounded companion and studied what certainly looked like quills that protruded from his thigh.

"They are in deep," Vincenc said grimly.

"And they burn like shit," Havel muttered. "Get the fucking things out."

Pavel took hold of one but he hesitated as the kid braced himself. "Won't it start the bleeding if we remove them?" he asked cautiously and kicked himself mentally for being stupid enough to forget the first aid box.

"I don't care," the wounded man said. "I'd rather bleed to death than live with this pain."

"They could be poisoned," the gamekeeper said after a

moment. "If each of us tear a sleeve off, we can pack the wounds and tie everything in place with his belt. That's probably the safest course to follow—if they are poisoned, the longer they stay in, the less chance he will have."

"Sleeves," Pavel snapped and glanced at their companions who had gathered around the unfortunate man. "And for Christ's sake, keep an eye on this bastard jungle. We don't need all of you to stand and stare while we take care of the problem."

His warning, unfortunately, came too late. One of the killer vines serpentined out of the tree behind the group without a sound and landed with its gaping maw over the head of the man at the back. He screamed, the sound muffled by the fleshy lips that closed around his neck. Blood trickled between them, no doubt when the razor-sharp teeth buried themselves into his flesh.

The two men closest spun and while one hacked ineffectually at the creeper, the other caught hold of their comrade and tried to pull him free.

"It's too late," Pavel yelled. "He's dead, for Christ's sake." Even if he wasn't, no one would be able to help him with his face already scraped clean—which seemed the most likely possibility. "Leave him and position yourselves around us in a circle back to back and watch the goddammed jungle. You can do that while you rip a sleeve off but take turns so someone is watching at all times."

He felt like the goddammed single parent of a horde of idiotic teenagers but tried to control his frustration. With a frown, he ignored Vincenc's raised eyebrow as he took the first of the sleeves and stretched them across Havel's stomach so they'd be at hand when needed.

"Are you ready?" the gamekeeper asked and the kid nodded, his face an odd shade of gray and his pupils dilated, which seemed to confirm the presence of a toxin. "Hold the leg down," he told Pavel, who complied in silence and grasped the limb firmly using his weight to anchor it so it couldn't move.

Havel shrieked as the first of the quills was extracted and he passed out before Vincenc could grasp the second.

"It's maybe for the best," Pavel muttered and tried to ignore the blood that welled immediately from the wound.

"Maybe. I only hope none have gone into the bone. If they have, I doubt any of us can pull them out."

"Do what you can and do it quickly. We need to get the hell out of this nightmare and if we have to carry the kid, it will slow us even more."

While they worked together to remove the remaining three quills—none of which had lodged in the bone, fortunately—he allowed himself a moment of sheer disbelief. This wasn't the kind of situation he could ever have imagined being an issue until now. Even though they worked with products from the Zoo, the possibility of it going this wrong had never occurred to anyone. He had always assumed that the people who handled it knew how to keep it clean and isolated so something like this could never happen.

"Where are we going?" Tomas asked once the boy was bandaged and semi-conscious, at least enough to carry some of his own weight if supported by a comrade on either side.

Pavel divided the group into pairs and instructed them to take turns with Havel so he wouldn't slow them unnecessarily by wearing his rescuers out. It would be tiring enough to push through the goddammed jungle without having a wounded man to contend with. As the only two men with weapons, he would position himself at the front and Vincenc would watch the rear of the group.

He grasped the shotgun tightly and looked around before he answered what should have been a very simple question—where the hell did they go now? The jungle continued to grow before their very eyes.

Aside from that, it seemed there was certainly a clear intention or some kind of will that made it change and adapt according to their efforts, which made it almost impossible to move toward the gate without regaining their bearings. The leaves overhead obscured the sun almost entirely, and with the way the growth continued around them, finding the right direction had become infinitely more complicated.

They'd had the rumble of car engines to guide them earlier—and reassure them that the gate wasn't that far away. Since then, however, they seemed to move farther from the gates rather than closer. The motors were silent now and somehow, even though it felt like they were still very much on Stepan's property, they were completely lost.

"We'll have to simply choose a direction and cut our way through," he said finally, his tone weary.

"Cut?" Tomas frowned at him

"We have knives, don't we?" he snapped and looked at the gamekeeper as he gestured in what he thought might be the correct direction. "And you have a hatchet. That's what it's for, right? We cut through the jungle and reach the gate one way or another."

He could attribute his sudden onset of courage to the fact that they hadn't heard anything more from what he could only assume were monstrous alien boars. It was a relief, honestly, as the squeals and screeches had been a sure trigger for panic.

The noise they made was unmistakable. He'd lived in the countryside long enough to know what a boar sounded like and he had no doubt that these were the twisted Zoo version of those same creatures, although they hadn't seen any of them through the trees or heard the heavy footfalls that usually accompanied the sounds. But any country boy could tell them that tangling with a boar in the bush would always be a bad idea given that they tended to use their tusks to disembowel their adversaries at any opportunity.

And whatever the Zoo had done to them would have made them worse. There was a time, he thought morosely, when he would have questioned whether this was even possible but any doubts were erased by the weird alien landscape.

"Fine." Vincenc took the hatchet from his belt and swung it at one of the branches. He paused along with the rest of the team and looked around as if waiting for the jungle to react.

"For fuck's sake. These are only trees and bushes. We need to start cutting to get them out of the way."

To his relief, no one questioned his authority and probably wouldn't from this point forward. All those with knives and blades of any kind began to hack and hew a path for them to follow. He'd chosen a direction for them to go in and they had to reach the end of the jungle eventually. The gamekeeper handed his hatchet to Tomas, who was by far the strongest of the group, which left him free to assist with watching for anything that might attack from the dense underbrush.

No one spoke as they pushed forward, their entire focus on the nightmarish task. More than once, someone stumbled and fell when a root thrust from the earth as if deliberately timed to trip the unwary. The vines above became more agitated and even those without mouths slithered out of the canopy and tried to snatch various members of their group. Fortunately, the pairs fell into a routine so one attacked the jungle while the other kept watch until the first man tired and they exchanged tasks.

Pavel spun on his heel when Havel screamed, a shrill, high-pitched keening that spoke both terror and delirium. The two men who supported him used their free hands to hack at what looked like three vines that had dropped suddenly and coiled around him.

"Get in there and help them," he shouted as he rushed closer and yanked his penknife from his pocket. It scared him more than anything to even consider the probability that these horrendous creepers were somehow sentient enough to discern the weak and wounded among the group to target.

It took six of them to finally free the kid, who writhed and flailed while he continued to shriek in utter terror— not unfounded, Pavel thought grimly, as one of the vines had secured itself firmly around his lower legs and began to try to hoist him up feet first. His two helpers hung on desperately while the other four hacked and sliced at the fleshy vines until they finally released him.

Perhaps even worse than the outright attack was the

way they hissed as they withdrew into the foliage as if angered that they'd been denied their prey.

"Keep moving!" Tomas shouted as they paused to catch their breath. He hacked the bushes with renewed determination and shoved the men closest to him through without bothering to clear the chunks away.

Pavel could understand his concern. With the vines now actively aggressive, it made sense to get the hell out of where they knew they were. Of course, the goddammed things could be anywhere given how closely the foliage grew, but if they remained on the move, they would hopefully present a less tempting target.

The way the vines moved made him think of snakes or even the tentacles of a monster that lurked in the branches, watched them, and waited for them to relax even for a moment so it could snatch them.

He had noticed small leaves extending from the vines here and there but honestly, nothing about them seemed truly plant-like. It was as if the Zoo had taken nature and twisted it into an unholy creature designed to attack from above under the guise of innocent creepers.

With a muttered curse, he flinched at the thunder of gunfire from close by. Vincenc had opened fire into the trees and everyone in their group came to an abrupt standstill to peer upward to see what he had unloaded two rounds of buckshot on.

"I...I saw something in the trees—eyes looking down on us."

"Are you sure?" Pavel asked while the man reloaded quickly with fingers that shook as he fumbled with the shells he carried in a pouch.

"Yes...maybe. I...the eyes were there."

The expressions on everyone's faces were sufficient evidence that each member of the team shared the feeling that they were being watched. Hell, Pavel conceded, he hadn't been able to shake it either but they were in a situation where resources were in short supply and it didn't look like the man had many rounds to spare in the small pouch strapped around his waist.

"Next time, be sure there's something there to shoot," he snapped and poked his finger into the gamekeeper's chest. "We don't know how much shooting will need to be done to get us clear. Besides, any more gunfire might draw the attention of—"

He lowered his head and shook it morosely. It was like the Zoo had simply waited for him to make the suggestion before the low, throaty squeals of the boars resumed not too far away—drawn to them by the sound of gunfire, no doubt.

"If we don't have enough bullets to fight the shits off, I'll find and strangle you in the afterlife." Pavel pushed past him roughly to join the others and used his irritation-fueled strength to shove branches out of the way so they could move along a little faster.

They all heard the monsters bearing down on them at a rapid pace and the sounds they made were more intense. While before, it had sounded like they were trying to find the humans in the brush but they now knew exactly where to hunt.

"I never thought I'd meet my death at the tusk of a boar," Tomas rumbled belligerently as he hacked the branches ahead of them with focused determination. He increased his pace despite the fact that anyone could see he was exhausted. "A proper predator would be better, like…a panther maybe."

"Boars are predators enough," Pavel whispered, dropped into a crouch, and tried to feel the vibrations of the ground that would indicate how close the creatures were. "Well, opportunistic omnivores, but it works out the same for the prey, wouldn't you say?"

"As long as you make sure you're shooting at the bastards when they reach us."

"What is that supposed to mean?"

"I'm merely thinking that it wouldn't be above you to shoot me in the leg and let them eat me while you escape."

Pavel laughed at that, a sound he didn't think would escape his lips while still in the goddammed jungle. "True, but given how many of them there are, I would be better served with you alive and using those impressive muscles to clear a path ahead of me while I cover your rear. In this case, I rely on you for survival more than you rely on me."

"And don't you forget it."

Another squeal seemed much closer and immediately held their attention as they continued their push toward what they hoped was the gate. He could feel the vibrations in the ground now from the beasts approaching. Even worse, he could feel them without needing to touch the earth with bare skin. The creatures were heavy and they were moving fast.

The first flicker of movement came from the left, although Pavel managed to rein in the impulse to fire immediately. The first lesson he'd learned about dealing with wild boars was only to take a shot when he had a clear one. They had a tendency to charge in directly, which meant this would provide his best chance for a shot that counted.

Finally, it appeared and he knew immediately that it was already mutated well beyond the average boar. A massive creature almost the size of a bear stopped abruptly and stared at him. The stubby legs, thick black fur, and powerful build made it look far more predatory and almost like a wolf. This perception was made even worse by the sight of what looked like fangs that extended downward almost as long as the tusks from the bottom extended up.

He could imagine what it would look like when both snapped shut around his torso. Beasts with tusks instinctively moved to disembowel, but he could only imagine what the monster he now faced had instincts for.

The huge beast moved suddenly and kicked dirt into the trees behind it. Logic shrieked that it was impossible for a creature that large to move that fast, but he was ready for it. He pushed the stock of the shotgun into his shoulder, raised the barrel, and squeezed the trigger to deliver a spray of lead into the jungle ahead of him.

For a moment, it didn't look like the shot had done anything as the monster continued its forward run, but a chunk of its head and skull fell away and splattered into the foliage around them. In the sudden silence, he heard shouts from behind them, too far away to be from their group.

Pavel took a moment to make sure the beast was dead before he snapped the shotgun open, ejected the spent shells, and slid two more in. He closed it and turned to see what was happening.

They were at the edge of the jungle. The trees parted unexpectedly and gave them space to move without the necessity to cut through the underbrush and he could see the gate. A handful of vehicles were parked outside and dozens of men with guns awaited them. Police officers, he realized from the uniforms, and some of the guards who usually patrolled the grounds. He could make Stepan out as well where he stood alongside his brother. All were armed with rifles and ready to help.

The welcoming group waved them forward, away from the trees and the danger.

"Let's go—move, people. We're almost th—"

The sentence was cut off when something collided with Pavel's side. The force of impact launched him off his feet and snapped him around to career into a nearby tree, which knocked the breath from his lungs.

Something large had bulldozed into him. He suddenly realized that he lay on his back, easy prey for the sounder of hogs that descended on them. Squeals and screams filled his ears and he watched helplessly as Tomas fell. The man's lifeless eyes stared at him and the lower two-thirds of his body was severed around the stomach a little below the ribs. Some of his organs were still connected to the top half.

Pavel's whole body ached and he knew something similar had happened to him. He tried to ignore the scene and the sounds the hogs made as they began to devour the fallen men. Their massive fangs seemed to bite through both flesh and bone as easily as a child might bite a boiled egg.

Finally, he looked down and groaned softly when he

realized that his right leg had been severed near the hip. His foot, ankle, calf, knee, and thigh were all gone and only a bloody chunk remained where a leg had once been attached.

He was supposed to be in shock by this point, but he felt only the pain that arced up his body in relentless waves.

"Crap," he whispered and stretched his hand to the remaining leg. It was mangled but at least still intact. If he could reach the gate, they would be able to reconstruct it or at least leave it in better condition than the one that was missing entirely.

The single quiet curse was enough to snap a massive hog's head around to look at him and his eyes widened as he cursed his stupidity. If he'd remained still and quiet, they might have left him alone. It was a theory he wouldn't ever put to the test as the monster closed on him, the elongated maw already dripping blood.

Perhaps the shock would kick in this time and it wouldn't hurt as much.

Anton looked away as the creature's jaw closed over the head of the one man who was still alive in the group. The hogs had made short work of the others and ripped through them to leave a bloody mess behind before they began to drag the bodies into the jungle where they could eat them in peace. As crazy as it seemed, they appeared to know they were at risk of being shot by the group that watched them from the other side of the gates.

A couple of the guards and the cops had managed to kill a couple of them but despite their size, they moved too quickly and too unnaturally, which made it difficult to hit them without injuring the survivors who tried to reach the gate. Not that it mattered now. All of them were dead and it might have been kinder to end them with a bullet.

He knew the last man who'd had his head crushed like an overripe watermelon and watched with helpless fury as his body was dragged away. The hogs even hauled their own dead from the killing field. As far as he knew, wild hogs were opportunistic omnivores, which meant they would eat almost anything. In fact, people regularly claimed that their diets were as varied as humans'.

Even humans were cannibals from time to time, he reminded himself in an effort to try to restore some faint thread of normalcy. It was sickening, and the fact that it wasn't even in the top five most disturbing things he'd seen happen over the last five minutes was probably the kind of thing he would need to speak to a therapist about.

For some reason, that thought pushed him beyond the point of control and he fell to his knees, doubled over, and heaved up the snack he'd had before coming to work. He wasn't the only one openly sickened by what they'd seen, although he was past caring about either that or what others might think of him.

Anton washed his mouth out with water from the bottle he always carried and drew a few long, deep breaths. The nausea persisted but at least he no longer had the urge to throw up. After a moment or two, he was able to turn to look at a jungle that could advance at about five or six meters in an hour. It was an unsettling thought even without the wild boars that could cut a man in half with a snap of their jaws.

His brain settled on the first thought he'd had when he'd arrived that morning—something had to be done. Fortunately, the police chief seemed to share the conviction and approached Stepan with a grim expression once everyone had recovered.

"We will not be able to deal with this," he stated emphatically and shook his head. "Not even with every officer under my command. We have to call in the military."

Of all the people in this area who did not want the military to wander around their property, the furrier probably wanted them the least. His conflicting emotions regarding the matter played freely on his face but he made no effort to stop the chief of police when the man turned to his car where another man waited with a radio.

"I have someone on the radio."

Anton turned to look at Ivo—Stepan's brother—who held the radio in one of their vehicles.

"Who?" Stepan asked and hurried toward him.

"Someone who's still in the barracks." Ivo held the headset out to his brother, who shook his head. "The connection is spotty but they say they are still alive in there."

"Tell them to stay where they are," the older man answered. He looked a little sick but possibly for reasons that had nothing to do with what had made the rest of the men present heave their guts out. "It might take some time but the military is on the way. We will do all we can to get them out."

CHAPTER TWENTY-ONE

It had to be donuts. Bobby insisted and Taylor was more than willing to oblige.

The team had all put in extra hours, which meant that a late breakfast was in order. Vickie especially had pulled double-duty to get the job done, and so had the freelancers. Splurging on serious junk food as a celebration for a job well done felt like the right thing to do.

They'd been lucky to get Tanya back without serious injury and they'd made sure to deliver retaliation in their usual excessive style so the message wouldn't be forgotten.

Celebrations all around were more than earned by this point. For the first time ever, donuts felt like they came in a little short of what was owed, although he knew it was a start, at least.

Bobby and Tanya sat together and it seemed like the mechanic would be a little clingy for the next few days. Sooner or later, of course, she would tell him to cut that shit out but she basked in the attention for the moment.

She whispered something in his ear that made him laugh and shake his head.

Niki leaned closer and kissed Taylor on the cheek. He turned to her, a hint of surprise on his face as she leaned back in her seat. He realized he'd been robbed as she took advantage of the distraction to snatch his rainbow sprinkle donut.

"Sneaky."

"You know it." She grinned and took a bite of the pastry. "Do you think this is the last time we'll have to prove our point to the local criminals?"

"Don't change the subject. You know I like the rainbow sprinkles."

"Sure, and you always hog them. I need to see what all the fuss is about. Anyway, who do you think we'll have to intimidate next?"

Taylor shook his head and chuckled. "We might need to deal with any new assholes who might think they have to confront the biggest guys in the yard to prove themselves to the rest of the gangs but hopefully, those bikers will spread the word that fucking with the McFadden and Banks team always ends badly."

"The McFadden and Banks team?" Tanya asked and raised an eyebrow.

"Sure. Why not?"

"Well, you guys are moving the McFadden and the Banks part of that to Italy, so maybe it might be time for them to realize that fucking with the Zhang and Novak team is as bad? Just saying."

"True." He stroked his chin thoughtfully. "But the McFadden and Banks brand is one people recognize around here, so deviating from that might mean you have to prove yourselves the same way we had to in the beginning."

"As long as there's no more kidnapping, I'm okay with that. It's been a while since we did some *Ocean's 11* robberies on mob bosses, so it's about time we get back on it. I think there are a couple of other casinos we could probably get away with stealing from, wouldn't you say?"

Taylor shook his head. "You're forgetting that we've effectively reached an understanding with both the mob and the Thirteens." It had been unexpected but very satisfying to find Juan-Pablo waiting outside the gate when they'd opened shop early that morning. At first, the team had been tense and prepared for trouble but the man had hastened to allay their concerns.

His purpose there, he'd told them without any attempt to beat around the bush, was to assure them that the Thirteens would make sure to keep their eye on the strip mall. Niki had bristled at this but he hurried to explain that it was with no expectation of reward. The gang was simply returning the favor the M and B team had done them by rousting the GAMC.

Besides, he'd added with a grin, it was in their interests to do so since the strip mall might attract more of their rivals in the future. It made sense to preempt any future attempts to muscle in on their territory.

"I still think you went easy on him," Tanya said with a mock pout. "Next thing you know, the rumor will be that you're best buds with the gangs and the mob."

Before he could point out that having their support only strengthened his position—and protected her, Bobby, and Elisa in their absence—he was interrupted by Vickie's almost feral growl, a sound that could only be described as massive amounts of frustration being unleashed.

"Fuck," she roared at the ceiling and let the single syllable of the word drag on for as long as her lungs would allow.

"Is there something you want to get off your chest, Vick?" Niki asked.

"Wait for it," was the hacker's cryptic response.

Taylor waited and a moment before he could ask what exactly they were waiting for, Desk spoke through the speakers in the shop.

"Chatter has us alerted to a possible Zoo incursion in the Czech Republic," the AI announced.

"Huh." He grunted. "Well, shit."

"Exactly," Vickie agreed and shook her head. "You'd think these assholes would know better by now but no, they will persist in the kind of dumbass behavior that unleashes the worst nasties imaginable."

"It might work in our favor," he commented and raised an eyebrow. "Is there any word on whether they want us to get involved at this point?"

"Yes. An officer in the Czech Republic army is attempting to contact the McFadden and Banks team through the official channels."

"Wait, we have official channels?" Niki asked.

"They are attempting to make contact through our connections in the Pentagon… Oh, it's coming through rather quickly and…there we go. We have a message from the Pentagon asking to make a connection between them and us."

"You might think we could do without a middleman," the hacker commented sourly.

"I could have interfered but it would risk allowing them to see my involvement. It would have made the connection about ten minutes earlier but I decided that safety is the better option given our current circumstances."

"It is." Taylor looked at Bobby. "Do we have somewhere to take this kind of call?"

"I put a smart TV in the break room," the mechanic answered with a nod. "You should be able to connect the call through there, right?"

"Can do." Desk cut out for a moment and they hurried to the break room where the TV was already on. "Someone is trying to connect on the other line. Let me know when I can put him through."

Taylor looked around to make sure everyone was in place before he focused his attention on the TV and folded his arms. "We're ready, Desk."

The officer in question had a very distinctive military look about him. His clean-shaven face and short hair both looked like they were maintained with almost religious diligence. He faced the camera squarely and raised an eyebrow.

"Hello," he said briskly, his arms tucked behind his back in the customary at-ease position. "Am I addressing the McFadden and Banks team in its entirety?"

"You are," Taylor answered. "And who are we addressing?"

"I am Captain Dominik Petru of the ACR," he answered quickly in decent English but with a heavy accent. "I have been entrusted with handling a situation that has developed in our country."

"Another Zoo incursion," he commented.

"Indeed. How did you know?"

"There could be no other reason why an officer in the Czech Army would contact us. We do possess a particular set of skills, after all."

"Yes." The man's gaze shifted and Taylor realized that while he put on a good show of being unaffected by the situation, a hint of worry intruded and made him look a little more hard-featured than he usually might. "A local rural area has been overtaken by a sudden incursion—one that is filling the surrounding landscape at an impressive and unsettling speed."

Desk immediately called up a map of the location where the outbreak was reported to have occurred.

"What's in the immediate location?" Taylor asked and studied the map closely.

"As far as we can tell, a handful of small farms and a leather tanning facility."

He'd honestly expected a lab, not farms and a leather tanning facility. That was something new. The Zoo, as impressive as it was, did not have the ability to teleport across the world. Something had brought it into the area and he had a feeling that Desk was already digging into who and what was responsible for the transition.

"Do you know what caused the outbreak in the area?" he asked, his brow furrowed as he studied the map a little more intently.

The captain tilted his head. "I'm sorry, am I to understand that you are interested in the job?"

"My responsibility is first and foremost to take care of any cryptid incursions outside of the Zoo," he answered. "The assumption is that the people involved are willing to pay our fees without the annoyance of trying to whittle our prices down. You know how it is."

"Of course." Petru didn't look like he was involved in too many financial decisions. As things stood, all he knew was that he needed help and he wasn't too particular about where it came from. "As to your question, we are not entirely sure where the incursion came from but have heard rumors that the tanning facility might have handled pelts from the Zoo as a way to make extra money. We cannot be certain of this yet but given the fact that the outbreak is centralized around the factory itself, the explanation seems a safe one."

"Right. I assume we should be there as quickly as possible, yes?"

"Correct. Our government is already planning a scorched-earth policy on the area but we need boots on the ground for better assessment. Further mission parameters will be provided as more intelligence comes in. At this moment in time, we are working blind and have no details on what is happening within the facility."

"It sounds like our kind of business."

"Correct. I have been informed by your Pentagon that should you take the work, an aircraft will await you at Nellis Air Force Base. Such is the urgency of the situation that we could not afford the time it would take to send one of ours. Our government has agreed to cover all costs regarding your transport and the fees charged by your team."

"You'll receive our invoice soon," Taylor answered with a small, tight smile. "I look forward to discussing the situation with you in person, Captain. We'll be at the base within the hour."

"It is an honor to work alongside someone of your reputation, McFadden."

The line cut out and they were all quiet for a moment. No one seemed surprised that they wouldn't be allowed so much as a moment's respite after dealing with a kidnapping and decimating an encroaching gang in their city.

He heaved an inward sigh of relief that he'd used his spare suit for the raid on the GAMC rather than his multi-armed one, which would be recognized instantly by anyone who might have seen them. Desk had managed to erase all signs of their presence from any footage in the area, and she'd also skillfully diverted law enforcement to provide enough of a delay for them to leave the location before anyone arrived to investigate.

That was a good thing, given how many of the alphabets and their hangers-on were interested in their activities, but it was more important that what he considered his "real" suit was in perfect working order. He'd long since moved past using a normal suit in Zoo conditions and would have been seriously pissed if he'd damaged it on a gang raid.

Niki shook her head. "Go!"

Her voice cracked through the room like they had all expected it to, and the group hastened to comply. The freelancers scattered with donuts and coffee in hand and immediately set to work preparing the suits for the operation.

Given that the unusual was their business, Taylor had a feeling that Chezza, Trick, and Jiro had adjusted to accommodate that kind of thinking to prepare themselves for almost anything they might encounter.

"Hold on," Vickie said quickly but no one paid her any attention.

"We need to coordinate with Nellis too," Niki pointed out. "We don't want them to be surprised by our arrival with a stash of military-grade weapons. I can call ahead to make sure we lose as little time as possible in loading."

"Wait!"

She and Taylor both turned to the hacker, who was still seated and looked tired and annoyed at the world in general. There wasn't much anyone could do about that, but something was on her mind and she needed to say it.

"Taylor said that we might be able to use this to our benefit, right?" she pointed out. "I know how we can use it. You'll have to take the goddammed server with you—the real one."

Her cousin looked at her in confusion. "What?"

"I can arrange for a car to meet the plane at the Czech Airbase," Desk interjected. "Vickie will need to be involved with the situation as an escort, of course, but I think it shouldn't be too much of a hassle."

Vickie had already rushed out to get the server packed, while Niki looked like a golden retriever with her head cocked to the side, absolutely confused by what was happening.

"Okay, from what I understand, we're letting the Czech Republic military cover the expenses of moving our AIs overseas," Taylor explained for her benefit.

"Oh. Where will we move it to from the airbase? We can't take it directly to Italy, I don't think."

"Probably not, no," Desk agreed. "We can say that Vickie is needed there as overwatch, and she can be responsible for keeping an eye on the servers at all times, no matter what."

"We might need her to…you know, keep an eye on us too," Taylor pointed out.

"Well, yes, but she's rather skilled at multitasking. For a human."

"It seems a little odd that you needed to include that last part," Niki pointed out. "We could probably convince the local authorities to fly the freelancers home while Taylor, Vickie, and I can escort the servers to where they'll be housed. We might need to take a commercial plane from there to the States but all told, it'll probably be a hell of a lot cheaper than if we paid for everything on our own dime."

"And it'll give us the chance to check on the progress on the property in preparation for our final move there," Taylor agreed. "Not to sound like a geek but make it so."

"Why…what?"

"Nothing." he shook his head. "Vickie would get it."

"I understood the reference," Desk said helpfully.

"I know but it's not the same."

As the ENSOL team entered the US base, Sam experienced a surprising wave of nostalgia. He realized that ironically—given the unnatural jungle that was the focus of everything in the area—this was as close to home as he would ever feel. After so much time living in Berlin for work, it was about as close to home as he would physically get in a long time.

The moment didn't last, though. They were at the end of their circuit around the Zoo and the reality was that he wished it would all come to an end so that they could leave without worrying about the monsters that had been so much a part of their recent experience, even if only by hearsay. It would probably take a while for the nightmares to go away but it must surely improve if they were far away, right?

Franklin was the easiest to speak to of all the base commanders, although Fix conceded that he was probably a little biased when it came down to it. As the American base commander, the man made him feel a little more comfortable with the chain of command for some reason.

"Is there something wrong with the reports?" Elke asked. "We are more than happy to clarify anything that might be difficult for you to understand."

She was as blunt as always but he appreciated that she was the one to address it. Franklin looked like he was trying to make sense of something on the tablet in front of him and was too stubborn to simply ask it outright.

"Your reports have been concise and interesting to read, as usual," he replied. "Your team has a talent for making complex engineering issues easy to understand, which is one of the reasons why I assume your group was selected for the job."

"So, there's…no problem?" Chen asked and raised an eyebrow skeptically.

"There is a problem but not with any of the reports." Franklin shook his head and drew a deep breath. "It looks like we have another problem with the Zoo trying to sink roots into a rural area in Eastern Europe. My contacts in Washington know what we're trying to do and picked up on a request for a military aircraft to fly specialists out to deal with the situation."

"The McFadden and Banks team?" Chen leaned a little closer and his eyes widened as a small smile appeared on his face.

The commander's eyebrows lowered. "Yes. How did you know?"

"I've been making vids on their work outside the Zoo for a while now and created a small series on it with the intel available to the public. Not much is official but there's considerable speculation to work with. From what I've learned, they are the people to call in when anyone has any Zoo-related problems that aren't in the jungle itself—and sometimes inside or around the Zoo too. Is it true that they were called in to help retake the Japanese base?"

"I won't ask how you know about that and will simply assume that someone talked about it around the bases you visited."

"Numerous people talked about it, including the usual bragging by the mercenaries, especially."

"I'd say it's an intelligence nightmare, but I don't think anyone cares that we're letting that story go around. It always helps with morale on the bases to know that the crazy redheaded bastard is still alive."

"Still, having the Zoo try to expand into Europe has to be an altogether different kind of nightmare," Sam pointed out and tried to not let them see that he had cold sweats merely thinking about it.

"Sure. No one wants the Zoo to expand anywhere outside the designated area, but there might be a silver lining to that. Whenever something like this happens—like it did with the Sustainagrow site—it generally means we get considerably more funding from the people who simply want the problems to go away for whatever financial or political reasons. It also means the naysayers tend to not disagree with any efforts to increase security, which means more money and resources."

"Still, the Europe situation probably means security problems that don't have much to do with wall construction," Chen pointed out. "The most obvious weak point would be the Sahara Coalition due to their lack of overall security, but there's no assurance that there aren't security leaks elsewhere along the wall."

The kid had a point. Wherever there were humans who wanted a little extra cash on the side, there was the possibility of security leaks. Still, Fix had a feeling that if there was any finger-pointing, it would be directed at the Sahara Coalition anyway. It would result in lip service being paid to security while nothing was changed because too many people made too much money from the lax security around the Zoo.

Of course, now there would be something else for them to focus on. The blame game would come later, especially if it provided a way to avoid greater commitment of financial resources or a curtailment of some activities.

"Well," he said finally, anxious to close the meeting, "you've received our reports, together with any supporting documents or footage. As per our brief, we've done a full inspection of Wall Two, highlighted the areas of concern and included the reasoning behind our opinion, and provided extensive recommendations. Some sectors will require more work than others, but that's all detailed in what we've submitted."

Franklin nodded. "The Pentagon—supported by other nations like the Russians and the Japanese—have already approached the member nations to obtain their commitment to the completion and reinforcement of Wall Two. They have also begun to put pressure on corporate groups with a vested interest in the Zoo to put their money on the table to assist with the financial implications. It might take a while, but with the recent tragedy of the Japanese base still fresh in anyone's minds…"

He let the sentence trail off unfinished. It didn't need to be said that disaster often provided the greatest opportunity for successful manipulation.

Fix nodded as he stood and shook the man's hand. "Well then, we'll wait to hear from you." He paused while his colleagues said their goodbyes, then smiled as he looked the commander in the eye. "But let me again state for the record that ENSOL, if they are awarded the work, will not be a party to compromises that bring the integrity and security of the wall into question. If we build your damn wall, it'll be done right—no politics, no bullying, and no offers under the table from anyone to shortcut the process and save a little money."

"Agreed," Franklin said and even looked relieved. It spoke volumes about how business was run at the Zoo—

yet another concern to keep in mind if they were awarded a project he wasn't entirely sure they wanted.

As promised, everything was loaded and ready to travel within the hour. There would be enough work to do in the plane regarding logistics and what they would do when they landed.

It would be a long flight and Taylor had already begun to prepare himself mentally for it.

Hopefully, once their trip to Europe was over, there would be fewer trans-Atlantic flights. Then again, with his luck, the US would suddenly develop a slew of problems and they would have to start flying there from Europe again.

"Taylor, I've made contact with Dr. Jacobs as requested," Desk told him once they were in the truck.

"Why are we talking to Sal about this?" Niki asked as he started Liz. "We don't generally talk to him when we head out to kill monsters."

"Because I have a feeling we'll have more than only monsters to deal with out there," he explained as he pulled out of the shop and glanced in his rearview mirror to confirm that the rest of the squad were behind them. A follow team from one or other of the alphabets would no doubt join them presently, but the idea was that they would be firmly stopped when they reached the airbase.

All kinds of things could go wrong in a situation like this, but he chose to work under the assumption that no one would want to mess with them when they were heading out to deal with a cryptid situation.

They certainly intended to take advantage of the situation but given that the assholes involved had taken advantage of the system set up to support their interests, it was only fair play for them to do the same.

"Hey, Sal, are you there?" he asked when the call come up on the truck's windshield HUD.

"I have to say I didn't expect to hear from you so soon," the researcher commented. "What can I do ya for?"

"Well, we didn't expect to hear about the Zoo erupting in the Czech Republic, so it seems like the whole world has problems."

"It always does. They called you in to deal with the situation in Eastern Europe, then?"

"Yeah. Did…did you know about it?"

"I heard some whispers that a situation was developing and even wondered if they would call us in for it given that we're a little closer. Of course, I prepared my speech about how I was needed in the Zoo and couldn't race around the world playing hero."

Taylor nodded. "So was it a good speech?"

"Yeah. The kind that makes me seem like I have better shit to do with my life without sounding like a complete and total asswipe."

"I love those. Okay, back to business. From what we've heard, the incursion started when pelts from the Zoo were brought in."

"Pelts?"

"Yeah, that's what the word says."

"I've never heard of pelts being able to transmit the

goop," Sal muttered and Taylor could hear him tap a nearby keyboard. "Not skins or pelts, no. As far as I know, it can only be transmitted via live body tissue. I won't outright say something's impossible, though, because nothing is when it comes to the Zoo. We all know that."

Taylor tilted his head and tried to decipher what seemed off about the younger man's voice. Whatever it was, it made him think there was something else on his mind and speaking on this particular topic somehow made it worse.

"What's the matter, Sal?"

"The Zoo seems like it's going into a new phase. It felt almost dormant before and now, we're watching it make the kinds of changes that we might not be able to adapt to quickly enough. This…well, this might be part of that."

"I'll go ahead and guess that no one's sure what to expect from the fucking place at this point."

"You would be correct in that assessment, yes."

They pulled up to a red light and Taylor checked the rearview mirror. Sure enough, it was easy to identify at least three cars tailing them.

"Well, I'll let you know about everything and anything we find," he assured the scientist. "It sounds like shit might be bad over there, though."

"If you're not able to put reports in, try to save the HUD feed recordings. Those might be more helpful."

"I'll see what I can do."

"Good luck, McFadden."

"Thanks," Taylor answered as the call ended. "I think we'll need it."

"What was that?" Niki asked.

"Do you think this will count as another trip into the Zoo?"

She narrowed her eyes as if she knew that wasn't what he had said but she wouldn't make any fuss over it. "Maybe. Maybe not. This might be a brand-new section of jungle so you can have two tallies running."

CHAPTER TWENTY-TWO

Eben leaned a little closer to his screen and tried to find out who had sent him this particular alert. Mostly, he wanted to make sure he wouldn't owe anyone else in the goddammed matter that seemed to plague him relentlessly. After a long moment, he decided it was merely something that came from spending as much time working as he did. People knew he was tuned into the investigation involving McFadden and Banks, nothing more.

This was simply people spreading the news that would reach him anyway. He sighed and studied the screen to decide what the hell was going on.

"Who the hell is letting them leave the country while they're a part of an ongoing investigation?" He skimmed through the paperwork that had gone through the pipeline. "Oh... Of course the Pentagon is involved. The goddammed military has no idea what they're doing these days."

Then again, maybe they didn't care. As far as the DOD was concerned, they already had the AI they had searched for and didn't want to spend any more time and money looking for something they already had. The fact that it was corrupted beyond recognition didn't seem relevant to them for some reason.

There was also the fact that they were dealing with a potential disaster on the other side of the world, but that wasn't his problem. He couldn't deny that McFadden and Banks were both essential when it came to dealing with a Zoo outbreak in other places in the world.

They were well-paid for their efforts, though, so he felt somewhat offended by the fact that he was forced to step aside and let them move around with what he assumed was the AI he'd tried so hard to find. Too many people had told him he was on a wild goose chase and that continuing was a waste of time.

Part of his frustration came from the fact that they knew how to game the system to their benefit. Eben was sure that Taylor did not possess the skills and knowledge himself and while Banks would have learned about how it worked when she was still with the FBI, he had to assume that other forces were at play that helped them get what they wanted when they wanted.

He wasn't one of those people who watched too many movies as a kid and decided that an AI would take over the world if they gave it the chance. At the same time, he was well aware that they were dealing with something that powerful, no matter what his bosses told him.

The fact that their official documentation was merely a prelude to a move to Italy convinced him of it. They were taking advantage of the fact that the Pentagon needed them to travel fast with considerable equipment to deal with an international problem. Unfortunately, they would get away with all of it.

With no other options on the horizon, he was forced to accept that the AI software he'd found was corrupted and beyond repair, but he was still convinced that they had a functional copy. That would allow him to get out from under Shane's thumb. If not on a server somewhere, it was probably in McFadden's suit given how it allowed him to operate four extra limbs like he was born with them.

Eben wouldn't call himself a good person and could acknowledge that in some cases, he could be a fairly nasty one, but he had never been dishonest and always kept his dealings firmly on the legal side of proceedings. His deal with Shane was the first time he'd ever crossed a line into a murkier area. He'd trusted the man's intentions to be honorable and had been screwed by it.

"Hey, are you in there?"

He jerked up from his seat, his eyes wide as he looked at the door of his office. One of the other agents stood there and looked a little confused by his reaction.

"You've been in here all night by the looks of it," she said as he settled into his chair. "I'm checking to see if you needed coffee or something before you start another day's work."

She was the same woman who had approached him before and again, he couldn't understand why she treated him better than the other agents.

"No...thank you."

"If you're done for the day, I wondered if I could entice you with a drink after work. We all need downtime after this. Don't think we haven't noticed that you've worked long hours and not eaten or slept much either. Unwinding is a healthy thing or so I've heard."

"I...I would but I still have a ton of cleaning up to do—all the paperwork from my time running a task force. Thanks, though."

"Another time, then." She smiled, slipped smoothly out the door, and closed it behind her.

"Another time," Eben repeated in a whisper and refocused on his screen. McFadden and Banks had put their possessions beyond his reach from a legal standpoint and were well on the way to making it physically out of reach as well. There was no real telling if it would ever work out for him in the end.

It had gone full circle and unless a miracle happened, he would have to face the consequences for his actions, one way or another. Time would tell if he had what it took to survive it.

It was one hell of a day to be called in to help. A couple of people had called in sick and she therefore had no choice but to head to the pelt facility to spend the day tending to the small farm they maintained on the property. It wasn't even a moneymaker but the owner, fucking Jakobec, wanted a source of food in the area rather than have to buy everything outside. The result was that the small fields of wheat, potatoes, and other vegetables needed regular attention to feed the workers in the barracks and the factory, the real source of income.

Now, they were stuck in the barracks, already abandoned by the other workers. She kicked herself for being tired enough to allow the other fieldhands to convince her to stay and leave in the morning. If she'd simply pushed through her exhaustion, she'd now be at home and hearing about this disaster from a safe distance.

At least they were trapped in the barracks and not out in the unbelievable jungle that had already surrounded the buildings before she woke early that morning. Two of the men she worked with had ignored the collective warnings and set off cheerfully, determined to go home. It hadn't been five minutes before the terrifying squeals of boars and their screams declared their fate. Since then, no one had suggested that they try to escape.

A few of the factory members were there as well, which helped to bolster their numbers and their courage, and they had all occupied themselves with improvising a few weapons from the kitchen utensils.

She envied those workers who had left the day before to enjoy their time off-shift with their families. All that those who remained could do was gather together in the largest of the four barrack buildings, seal the doors, and hope some kind of rescue attempt would be made.

They had been given the assurance that it would be before the signal disappeared but as time dragged on, the likelihood that this would be successful faded. It was like they were out in the middle of nowhere, cut off from the world and unable to determine if anyone even cared enough to help them. Given the lack of reception, their cell phones might as well have shown negative bars.

"They're attacking again!"

When the boars squealed outside for the umpteenth

time, she rushed to the door and leaned her full weight against it. The creatures had tried repeatedly to batter their way in and although they'd had little success, it was surely a matter of time before the structure gave. The trees—that still grew alarmingly—had weakened the walls but the holes were still too small, which left the door and windows as possible points of ingress.

Her companions hefted the chairs and held them ready as they waited for the squeals to start again.

The shattering of glass alerted them to the next attack, and a couple of men in the group dragged the heavy tables to the shattered pane and pushed them into place to seal the attempted entry.

The jungle growing outside made it difficult to see the monsters but it was clear that they were not the wild boars Hana's father had hunted in her youth. These were the size of bears and had fangs as well as tusks. She'd seen the effectiveness of the combination when they tried to patch Nikolas' mangled leg, even though most of it below the knee was missing.

He'd been attacked by a single boar when he darted out to retrieve a hatchet from the stump where they split wood. The others had managed to drive the beast off but there was nothing for them to do except bind his wounds and ration him with what few pain meds were available for them to use as a way to ease his passing.

Hana rushed to join the others as they heaved a table up to block the window. She shuddered when she felt the power of the beast that attempted to break in.

The concerted effort of all fifteen of them was barely enough to hold the furniture against the aperture until the

The man made a good point and she shook her head.

"Probably not but we won't make it easy for them."

"We shouldn't let them get to us at all," he snapped. "The gas lines are still open. We should burn this whole place and ourselves with it. Maybe we can't burn the jungle but failing that, we can as sure as hell deny them any and all possibility of feasting on our lifeless corpses."

"We won't even consider that."

"We should!"

Hana caught the man by the collar, dragged him closer, and made sure he was looking at her when she spoke.

"We won't consider that. Understood?"

He nodded. "Won't consider that. Understood."

She let him go and the group returned to work. Still, she knew he wasn't alone in wanting to be the master of his fate at the very last. It wasn't despair but was still far from the optimism she'd hoped for. Then again, they were isolated from the world and while the rescue party had been promised, the cell phones had stopped working and she knew others wondered like she had whether anything would be attempted or not. Everyone knew the only real option to deal with the Zoo was to bomb the absolute shit out of it, regardless of the human casualties that might result.

In that case, mass suicide wouldn't be necessary. Someone else would put in the hard work to see it happen.

CHAPTER TWENTY-THREE

"So plane rides are still rough for you, huh?"

Taylor scowled at Vickie as he pulled his helmet on. He'd thankfully had time during the hour's drive from the small military airstrip at Ostravice to the middle of nowhere to regain much of his equilibrium. "No, I think I've taken control of the phobia, turned it around, and made it my bitch."

"Honestly?"

"Hell no. And it's insensitive of you to constantly bring it up. Come on."

She shook her head. "It's not like you have much else we can make fun of you over. I could start making comments about how you're a ginger and don't have a soul but that would be racist shit. Why do you want me to spout racist shit, Tay-Tay?"

"Let me guess—you've spent time on Twitter again?"

"It's tough to stay away sometimes. People are so easy to jerk around, even after all these years."

He grinned and donned the rest of his suit. It felt

vaguely odd since he'd used his older suit for the battle with the gang and hadn't had Nessie in it with him. The experience had been interesting and he'd adapted quickly to the necessity to revert to what he'd once been used to.

While it had been strange to work on his own, they had been dealing with regular-assed humans with no military-grade equipment and he hadn't honestly missed the programs that went into controlling the limbs that extended from his back.

Hopefully, now that he and Nessie were together again, he would be able to take full advantage of the benefits she brought to the suit, although they still hadn't been told what exactly people expected them to do in the area. It was a given that they could move in and kill a horde of monsters—which would be all kinds of fun—but that wouldn't solve the overall problem.

For the second time in history—that he was aware of anyway—the issue of most concern was that the monsters were supported by a complete biome growth. This meant that either they would give him a big fucking ax to fell all the trees with—or hopefully a plasma thrower—or they had something else in mind for the M and B team to do.

"Where will you be?" Taylor asked as he settled into the suit and rolled his shoulders to get used to the movement again.

"There's a little hotel nearby that I can operate from," the hacker informed him. "They have good security and storage space, so that's where we'll keep the server."

"Will the AIs be safe there?"

"As safe as possible. Besides, we're only storing it there. It will be disconnected from everything including a power source so no one can make use of it without alerting us. On top of that, neither Nessie nor Desk will be on it, which means that if anyone did try, they would find nothing except Desk masquerading as security programs to make their lives a nightmare."

"Wouldn't that alert them to the fact that she is there?"

"It might, except she's exceptionally good at hiding her identity. And she would want to make their lives a living hell." Vickie jumped off the crate she was seated on and patted him on the shoulder. "Are you good for this?"

"Always. Besides, what would I be able to do even if I weren't good for this?"

"You're always worried about me. I'm merely letting you know that I worry about you too, no matter how big and monstrous you might be."

"Well, I'll make sure I'm alive at the end of it to give you a proper response to that." Taylor keyed into the commlink with the rest of the team. "Niki, do we have our marching orders?"

"To start with, they want us to do a quick sweep of the perimeter. The teams they planned to send in to do that have no Zoo experience and the jungle is growing too fast, so they want us to give them a decent view of what's happening on the ground. Thus far, they've only been able to view what's happening from above."

"Right, then. Let's get moving."

It was clear that they were very much needed in the area, even if they only provided the locals with additional support. The military was completely and utterly out of their depth, which suggested that the situation might well require them to intervene more fully. That aside, other problems were in evidence as well. The local populace had made an appearance, for one thing. Friends and family of the fallen and those they assumed were still alive while trapped inside had gathered, their ranks swelled by curious bystanders. The soldiers would have a real challenge to keep them away from the expanding jungle.

Without needing to zoom in close to see what was happening at the perimeter, Taylor almost immediately identified more than a handful of the now-familiar red-and-blue Pitas. He had come to expect them along with what had begun to feel like a more cohesive and determined attempt to establish a Ground Zero outside the Zoo and expand from there.

This event appeared to represent a new development and his instincts suggested that it was different from the somewhat random outbreaks they'd dealt with in the past. He sensed that it had a definite strategic purpose, although he couldn't tell precisely what that was.

"The military looks like they're having a tough time," Chezza commented as she checked her rifle. While the team did their level best to ignore the bystanders, they could feel the eyes of the locals on them.

Given how the heavy combat suits stood out from the standard military attire, he wasn't surprised that they were the focus of speculation and avid attention but the woman was right. The local military was stretched thin in their efforts to maintain a perimeter without moving in too close. Dealing with the locals and the possibility of the Zoo breaking out and attacking them would certainly be wearing on their morale already.

Taylor recognized Captain Petru when the man

approached at a slight jog and made sure to look around and study the effects of the new arrivals on his men.

Two men accompanied him. They appeared to be locals but wore expensive watches and boots and carried rifles in their hands. While undoubtedly civilians, they certainly weren't the poor farmers the other civilians appeared to be.

"Your fast arrival is most fortuitous," Petru noted. "Thus far, there has not been much activity outside the jungle but it has continued to grow at an impossible rate."

"Not much is impossible when it comes to the Zoo," Jiro interjected and Taylor smirked as the freelancer drew his knife reflexively, flicked it up, and caught it without so much as a pause.

His fine motor skills were something to be admired, and he wondered idly if he could do what the man accomplished with apparent ease.

"That is true enough, as we are discovering." The captain shook his head and removed his beret to scratch his scalp before he replaced it. "From what we have heard, there are still a few people inside one of the buildings, although we lost communication with them a while ago."

"The jungle will be looking for something to feed on," Taylor asserted quickly. "Something to increase the biomass that allows it to expand. Once it has that—and it will certainly focus its effort on those trapped within as an easy source—you'll see it grow one hell of a lot faster."

"There is a great deal of anger and fear around here already," Petru whispered and moved a little closer to try to keep their conversation as private as possible. "We've managed to prevent the bolder ones from advancing but I don't think we can do so for long. I've been told there might be an issue with those who have a mind to kill the monsters, even if it means entering the jungle."

"You might want to put more effort into that," Niki suggested. "Remind them that all those who die inside will only increase its growth. That should do the trick."

"Probably," one of the rich farmers noted and hefted his rifle a little self-consciously.

"And who are you?" Trick asked. "I suggest you rejoin the civilians. Make yourself useful and stop them from heading in and making everyone's job more difficult."

"These are Stepan and Ivo Jakobec." Petru introduced the two men stiffly. "They are brothers and co-owners of the land that has been taken over."

"You're the ones who brought the pelts in from the Zoo?"

The two men shared a glance and Taylor could see that it had not been an intentional act on their part or at least didn't look like it.

"We've imported the pelts for a while and from a variety of sources, some legal and some not," the older brother explained. "We have used the same operational procedure, which is essentially that they are processed and cleaned of all non-inert biological materials through the procedures approved and implemented by the larger corporations that do the same in the area."

"Did you get them through the smugglers there?" Niki asked bluntly.

"Well, yes, but they were processed by the professionals on base. Any criminal activity ended when they reached the nearby bases. The items were cleaned and processed in monster eventually lost interest and vanished into the shadows of the jungle.

"Shit!" She looked around as a few of the men moved away as if it were safe to relax. "We need to keep the table in place to seal it. Come on!"

They responded without argument and added chairs and duct tape to seal the aperture. There was no guarantee that it would be effective but they had no other options.

Hana smiled as a couple of the others rushed forward to carefully pick up the shards of glass that had fallen and use the duct tape to attach them to pieces of wood. They didn't have much in the way of weapons and what little could be improvised was welcome. Although she doubted that the little glass knives would do much to slow the boars, it would feel better to think they had some means to defend themselves against the jungle that continued to close in around the barracks.

She pulled a few strands of blonde hair from her face and tied it back with a band before she joined the group. Someone had directed them to gather the rest of the tables from the mess hall and they now used them to seal the windows that remained.

It was encouraging that she didn't need to instruct them to do it. They were all tired but none were at the point where desperation had turned to despair.

"Do you think those creatures will eat us?" one of the others asked.

"Boars eat anything and everything that they can," she pointed out as she helped one of the factory workers to tape a chair into place. "But not us."

"Do you think these walls will stop them?"

the manner deemed acceptable by most corporations in the region. If they were unsafe, don't you think there would be dozens more of these...uh, jungles manifesting around the world?"

"In fairness, they kind of are," she pointed out.

"I checked the paperwork," Petru added and folded his arms. "The importers ran tests as well to ensure that no live tissue from the Zoo was imported."

There were numerous points at which all those checks could go wrong, however carefully they were prescribed and implemented. Taylor wouldn't put aside the possibility of human error for the moment, but he couldn't shake the sense that too many things had to go wrong for this to go right for the Zoo and maybe that was the plan. It had a way about it that seemed almost beyond the realm of simple opportunity when the right conditions favored it.

Every instinct in him insisted that this incursion was indicative of something more sinister. It was possible that circumstances had simply conspired to improve its odds, but maybe the Zoo was increasing its efforts to the point where, statistically, something had to work for it.

The fact that he was seriously considering whether a jungle was able to engage in statistical analyses was absurd, but such was the world they lived in at the moment.

"See what you can do to make the crowd disperse." Taylor directed his attention to the captain. "We don't need anyone to charge in or try to be a hero. That's what we're here for, and we're paid more for it and are much better equipped for the job."

"Understood. What about the possibility of survivors?"

"Our priority will be to get them out," Niki assured him

in a tone that brooked no argument. "Not only because saving human life is why we're here but also to ensure that there is no more biological material for the jungle to convert to biomass. Right now, those survivors represent a handy and relatively easily accessible larder so depriving the Zoo of that is essential. We need a layout of the area to make sure we don't run into any walls or any obstacles that might make rescue more difficult."

"We'll send them to you presently," Ivo said. He had been quiet and subdued for most of the conversation but seemed to be the more approachable of the two brothers.

"Do you have plasma throwers on the way?" Taylor asked the captain.

"We do, as per your request."

"When they arrive, have your people start to push the perimeter back. For now, though, your efforts to keep the people away from the jungle will be your highest priority. See if you can convince them to leave on their own without needing to make a scene about it."

"Understood. What will you do in the meantime?"

Before he could answer, the attention of all those present was immediately drawn to the jungle, where the loud squeals of monsters within provided a discomforting indication of what they could expect. Taylor wasn't sure how, but the noises reminded him of pigs.

"Check to make sure your superiors are sending bombers in but give us three hours," he said curtly and avoided the question. For the moment, he wanted to keep their priorities loose, play the situation by ear, and remain open to changes in case something happened to necessitate flexibility in their plans.

"I shall do so," Petru responded without hesitation.

"Why do they need bombers?" Ivo asked.

"Because we will clear the mutants out but the vegetation will remain," Niki explained. "That means the goop remains too and will simply make more monsters. We'll have to utterly destroy every last piece of leaf and root."

"You cannot do this," Stepan protested. "This is our homeland. Our family has tilled this land for fifteen generations!"

"You can rebuild," she snapped quickly. "Unless you want to head in there and clear all the vegetation by hand, which we both know you can't do and certainly not in time to avert greater disaster. The jungle will continue to grow until it finds a larger source of biological matter to feed on and you'll see an explosion that will cover the entire country within a day.

"Assuming we can contain that shitshow—which, let's be honest, is very unlikely—people around the world will want to know who to blame. So at the very least, you'll have to face a world court that will probably slap your entire family into prison for the next fifteen generations—or the end of Europe as a human-habitable zone thanks to the Zoo. Which would you prefer?"

Petru and the two owners paled and immediately moved away to shout orders in the local language that spurred the required action. As the soldiers responded to their orders and relayed the facts of the conversation in their language, the implications of the situation struck home and many of the bystanders began to leave of their own accord.

A few even increased their pace, reluctant to be caught by whatever made the squealing noises inside the jungle.

"You always did have a way with words," Taylor commented and checked to make sure his team was ready. "Vickie, have you been able to hail anyone from inside the jungle area?"

"That's a big ol' negatory," the hacker answered over comms. "The interference is doing one hell of a job to make the whole region a dark zone. I'll keep trying, though. Anja sent me some data on their efforts to find a way around the Zoo's natural interference so I'll try that, but she did stress that even things that seemed promising seldom made any lasting difference."

"Do that." He rolled his neck, still a little uncomfortable in the suit without Nessie with him. It was extremely odd that the Zoo generated that much interference for a smaller growth area. Most radios in the Zoo proper were able to work across the distance covered by the incursion and yet they had encountered what felt like a direct act by the jungle to ensure that their captives could not communicate with the outside world.

"Are you sure that three hours will be enough?" Chezza asked as they began to advance on the jungle. "I have all the confidence in the world about our abilities and shit but if we're a little late, we might be roasted by the bombing runs to clear the jungle."

"If we let it grow any longer, we risk it finding another source of biological material and it'll boom anyway. At this point, I'm tempted to simply leave the people inside to fend for themselves and focus on containing the jungle on the perimeter, but..."

"That would make you a psychopath," Niki stated bluntly as his voice trailed off.

"We have enough of a buffer to try to reach them," Jiro pointed out practically. "If not, we will have to leave those inside to die and that is the truth."

"And we already know you're a psycho," Chezza retorted and patted the man on the shoulder.

"Right." Taylor raised his weapon when he heard the soft chime that told him that Nessie was being uploaded to the suit. It was a short and seamless process, and it wasn't long before he felt the AI take control of much of the movement so he could move faster and smoother than before.

"It's a pleasure to be aboard again." Nessie sounded a little petulant. "It's been too long."

"We've been protecting you so don't make too much of a big deal about it."

Before he could say anything else, the squeals from inside the jungle seemed to gain a more frenzied edge.

Chezza stopped for a moment and tried to gauge where the noises were coming from. "Is it only me or are those exactly where the barracks are?"

He had thought the same thing but he didn't want to say it outright. If the monsters were attacking the buildings, the chances were that there would be no one left alive inside to rescue.

Still, they had to try. Taylor increased the pace and led the team away from the fences that signified where the brothers' lands began. They headed directly toward the jungle and as they approached, something else moved at the top of the trees.

He narrowed his eyes and focused on what appeared to be wings flapping. Within a few moments, he was able to determine that creatures the size of pterodactyls watched them from the tree cover, although none made any attempt to attack yet.

"I thought they said the monsters spotted inside looked like wild boars, but bigger," Chezza muttered, clearly picking up the same readings as he did.

"The Zoo loves making and breaking the mold with their creatures," Niki answered as she aimed at the targets in the trees and tried to track them. "We might as well assume that the pig monsters might be the only ones that were seen thus far."

Before she'd finished her sentence and as they reached the outermost Pita plants, a handful of the mutants leapt from the branches to circle on massive wings as if in warning. They glided easily above them before they settled into the canopy again.

"What in the living fuck is that?" Trick whispered and lifted his rifle.

"Death on wings," Taylor answered grimly and prepped his rifle. "Fast, lethal, and hard to kill. This should be a blast."

"If you say so."

"I do."

"And who was the psycho here again?"

"Me," Jiro interjected as he drew the sword he carried on his back.

"All of us. Let's be honest," Chezza added.

"Speak for yourselves," Niki retorted.

CHAPTER TWENTY-FOUR

The creatures were some of the most interesting that Taylor had seen in a while. They had six limbs but were very different than the insect-like creatures they had faced in the other incursions. These appeared to be a hybrid of wolves and bats, although they clung to the trees with the kind of ease that came from using sharpened claws or talons.

He'd seen something similar in the Zoo before, although only once or twice. They were rare and seemed to prefer certain areas of the jungle, which might explain why the freelancers didn't recognize them. These looked slightly different, however. With powerful jaws and large fangs, they appeared to have been created from the wolves that were prevalent in the area. The claws on the forelimbs allowed them to hang like bats from the trees when they wanted to.

On the surface, it looked like the jungle had simply used the DNA of local creatures. Some researchers insisted that there was enough evidence to support the idea that where there wasn't much DNA to draw on to begin with, the Zoo was compelled to simply build on what it could find.

Taylor doubted that was the only reason, though. It made more sense that it could somehow adapt to the different areas of the world where it gained a foothold and made itself increasingly dangerous as it expanded.

"Should we get into the tree line?" Chezza asked, her focus on the creatures that flocked all around them.

"It might be as much cover as we can get," he whispered and motioned them forward, directly into where the creatures appeared to have established their nests or roosts.

The approaching team was immediately greeted with a cacophony of howls that was a warning for them to stay the hell away. As much as he wanted to give the beasts a wide berth, he didn't intend to waste any time, not when their clock ticked inexorably toward a massive series of explosions that would kill them as well as the monsters if they couldn't get out in time.

"Trick, I need you to clear us a path when they start to attack us," Taylor called as the creatures launched from the trees and began to circle the group from an elevation he guessed was a perfect height from which to rocket into a combined assault.

"Shit, that's a terrifying noise," the freelancer whispered. "Do you want me to lay out some explosives to clear a path ahead of us?"

"Maybe save that for the grand finale. I thought you could make your trick shots work in our favor to stop them from swarming us."

"Oh. Okay. I'll get right on that shit."

They would all be able to open fire on the monsters

when they started their dive but Trick had the ability to find the shots that would knock the impetus out of any attack. It was another skill Taylor wished he had but all he could do was rely on others and hope they had the same tactical sense he did.

"They're coming down," Niki warned, raised her assault rifle, and opened fire at the monsters. The airborne attackers seemed unconcerned that they were diving directly into the trees and simply twisted their massive bodies like corkscrews to navigate the branches without so much as slowing.

They displayed impressive reflexes, even for Zoo creatures, but Trick opened fire on one of the trees instead and shredded the trunk, which made it topple and force the initial ranks out of sync with the rest of the group. Their dive was disrupted and a handful of them was impaled on the branches as the tree continued to fall.

"I have to give it to the guy," Niki muttered as she reloaded her rifle. "He does know how to get the job done."

Taylor grinned in approval as Jiro bounded up and fired at the mutants that approached them while he hacked at the trees as well. His efforts cleared a little more space for them to shoot through as the creatures continued to attack.

It felt like old times, a remarkably familiar experience of standing his ground while the mutants threw themselves into their line of fire as if they hoped the humans would run out of bullets before they ran out of bodies.

Maybe there was more to the tactics involved but in the end, it didn't matter. It was the kind of simplicity he'd missed although he hadn't realized it.

Jiro made short work of the beasts that perched on the

branches and tried to regain their bearings after their initial assault failed. Trick managed to knock a couple more trees down and effectively denied them cover while Taylor, Niki, and Chezza focused on eliminating those that were still in the air.

"Be advised, you have movement headed your way on the ground," Nessie alerted him, and Taylor turned his attention to the jungle floor. The AI relied on their motion sensors, although he was surprised that there had been no squeals to alert them that what he assumed were the boar-like mutants were advancing. Then again, it was possible that the howls from above had effectively drowned out any earthbound noises.

Either way, they needed to prepare for this new threat.

He twisted to avoid one of the giant boars when it tried to gore him. Nessie stabilized his movement with the limbs jutting from his back and lifted him quickly out of the way of the next attack. One of the limbs latched onto a nearby tree to anchor him above the other mutants.

Frustration surged when he realized his mistake. He should never have disregarded the very real threat that the boars would attack. His focus on the bat-wolves had put Niki in a position where she had difficulty keeping the ground adversaries at bay.

All he could do in response was drop a grenade into their path. The powerful whoomph shook the earth and the trees as well and left three or four of the monsters dead around it. The remainder of his team were now mostly in the clear and he opened fire on those creatures that continued their charge.

"Trick, Jiro, Chezza, keep your attention on the attacks

from above," he called as he dropped from his perch. Nessie took possession of his sidearm and his combat knife, pushed a handful of boars back quickly, and killed the two that would not move.

"The bat-wolves are moving away," Trick stated with almost unnatural calm as he manually snapped a new magazine into his assault rifle. Perhaps it was simply reflex or maybe he thought it was faster to do it that way. "They are moving in the direction of the barracks!"

Taylor scowled and studied their surroundings for a moment. There wasn't much of a choice in this particular situation. They had to press forward and hope that they didn't barrel head-first into a group of the monsters they couldn't clear out of the way quickly. The boars were fast and from the way they moved, he had a feeling their tusks were capable of doing more than enough damage to any suits they encountered.

"And we have more movement on the ground," Niki added as she opened fire on another sounder that advanced from the left as if to flank them.

Almost on a whim or perhaps as a precaution, he unclipped one of his grenades from his belt, tossed it in the direction in which they were heading, and watched it bounce into a tree and disappear into the thick bushes. A few seconds later, the explosive detonated and it was immediately followed by a cacophony of shrieks and squeals from the beasts that had been hiding in the underbrush.

"Did you know they were in there?" Niki asked and let her suit reload as they pushed forward again and past a small sounder of the beasts that now lay dead around the blast area.

"I had a weird clever-girl moment," Taylor explained absently, most of his attention on movement approaching them that his sensors had picked up. "It's not the kind of thing you would expect from animals, but the only reason I can think of that they would try to flank us would be to divert attention away from something waiting for us."

"A...clever-girl moment?"

"You know—that moment in *Jurassic Park Two* where the hunter gets..." Taylor shook his head and let the sentence trail off. "Vickie knows it better than I do. Vickie, are you still there?"

The comms already manifested the usual Zoo interference and there was no sign that the hacker could hear them. When he checked, her name was no longer included in the connected names on their group link.

"Fucking hell," Niki whispered. "Is the jungle being that much more difficult simply because it wants to?"

"It might be. Or it's simply trying to keep any and all human communications out to make sure that anything in here is killed. Anyway, it was from the movie."

"I've never watched any of those dinosaur movies."

"I—what?"

"What?"

"You never watched the *Jurassic Park* movies?"

"Of course not."

"I watched them," Trick announced. "In fact, Jiro, Chezza, and me were at the marathon they ran last month. It was an all-nighter and a shitload of fun."

"It sounds like you're all a group of kids who love

dinosaurs too much," Niki grumbled as they formed up again. "Or have you assholes forgotten that we all dealt with an actual dinosaur not that long ago?"

"Hell yeah," Trick answered with a laugh and opened fire on the mutants that attacked from the front while Jiro and Chezza kept an eye open for any attempts to flank them. "Why the hell do you think we went to watch the movies?"

"Nostalgia?"

"It's easily like...the third biggest moneymaker in the world. The biggest in the world when it comes to the entertainment industry."

"I'll need some sourcing on that."

"Yeah, let me get right on that...wait for it... Oh no, my Internet is down."

Taylor grinned and shook his head as they focused on the trees again and waited for something else to make an attempt on their lives. Trick had brought up a good point, though. Maybe the guy didn't mean to but it was still there. The fact that they had no communication with Desk, Vickie, or anyone in the outside world would be a problem if the military decided to start dropping bombs on the area.

They needed to get a move on. He increased their pace and kept them moving through the ever-changing jungle ahead of them. Thankfully, Nessie was on board with her ability to direct them toward the barracks using the map Ivo had provided.

There were more signs of the bat-wolf bastards in the air above them, but Trick did a good job to ensure they wouldn't swoop into an assault and from what he could tell, the beasts appeared to have learned their lesson when it came to trying to launch an airborne assault against the humans.

"The barracks are just ahead," Niki called as the buildings came into view through the heavy tree cover. "How do we know anyone's still alive in there?"

Taylor tilted his head and took a few steps closer as he detected another sounder of boars. It looked like they'd worn a rut around one of the buildings when they circled it to try to find a way in. They weren't the brightest of creatures given that they likely had enough power to simply burst through the walls if they wanted to.

Or maybe they were smart enough to keep looking for a weak area in the building so they wouldn't injure themselves. Despite the tendency of the lower species to simply fling themselves like grist in the mill, an instinct for self-preservation wasn't entirely common among other Zoo mutants.

"I'd say the fact that there are monsters around here and that the walls are still up means there is hope that someone is alive inside," he answered and checked his belt for another grenade. There weren't too many left and he wanted extra firepower to blast their way out if the need arose. They waited for a moment while Niki and Chezza checked the first three structures and confirmed that they were empty—a fact that explained why the mutants had congregated around the last of the buildings.

"Trick, clear us a path through the bastards." Taylor motioned for the team to be ready to move when they had an opening.

"The explode-y kind?"

"No, damn it. I'll tell you when it's time to break out the explosives."

"Kill-joy." The freelancer's tone suggested a dramatic eye-roll as he raised his rifle and felled a few of the boars before they even realized they were under attack.

Jiro had a handful of knives ready, and it looked like he'd fiddled with the mechanics of his suit—no doubt with Bobby's connivance—since he fitted the blades to launchers that attached seamlessly to the back of his hand.

He couldn't have worked that shit out on his own, Taylor decided. Bungees must have been involved somehow, but the idea no doubt came from the freelancer. He was the only one both crazy and blade-obsessed enough to think of it.

Further proof of the mechanic's expertise was the fact that the launchers worked. They snapped the knives forward at a powerful speed and buried each one to the hilt in the skulls of the beasts that remained.

"I...kind of want me one of those," he whispered.

"Why?" the man asked casually. "You only have one knife."

"I could get more. And it might be something for Nessie to operate—something to help her without adding another rifle."

"It's an interesting solution," the AI concurred as they approached the last building. "Another might be to give me a proper rifle."

"I need as many of your hands as free as possible in case I need them for mobility and shit. If we could fit one of those launchers to them without compromising your ability to move and grasp things, it would be a useful hybridization of your abilities."

"Interesting."

Before Niki approached the door, she tried to peer through a window that had been shored up and blocked by a variety of chairs and tables.

"We should have brought Tanya for this," she whispered.

"Why?"

"Well, she…uh, speaks the language. I think."

Taylor wasn't sure if there was much overlap between Czech and the languages Tanya spoke, but a knock on the door was as universal as a human greeting and certainly—hopefully—not alien.

Niki tapped gently on the wood. "Hello? Anyone in there?"

A voice replied from inside, speaking Czech, and sounded more than a little terrified.

"We're all humans out here," Chezza shouted and let the suit's speakers carry her voice. "We are the rescue team."

The voice went silent for a while and Taylor wondered if anyone in there could speak English. After a few seconds, the chairs and tables began to move to allow them to open the battered doors.

"More problems," Jiro pointed out quietly, although he had the good sense to keep the comment on the commlink.

He wasn't wrong. It looked like almost fifty people were huddled inside. They appeared to all be healthy and able to walk and run if needed, but none had any weapons or armor to speak of.

"Dammit," Taylor whispered. "Chezza, run a quick check and make sure everyone's alive and well."

"Yes, boss."

He switched the external speakers on and directed his attention to the small crowd of terrified humans in front of him. "Does anyone here speak English?"

A look of confusion was exchanged between members of the group before one woman stepped forward. She was short and stout with a weathered look about her and she faced them squarely as she pushed her blonde hair out of her face and captured it in a band.

"I am Hana. I speak some English."

"Some English is all we need. We have to move you all out of here immediately."

"We have no argument with that. But why?"

"Well, not to put too fine a point on it but this property will be bombed to kingdom come and none of us will want to be around when that happens."

"I don't know. We could always drop a helicopter on you, Taylor," Niki muttered.

She would never let him forget that one time. Never.

"Okay, what are our options?" he asked and looked around.

"Options?" Trick tilted his head and regarded him steadily. "We'll get these people out of here as alive as we can keep them. That's our options."

"In case you haven't noticed, there are only five of us and fifty of them," Taylor responded.

"Forty-seven," Chezza corrected over the commlink.

"Right. Our usual way to move unarmed civvies out is to form a human barrier between them and the monsters. That won't work here."

"Can we request an air-evac?" Niki suggested.

"That's not practical," Jiro replied quickly. "Even if the comms weren't a problem, the bat-wolves outside will attack anything that flies in close. They will swarm planes or helicopters that attempt to land anywhere near the jungle."

It did beg the question of what they would do if they were able to fly clear of the tree line. The chances were that they did not enjoy hunting in the sunlight, given that both bats and wolves were nocturnal and the instincts would likely affect how the monsters behaved.

He had a feeling that the beasts would turn the surrounding countryside into a nightmare the moment that nightfall arrived. This immediately became another ticking clock, as if one wasn't enough.

"Our best hope will be for the military to begin the bombing run on the vegetation and force the mutants out into the open," Taylor muttered.

"We might need comms for that," Niki protested.

"We know you are speaking," Hana interrupted. "But not to us. What is happening? Why are we not yet moving?"

"We're discussing our best course of action," he answered quickly. "While we do that, pick up the tables and what weapons you have. It will be incredibly dangerous outside and anything you might be able to use as a shield or to defend yourselves will be helpful, understood?"

She nodded, turned to the others, and translated the orders. They seemed to follow her instructions without a fuss and immediately gathered what they could. He noticed that they had already improvised knives and spears from broken glass taped to handles that could be used.

It wasn't much but it was better than nothing.

"Comms." He sighed and shook his head. "We'll have to get creative. Trick, now's the time."

The man uttered an evil laugh that made Taylor immediately regret his words.

"What you need me to blow up, boss?"

"The other buildings. Do you have enough on you to demolish them?"

"I have enough firepower to level half this goddammed jungle if I do it right. What's the plan?"

"Start prepping the explosives. Niki, Chezza, help the locals to gather whatever weapons and armor we can improvise. I don't care if it looks or feels stupid as long as it works. Jiro, you and I will lay down some cover for Trick."

They worked quickly and the demolitions expert moved from building to building to lay the explosives and set the charges to detonate in a string. Taylor had a feeling that things would move considerably faster if Trick only had to blow the whole area up, but it took a fair amount of work to make sure he didn't flatten the building their survivors were in.

Once they returned, it looked like the whole building had been stripped clean of anything and everything that could be used. Some of the workers wore improvised armor and weapons made from pots and pans while others had made shields cut from the tables.

They didn't seem too optimistic about their chances but their steely determination was impressive. They were civilians but seemed to have decided that dying while putting up a fight was better than dying trapped and helpless.

"Are we ready to move?" Niki asked as she handed her

pistol to one of the group so they would have something more in the way of weapons.

Chezza and Trick had done the same and even Jiro had surrendered his sidearm and a couple of knives.

"About as ready as we'll ever be," Taylor responded. They should perhaps have prepared more and come in with suits and weapons to give them more of a fighting chance.

The reality, though, was that they simply did not have the time. Each moment they used to deliberate and gather resources before they entered the jungle was one less for those trapped inside. It was already surprising that the mutants hadn't managed to reach them, but they'd no doubt been distracted by the workers from the factory and the M and B team. If not for them, it was unlikely that anyone would still be alive to be rescued.

Preparation was always first prize. Mostly, though, they had to work with what they had.

"Trick, fire when ready."

"Roger that."

The freelancer connected to the charges through his HUD. It looked as though the interference that affected their comms with the teams outside hadn't affected the team, thank goodness. Still, Nessie monitored their links constantly to ensure that the comms between them remained stable and they weren't caught by surprise.

Taylor sucked in a deep breath as the first of the explosives detonated. The earth shuddered and the force struck him in the gut even though he wore full armor. Trick had not exaggerated and he would have to chat to the guy about carrying that many explosives on him while they walked around and engaged in firefights.

They were already moving out of the building when the second string of explosives went off and sparked a massive fire in the jungle. This was quickly followed by the third, which did the same.

The fire caught the immediate attention of the monsters and pushed them back and away. A veritable cloud of the bat-wolves rose from the trees, a handful of them aflame. Dozens more plummeted earthward, injured and dying although they attempted to fly clear.

He felt the fourth explosion more than heard it. It thumped into the soil like a meteor had landed and all he could be thankful for was the fact that none of them were close enough to feel the shockwave, which felled several trees in the vicinity.

"You weren't exaggerating," he commented and high-lighted a few sounders of the boars that his HUD sensors had alerted him to. "Next time, we might blow the whole jungle up and leave the bombing runs for another time."

"I keep saying that and no one believes me."

"It might be because no one wants to think about how crazy you have to be to carry that many explosives on your person," Chezza pointed out.

"You know that those explosives are about the most inert substances on earth unless the perfect conditions allow them to blow up, right? Fucking candlewax is more dangerous to carry around."

"Sure, and those conditions happen to be in your pouch with you, right?"

"It's not like that and you know it."

Taylor would have told them to focus a little harder on the monsters that had begun to turn their attention to the group that tried to push through the jungle as quickly as possible, but they already had opened fire on the mutants. Their volleys cleared a path ahead while he and Niki had the task of making sure nothing came in from behind.

It wasn't a particularly enviable job but it carried the most responsibility, given that it was the most difficult and also the fact that sneak attacks from the rear were generally effective because no one anticipated them.

Jiro covered the flanks well but when Taylor noticed two sounders advancing rapidly from both sides, he pulled two grenades out and handed them to Nessie to drop into the paths of the charging boars.

The explosives did a fairly effective job but one of the beasts pushed through. Its jaws snapped shut and in a single moment of horror, one of their survivors was cut in half before Niki felled it with two rounds to the head.

"Damn, these things are terrifying," Chezza whispered.

He couldn't tell if she was talking about the bat-wolves or the boars—maybe both, but it didn't matter. A sound caught his attention and he looked up reflexively. The low drone of planes in the distance could be clearly heard now. They were about a half-hour too early but at this point, he didn't mind that someone had jumped the gun.

"Chezza, Trick, send up some flares to let them know where we are," he shouted as he ducked under a mutant that attacked from above. Nessie gunned it down quickly, which left him to fend off the assault of another sounder of boars.

There hadn't been this many of them when the team

first entered. The jungle seemed to pump them out when it realized it was in danger, which left the survivors no other option but to fight toward the perimeter.

"Do you think they'll know to maintain their altitude higher than what the flying fuckers can reach?" Niki asked as she hauled up one of the survivors who tripped over a bush that appeared out of nowhere. She carried him for a few steps before she deposited him on his feet to run on his own again.

"If not, they'll find out fast."

As if on cue, the bat-wolves immediately banked from the group and left them with only the boars to deal with for the moment. The earth shuddered violently, and this time not because of whatever ordnance Trick happened to have in his pocket.

Explosives being dropped from above was probably a good thing, but it introduced additional elements of danger they had to be aware of. Top of the list was the hope that the bombs wouldn't be dropped on their position.

Another problem arose almost immediately when a cloud of thick, black smoke began to fill the jungle around them.

Those in suits wouldn't have too much difficulty with it given that they were fitted with air filters that would make the conditions survivable.

But those without suits would have trouble breathing as they continued to press forward.

"We can only hope they saw the flares!" Jiro shouted and ended it with a curse when two of the bat-wolves circled and swooped into a surprise attack. He cut one in half with his sword and felled the other one that targeted the survivors with two precise shots.

It was still alive, if only for a few seconds, and the claws impaled one of the men and pinned him to the earth. Both were dead before anyone could reach him to help.

All they could do was cover their faces and push on into the smoke, despite the coughing. A few more tripped as it now became difficult to see, but Taylor and Niki bullied them to their feet and into a jog in no time.

"McFadden and Banks team, do you copy? Repeat, do you copy?"

It was a surprise to hear any voice but their team members through the mess of static.

"Nessie, did you find a way to get rid of the interference?"

"Unfortunately, no. Although on the bright side, this must mean we are close enough to the edge that signals are seeping through."

Niki immediately keyed into the incoming frequency. "This is the Bravo-Mike team. We read you loud and clear."

"Why Bravo first?" Taylor asked.

"It's alphabetical, so shut up," she snapped in response. "Outside teams, do you read us?"

"Lots...static, but we...hear you." It was difficult to make out who it was but they spoke English with no accent. "What is your position?"

"We're close to the edge and have survivors with us. We'd appreciate it if you didn't bomb the crap out of us."

"We assumed that was what the flares were supposed to mean."

Chezza launched another bright red flare through a crack in the tree cover.

"You're very close to the edge. Continue to move west and we'll clear the fences for you."

There was nowhere else to go. Taylor's sensors had gone ballistic to warn him of movement and fire all around them. It had become extremely difficult to push through without running their survivors directly into a wall of flames.

In the next moment, the trees were gone. Ash was strewn all over the surface of the soil and smoke filled the air but they were free and clear. Without any need for orders, the group increased their pace and sprinted from the tree line.

The freelancers circled to cover the rear of the group alongside Taylor and Niki as they continued their retreat.

"Taylor, you idiot Neanderthal!" Vickie's voice broke through the static. "Where the hell are you? If I have to come in there to find you, bet your ass you'll prefer the monsters."

He grinned. "And it's nice to hear your voice again too. What's our situation?"

"Can't you see?"

"I see a shit-ton of smoke."

"Right...uh, stay on your current trajectory. You have a little help waiting for you."

As the smoke cleared, his surprise made him stop so suddenly that Chezza had to leap to the side to avoid him. Her caustic comment was preempted by his deep belly laugh.

"Well, shit." He stared at the three tanks—backed by

heavy artillery—lined up with almost perfect precision at the estimated exit point. Two of them were fitted with anti-air weapons and had trained their guns skyward above the group to deal with any bat-wolf creatures that broke from the trees.

The third was a little more standard and had aimed its single massive gun directly at the trees. There was no way to mistake the intention to blast the absolute crap out of any and all boars that thought they could attack the McFadden and Banks group.

Better still, dozens of paramedics had already begun to give the survivors oxygen, although when Taylor ran a quick count of those still with them, it looked like they'd lost eight all told.

It wasn't the best outcome but it was about as good as he had any right to expect, given what they had been through to get out.

"All humans are clear of the jungle," Petru snapped over the radio. "Turn that jungle into a crater."

Why he spoke in English was a mystery but it was no less effective than his home tongue. Two fighters darted out of the thick cloud cover and immediately swept the edges of the jungle with napalm.

"I think we might need to bring extra suits and shit on our next rescue mission," Niki commented as she ran checks on her suit.

Taylor nodded. "That would be ideal, yeah."

CHAPTER TWENTY-FIVE

Eben's phone rang and while he didn't want to look at it, he knew it would continue to be a pain if he didn't give it his attention.

He scowled and finally shifted his gaze from his computer screen to the device on his desk. Something cold and annoying slithered up his spine when he saw the name that taunted him from the screen.

It took effort but he quashed the feeling immediately and drew a deep breath, closed his eyes, and found some semblance of a happy place before he answered the call and put it on speakerphone.

"I don't know why you've avoided my calls, Eben," Shane said curtly. "It's almost like we're no longer friends, man."

The meaningless—and manipulative—reference to their non-existent friendship made him pause to fight back the wave of nausea again. He smiled at nothing in particular and hoped that it would miraculously manifest in his voice. "Work has been a little overwhelming lately."

"I suggest you take time off to rest and recover. Things have been stressful around there, I know. You might want to head to Cancun."

Eben's eyes narrowed as he picked the phone up off his desk and turned the speakerphone off. "Cancun?"

"I'll be blunt. I have a valuable shipment en route from Mexico and I'd appreciate it so much if you were to head down there to make sure it goes through unhindered."

"I'm not with customs."

"Of course, but I'm sure the FBI's wonderboy has some clout—enough to push it past any pesky assholes who might want to search it. Hell, if you're good enough, you might be able to work out a nice little system that'll help you deal with future shipments."

There was no real debate there. Future shipments would occur and he would have to help them clear customs every time.

"What are you bringing in?" he asked and rubbed the bridge of his nose.

"Think of this as one friend telling another friend that he doesn't want to know what's in the shipments." Shane laughed. It was an ugly, dry sound that made Eben shiver. "Call it...what's the term? Oh, right, plausible deniability. I heard law enforcement people need that for some reason."

The call ended abruptly and he stared at his phone for a few long seconds while he tried to decide if he was simply imagining the sound of his career crashing down around his ears or if it was real.

His first reaction was a faint stirring of hope. Perhaps it wasn't as bad as he imagined. He could attend to this shipment and buy time to find alternative employment. If he cut all ties with the FBI, his so-called friend couldn't demand that he facilitate any more of his contraband shipments because he would no longer be in a position to do so.

That brief glimpse of a way out shriveled as soon as it was conceived. Shane wouldn't care if he took a job trying to sell sexy lingerie to Eskimos. He'd expect his pound of flesh no matter where he was or what he did. Nor could he hope that it would be a one-time deal. The bastard had rubbed his nose in the amount invested so often that it wasn't a stretch to believe he'd have to continue to pay for the rest of his goddammed life.

Eben scowled as he faced the harsh reality he had known for a while would come. He was out of options and it was time to take a hard look at his future—or rather the lack of it—and for once, make the right choice.

There were some things he would never involve himself in. He'd already stepped over his personal line but honestly, it was a small jump rather than a giant leap. Repercussions would follow, of course, but he'd face those like a man and retain his self-respect—after all, everyone fucked up now and then.

Given Shane's vague talk about plausible deniability, it could only mean he was importing something highly illegal and extremely profitable. Common sense told him that an agent would go to jail for any involvement in that, although he might claim plausible deniability to get a reduced sentence and a better deal from a judge to keep him out of the maximum-security facilities.

Drugs, most likely, he reasoned morosely, or maybe human trafficking. Both were absolute deal breakers for him, even if he was willing to admit that he'd brought all this on himself due to his stupidity.

Eben sighed heavily as the various pieces coalesced into one simple truth—he absolutely couldn't do it. That left him with only one option. A little dazed by how suddenly it had all come together, he stood and walked to his boss' office. His senses prickled like every gaze watched his progress and he wondered vaguely what they saw. Most likely, he reasoned bitterly, it was the broken shell of an agent who had once, long ago, had a promising start to his career.

All he could think of was that this was a weird way to end it.

He stepped into Harv's office and closed the door carefully, then the blinds. The man was on a phone call and watched curiously as the younger agent dropped into a seat without waiting to be invited.

"I...I'll call you back on that," his boss said, his eyes narrowed as he replaced the receiver in its cradle with exaggerated care. "Do you have something on your mind, Taggert?"

He nodded slowly. "Yeah."

"Is it something you want to share with the rest of the class?"

For a moment, all he could do was nod. The words seemed to stick in his throat and he had to clear it a couple of times before he could speak. "I fucked up, Harv. Bad."

"How bad?"

"I'm going to jail bad."

His boss nodded and leaned back in his seat. "Do you need me to get you out of hot water?"

"No." Eben couldn't help a soft, bitter laugh. "No, I don't think there's any way to get me out of this particular situation without you burning yourself too. But...well, before you fire me, I'd like to help you take down a rich asshole who needs to be stopped more than anyone else I know."

Harv studied him for a moment from beneath the thick, bushy eyebrows and scowled deeply before he leaned forward. "I'm listening."

"Do you think it's a bad sign that the caretakers didn't want to come down here with us?" Vickie asked.

Taylor shook his head. "Any sign of cryptid activity has been thoroughly expunged from this place. In fact, I might even suggest that it's a good thing."

The hacker turned and folded her arms. "A good thing that the caretakers believe coming into our new server room means they would run into some ghosts?"

"It's not that bad. They still worked on the place," Niki pointed out. "The renovations have progressed according to schedule and our requests are all but completed by this point with the exception of parts of the perimeter wall."

"Right, but I still don't see how it's a good thing."

"It means that the locals won't lurk around here given that it's where the old don met his maker."

"You're not his maker."

"No, but I did punch his ticket for the one-way trip." Taylor shook his head. "No, what I mean is that the locals won't be a problem given that we'll move a considerable amount of dangerous equipment down here. We also won't need to worry about anyone sniffing around for an AI and if someone does, they'll be very, very easy to detect."

Vickie tilted her head in thought and finally smiled. "You know, that is a good thing."

"Right?"

Niki shivered. "I won't lie. This gives me the creeps too. When does our plane to the US take off?"

"As soon as we finish installing the server," Taylor replied and turned to the hacker. "How's that going?"

"Oh, were you waiting for me?" She wiped her hands on her pants. "I was finished fifteen minutes ago."

"I guess that means the plane will take off as soon as we get there," he responded. "They should hopefully be ready and waiting for us given that we commissioned the damn thing."

Niki stepped closer to him, her expression suspicious. "Why are you in such a good mood when you have to board a plane?"

"I managed to get my hands on some Ambien so I'll catch up on much-needed sleep on the journey."

"Damn," Vickie grumbled as she locked the heavy security door into the server room behind them. "It's always a highlight of our trips to tease you about your crippling phobia."

"You'll simply have to do that while I'm snoozing."

"Sure, but it won't be as much fun."

Taylor, Niki, and Vickie arrived at the workshop after the long flight and exchanged a glance that confirmed that all of them noticed that Bobby and Tanya were acting weirdly.

They would always be a little strange but something seemed unusually off about them both. Taylor didn't know what to think of it but given that they were in the middle of a move and he was jet lagged all the way to hell, there was no real incentive for him to question them on the topic.

Besides, they had their work cut out for them and there simply wasn't time to dissect the idiosyncrasies of his friends—although he did wonder if it had something to do with the fact that this was essentially the end of a chapter. Maybe they were unsettled by the fact that the big change was finally happening and weren't sure how to deal with it.

The M and B team, minus the freelancers, would fly to Italy in the morning, which meant that everything that wasn't included in the first trip there would have to be shipped with them.

He had always prided himself in packing light and Niki didn't own much either. Vickie, on the other hand, had all kinds of equipment that she was adamant could not be left behind.

She and Niki snapped constantly at each other and once or twice, he'd had to step in to avoid an outright humdinger of an argument. As a result, none of them had the time or the energy to devote to the odd behavior of their friends. Even Elisa seemed to have retreated to God knew where.

Finally, they packed the last of the items into Liz and

when he turned, he realized that Bobby was dressed in a clean and neatly pressed black suit.

Not only that, but he stood beside a stack of pizzas and donuts.

"Hey...uh, Bungees?"

"Yeah, Taylor?"

"Your... There's a... What's with the suit?"

"Oh, you noticed it?"

"Well, yeah. And the pizzas and donuts. Do you have something on your mind?"

"Yeah, but I'm—hold on."

He turned quickly as Elisa pulled up in her car. She was also dressed much better than usual and she dragged a harassed-looking chap into the shop behind her.

"And...who is he?" Niki asked. Taylor could only assume that she was similarly distracted and jet lagged and had only realized that something was up when he mentioned it.

"He is Father Mark Florence," the man snapped and shook Elisa's hand from his shoulder.

Taylor's eyes narrowed. "Father? As in...forgive me, Father, I've been a bad boy?"

"That's not—"

"I know what I said."

"Father as in a wedding officiant."

They all turned to Tanya, who wore a well-cut but feminine pantsuit, something she had certainly never worn before. To see her in any kind of formal wear at all was confusing enough but the fact that it was all white made Taylor's eyes widen with sudden insight.

She looked more comfortable in a pantsuit than she

would in a wedding dress, he had to admit, although her cheeks were a little flushed.

"What?" she snapped when she realized that everyone was staring. "They didn't have any wedding dresses that fit me so I went with something a little more stylish."

"It... I mean, it is very forward-thinking," Niki agreed. "Real quick, still processing this, give me a second. You guys are getting married?"

"Crap, I was supposed to tell you guys on the plane," Vickie interjected. She had appeared almost miraculously in what could only be described as a goth's version of a pantsuit maid of honor outfit, although Taylor wasn't sure where she'd even found something like that. "I dropped the ball there. That's my bad—sorry, guys."

"You got a Catholic officiant, though?" Taylor asked. "Aren't there, like...millions of other people here in Vegas who can perform this kind of ceremony?"

"Oh, right." Bobby grunted and adjusted his tie. "We did have this Elvis impersonator officiant in mind but he...uh—"

"Don't," he warned. "Don't do it, Bungees."

"He left the building."

"I warned you. It would be a huge problem to have to kill a man on his wedding day but I'm gonna."

"You are not gonna." Tanya took Bobby's arm. "I've been through the song and dance of a so-called proper wedding before and I gave it a pass this time. We wanted something a little more informal with friends, pizza, and donuts. You kind of pushed us to make it before the move to Italy, so this is on you. Anyway, Father, would you like to begin? Maybe you'd like some bubbly to settle the nerves?"

The man smiled and shook his head. "That will not be necessary. Are all those needed present?"

"I'm not dressed as a best man but sure, I'll do it." Taylor patted Bobby on the shoulder. He could understand why they would want to do something like this given all they'd been through lately. It also explained why his friend wanted to move into the cottage on their Vegas property, he realized.

"I'm glad to have you, man," the mechanic whispered as the officiant drew himself tall, ready to begin.

"Sure, but I never got to throw you a bachelor party—"

He was cut off when Niki hammered her elbow into his ribs.

"It's probably for the best," Bobby whispered. "This being Vegas and all."

"Yeah. You're right, it's probably for the best."

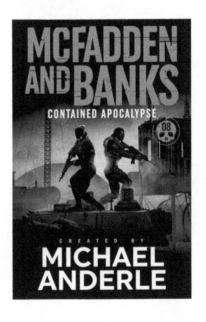

AUTHOR NOTES - MICHAEL ANDERLE

JUNE 18, 2021

Thank you for not only reading this story, but these author notes in the back.

This is going to be a rant.

Many of you might or might not know, but I have a penname which has adult humor and occasional adult situations.

That name is Michael Todd (my full name is Michael Todd Anderle).

One of my new series is Unlikely BountyHunters (no space.) This is a very bro-humor focused story and the covers and titles of the story. Unfortunately, my bro-humor title doesn't sit too well with either the VP of Operations (Zen Master Steve®), VP of Marketing (who is also my wife), and the new President of LMBPN Publishing.

Our first title is 'CODE BLUE: ALIEN JAIL BREAK.' This title doesn't offend anyone.

However...

The second title is 'Alien Probes Suck Ass.' For some

reason, this title (for a science fiction bro-humor, save the aliens sort of story) seems to raise a lot of eyebrows.

I think it's hilarious.

You would have thought that the title I chose suggested we kill a lot of puppies or something. No puppies were harmed during the making of this book, I promise.

Zen Master hates this title so much he did an under-handed, back-stabby trick to make SURE the VP of Marketing saw the title, and yes, she saw it.

>>*Zen Master Steve® note:* Eyeroll<<

I received 'questions' about the title and have been on the hot seat for the title for months now. Finally, I stomped my proverbial foot and crossed my arms across my chest, and refused to discuss the point any more.

So, all I have left is to rant to some fans in an author note and 'woe is me' about an (admittedly) risqué title which I find funny.

I hope to God this doesn't give Steve, Judith, and Robin ammunition to roast me with for the rest of 2021.

Have a fantastic week.

Ad Aeternitatem,

Michael (Todd) Anderle

CONNECT WITH MICHAEL

Connect with Michael Anderle

Website: http://lmbpn.com

Email List: http://lmbpn.com/email/

Social Media:

https://www.facebook.com/LMBPNPublishing

https://twitter.com/MichaelAnderle

https://www.instagram.com/lmbpn_publishing/

https://www.bookbub.com/authors/michael-anderle

OTHER ZOO BOOKS

BIRTH OF HEAVY METAL

He Was Not Prepared (1)

She Is His Witness (2)

Backstabbing Little Assets (3)

Blood Of My Enemies (4)

Get Out Of Our Way (5)

It All Falls Down (6)

Justice Comes Due (7)

All's fair In War (8)

APOCALYPSE PAUSED

Fight for Life and Death (1)

Get Rich or Die Trying (2)

Big Assed Global Kegger (3)

Ambassadors and Scorpions (4)

Nightmares From Hell (5)

Calm Before The Storm (6)

One Crazy Pilot (7)

One Crazy Rescue (8)

One Crazy Machine (9)

One Crazy Life (10)

One Crazy Set Of Friends (11)

One Crazy Set Of Stories (12)

SOLDIERS OF FAME AND FORTUNE

Nobody's Fool (1)

Nobody Lives Forever (2)

Nobody Drinks That Much (3)

Nobody Remembers But Us (4)

Ghost Walking (5)

Ghost Talking (6)

Ghost Brawling (7)

Ghost Stalking (8)

Ghost Resurrection (9)

Ghost Adaptation (10)

Ghost Redemption (11)

Ghost Revolution (12)

THE BOHICA CHRONICLES

Reprobates (1)

Degenerates (2)

Redeemables (3)

Thor (4)

CRYPTID ASSASSIN

Hired Killer (1)

Silent Death (2)

Sacrificial Weapon (3)

Head Hunter (4)

MCFADDEN AND BANKS

CPSIA information can be obtained
at www.ICGtesting.com
Printed in the USA
LVHW021310090721
692259LV00004B/225